THE

ALMOST

MOON

Alice Sebold is the author of the multimillion-copy
bestseller *The Lovely Bones* and the memoir *Lucky*. She lives
in California with her husband, the writer Glen David Gold.

Praise for *The Almost Moon*

'The spell cast by Alice Sebold's new novel begins in the very first sentence . . . As an outstanding piece of writing, it is exhilarating, unforgettable. There is a forensic ease about the prose that simply insists every sentence is weighted and committed to memory. This is a remarkable novel in which every word is vital, each nuance felt . . . *The Almost Moon*, comparable to Jeffrey Eugenides's outstanding debut, *The Virgin Suicides* (1993), is a candid, gut wrenching, at times horribly funny and often beautifully touching exploration of one woman's realisation that her life has been swallowed, or rather cancelled . . . The genius which guides *The Almost Moon* is its absolute, horrible, multiple truths; its staggering clarity'

Eileen Battersby, *Irish Times*

'Chapter by chapter, Sebold peels away the layers of her narrator's misery and self-deception, and creates an extended and sometimes blackly comic critique of a popular literary genre . . . At the core of this novel Sebold asks a profoundly interesting question about Helen's failure to recognise the authenticity and inviolability of others . . . Sebold writes brilliantly about the dangers of a narcissistic and victimised identity; about murderous self-pity and its overweening sense of entitlement . . . *The Almost Moon* is a mature, salutary and timely novel.'

Helen Dunmore, *The Times*

'This will be welcomed by admirers of Sebold's dirty realism, quasi-poetic style and helter-skelter storytelling gifts. Amazingly, she manages to make her gothic tale as moving as it is unquestionably gripping'

Observer

This is a powerful, intricate and beautifully written novel. It more than lives up to the publisher's description of it as a "challenging, moving, gripping story, written with humanity and fluidity" . . . *The Almost Moon* is a story of real people, in extremis, beautifully told by an accomplished writer. It is a worthy successor to Sebold's bestseller *The Lovely Bones*. It makes for an absorbing, if painful read'

Sunday Herald

'Sebold is one of the most talented and original voices around, producing thought-provoking books every woman wants to read . . . This brilliant, breathtaking, claustrophobic novel will leave you reeling as Sebold takes you on a journey of emotions that's shocking, brutal, tender and moving'
Glamour

'Brilliantly paced, it's brutally honest, and the Gordian knot at its core – an abusive mother and her traumatically attached daughter – is depicted with such generous intelligence that the fineness of the novel more than surpasses its own horror-show of circumstance . . . Along with its terrifying truths and vortex of ambivalence, *The Almost Moon* can be mordantly funny . . . Haunting, searing'
Boston Globe

'Biting yet dreamlike . . . Anguish, perseverance and sly dark humor permeate this exploration of a complex love–hate, mother–daughter relationship and how particular relationship tics are perpetuated from generation to generation . . . Along with its buoying dark wit, it is this eerily familiar blurred line between sane and insane that makes *The Almost Moon* simultaneously uncomfortable and absorbing'
San Francisco Chronicle

'From the opening line of *The Almost Moon* . . . we recognize Alice Sebold's hand: her sensuous yet impeccably direct language, her world where the poignant and the gruesome intertwine. Sebold has a track record of writing so movingly about chilling subjects that she has become something of a cultural bard. Her articulate, disquieting stories of horror – the horror of the unthinkable, of the right next door – resonate with a staggeringly large readership . . . An intensely compact and suspenseful story . . . [In *The Lovely Bones*] Sebold's brilliant descriptions of heaven and her nuanced observations of a grieving family made for some of the loveliest writing I have ever come across . . . Sebold writes just as beautifully here, with the same knack for stating truths page after page'
Houston Chronicle

THE

ALMOST

MOON

A NOVEL

Alice Sebold

PICADOR

First published 2007 by Little, Brown and Company, USA

First published in Great Britain 2007 by Picador

First published in paperback 2007 by Picador

This edition published 2010 by Picador
an imprint of Pan Macmillan, a division of Macmillan Publishers Limited
Pan Macmillan, 20 New Wharf Road, London N1 9RR
Basingstoke and Oxford
Associated companies throughout the world
www.panmacmillan.com

ISBN 978-0-330-52102-4

1 3 5 7 9 8 6 4 2

A CIP catalogue record for this book is available from
the British Library.

Printed and bound in the UK by
CPI Mackays, Chatham ME5 8TD

Visit **www.picador.com** to read more about all our books
and to buy them. You will also find features, author interviews and
news of any author events, and you can sign up for e-newsletters
so that you're always first to hear about our new releases.

Always, Glen

THE

ALMOST

MOON

ONE

When all is said and done, killing my mother came easily. Dementia, as it descends, has a way of revealing the core of the person affected by it. My mother's core was rotten like the brackish water at the bottom of a weeks-old vase of flowers. She had been beautiful when my father met her and still capable of love when I became their late-in-life child, but by the time she gazed up at me that day, none of this mattered.

If I hadn't picked up my ringing phone, Mrs. Castle, my mother's unlucky neighbor, would have continued down the list of emergency numbers posted on my mother's almond-colored fridge. But within the hour, I found myself rushing over to the house where I was born.

It was a cool October morning. When I arrived, my mother was sitting upright in her wing chair, wrapped in a mohair shawl, and mumbling to herself. Mrs. Castle said my mother hadn't recognized her that morning when she'd brought the paper to the door.

"She tried to slam the door on me," Mrs. Castle said. "She screamed like I was scalding her. It was the most pitiful thing imaginable."

My mother sat, a totemic presence, in the flocked red-and-white wing chair in which she'd spent the more than two decades since my father's death. She'd aged slowly in that chair, retiring first to read books and work her needlepoint, and then, when her eyes began to fail, to watch public television from dawn until she fell asleep in front of it after her evening meal. In the last year or two, she would sit in the chair and not even bother to turn on the television. Often she placed the twisted skeins of yarn that my older daughter, Emily, still sent each Christmas, in the center of her lap. She petted them the way some old women might pet cats.

I thanked Mrs. Castle and assured her I would handle everything.

"You know it's time," she said, turning toward me on the front stoop. "She's been in the house alone an awfully long while."

"I know," I said, and shut the door.

Mrs. Castle walked down the steps of my mother's front porch with three empty dishes of various sizes she had found in the kitchen and that she claimed to be hers. I didn't doubt it. My mother's neighbors were a godsend. When I was young, my mother had railed against the Greek Orthodox church down the road, calling its parishioners, for no reason that made sense, "those stupid Holy-Rolling Poles." But it was this congregation that had often called upon its ranks to make sure the cranky old woman who had lived forever in the run-down house got fed and clothed. If occasionally she got robbed, well, it was precarious to be a woman living alone.

"People are living in my walls," she had said to me more than once, but it was only when I found a condom lying beside my childhood bed that I'd put two and two together. Manny, a boy who occasionally repaired things for my mother, was bringing girls into her upstairs rooms. I had talked to Mrs. Castle and hired a locksmith. It was not my fault my mother refused to move.

"Mother," I said, calling the name only I, as her sole child, had the right to call her. She looked up at me and smiled.

"Bitch," she said.

The thing about dementia is that sometimes you feel like the afflicted person has a trip wire to the truth, as if they can see beneath the skin you hide in.

"Mother, it's Helen," I said.

"I know who you are!" she barked at me.

Her hands clasped the curved ends of the armrests, and I could see how hard she pressed, her anger flaring up and out at me like involuntary claws.

"That's good," I said.

I stood there a moment longer, until it felt like an established fact. She was my mother and I was her daughter. I thought we could go forward from this into our usual unpleasant encounter.

I walked over to the windows and began to draw up the metal blinds by the increasingly threadbare cloth tape that bound them. Outside, the yard of my childhood was so overgrown it was difficult to make out the original shapes of the bushes and trees, those places I had played with other children until my mother's behavior began to garner a reputation outside our house.

"She steals," my mother said.

My back was to her. I was looking at a vine that had crawled into the huge fir tree in the corner of the yard and consumed the shed where my father had once done carpentry. He had always been happiest inside that space. On my darkest days, I had come to imagine him there, laboriously sanding the round wooden globes that had replaced all his other projects.

"Who steals?"

"That bitch."

I knew she was talking about Mrs. Castle. The woman who daily made sure my mother had woken up. Who brought her the *Philadelphia Inquirer* and not infrequently cut flowers from her own yard and placed them in plastic iced-tea pitchers that wouldn't shatter if my mother knocked them over.

"That's not true," I told her. "Mrs. Castle is a lovely woman who takes good care of you."

"What happened to my blue Pigeon Forge bowl?"

I knew the bowl and realized I had not seen it for weeks. In my youth it had always held what I thought of as imprisoned food— walnuts and Brazil nuts and filberts that my father would crack and dig out with a tiny fork.

"I gave it to her, Mother," I lied.

"You what?"

"She's been so wonderful and I knew she liked it, and so I just gave it to her one day when you were napping."

Help doesn't come free, I felt like telling her. *These people owe you nothing.*

My mother looked at me. It was a horrible bottomless look. She pouted first, her lower lip jutting out and then quivering. She was going to cry. I left the room and walked to the kitchen. Whenever I came, I found good reason to spend many of the hours I was supposed to be with my mother in every room of the house but the one in which she sat. I heard the low moan begin that I'd been hearing all my life. It was a moan the notes of which were orchestrated to elicit pity. My father had always been the one to run to her. After his death, it fell to me. For more than twenty years, with greater or lesser diligence, I had been attending to her, rushing over when she called saying her heart would burst, or taking her on increasing rounds of doctors' visits as she aged.

Late in the afternoon of that day, I was in the screened-in back porch, sweeping out the straw mat. I had left the door open a crack so that I could hear her. Then into the cloud of dust that surrounded me came the unmistakable odor of shit. My mother had needed to go to the bathroom but couldn't get up.

I dropped the broom and ran to my mother. She had not, as I may have momentarily hoped, died and suffered the resultant loosening of bowels. Dead in her own home as she might have wished. Instead, she sat in her chair, having soiled herself.

"Number two!" she said. This time, the smile was different than the smile of Bitch. Bitch had had life to it. This smile was alien to me. It held neither fear nor malice.

Often, when I recounted to my youngest, Sarah, the events of a given day, she told me that no matter how much she loved me, she wasn't going to strip and diaper me when I grew old. "I'll hire someone," she said. "I've never heard a better incentive for hitting the big time than avoiding that."

The smell had filled the room within seconds. I walked back to the porch twice to take in huge drafts of dusty air and could think of nothing else but presenting my mother in the way she would have wanted to be seen. I knew I was going to have to call the ambulance. I knew, as I had for some time, that my mother was heading out of this life, but I did not want her arriving at the hospital caked in shit. I should say I knew *she* would not want that, and so what had mattered most to her throughout her life   appearances — became what mattered most to me.

I took a final breath out on the porch and walked back to her. No longer smiling, she was agitated in the extreme.

"Mom," I said, certain as I said it that she did not recognize the name or the daughter who said it, "I'm going to help you clean up, and then we're going to make some calls." *You'll never make a call again,* I thought, and I didn't mean it cruelly. Why is it that pragmatics are so often interpreted this way? Shit is shit and truth is truth. Done.

I knelt down in front of her and looked up into her face. I hated her more than I'd ever hated anyone. Still, I reached up, as if I were finally allowed to touch a precious thing, and ran my fingers down her long silver braid. "Mom," I whispered. I said it because I knew it would be still in the air. No reverberations, no response.

But the wetness was making her unhappy. Like a snail trapped in sunlight, say—anxious to get away from an element that caused pain. I went from kneeling to half bending over. I placed my shoulders against her shoulders, careful not to put any weight on her. I leaned in like a football player on a tackle and then lifted up. She was both lighter and heavier than I'd expected.

I got her to standing with ease, but once she was upright, she collapsed in my arms. It was all I could do not to drop her, bringing both of us to the ground. As I adapted to the balance of holding her full weight, I could not help but think of my father, how year after year he carried the burden of her, apologized to the neighbors, dried her copious tears, and how this body had folded into his over and over again like so much batter until the two of them became one.

I felt like weeping myself then. We were near the end of us and of the secrets of the house. I was forty-nine and my mother was eighty-eight. My father had been dead for almost the entire lifetime of my younger child—a few months after she'd turned four. Sarah could never know the full measure of his sweetness, or play in the workshop among his thrice-glued carpentry. I thought of the mutant rocking horses rotting in the shed, and my arms, with my mother in them, weakened dangerously. How the house and my life had changed after his death.

I dragged my mother, with her trying, I could feel, to help, over to the staircase leading up to her bath. I questioned my sanity. How, I wondered, did I think this feat was possible? She had to weigh at least a hundred pounds, and despite my midlife fitness regime, I had never lifted more than sixty. It was not going to work. I collapsed onto the stairs, with my mother soiled and damp on top of me.

I panted on the carpeted steps but did not give up. I was determined to clean my mother and to dress her in fresh clothes before I called the ambulance. As we lay there and her weight grew familiar, like the strange feeling of being pinned by a dozing lover, I thought of the alternatives. I could bring her to the bathroom in the back and try to wash her from the sink. There was also the kitchen. But where would I prop her up? How to hold her and wash her at the same time, not to mention the mess of water all over the floor and the potential for slipping and cracking both our skulls.

My mother began to snore. Her head tilted back over my shoulder so that I could see her ancient mottled face and neck. I looked at her cheekbones, as sharp as they had always been — almost painful now in her cadaverous flesh. *Who will love me?* I thought, and then banished this question by looking out at the birch leaves in the fading sunlight. I had been there all day. I hadn't even called to cancel at Westmore. I saw the empty space on the platform in Life Drawing 101 and the students, at their easels, staring at my absence, the useless charcoal in their hands.

I knew that if I did not move, my mother might sleep for hours, and darkness would come. I pictured my friend Natalie looking for me in the halls of the art building, vainly querying the students in class. Natalie would call my house — perhaps drive over alone or with Hamish, her son. The doorbell would ring in the empty house, and then Natalie would imagine that something must have happened to me or to Sarah or to Emily.

I lifted my arms up under my mother's arms and raised them slightly off the carpeted stairs. First one and then the other, like manipulating a life-size doll. To have controlled her as easily as that, impossible. I had to get through this without calling my daughters. This was something to be done on my own. I twisted out from under her, and she moaned like a collapsing bag of air. I sat by her body on the stairs. The house had a weight and a force that I knew could crush me. I had to get out of there, and I thought, suddenly, of the bathtub among the rocking horses in the shed.

I left my mother dozing and turned and ran up the stairs, darting into her cluttered bedroom for blankets, and the pink powder room for towels. In the mirror over the sink, I checked myself. My eyes seemed smaller and even bluer than they had been, as if the intensity of the situation affected color and its perception. For years now I'd kept my hair so short that I could almost see my scalp. When I'd walked into my mother's house, she'd taken one glance and said, "Don't tell me you have cancer too. Everyone has cancer these days." I explained that my haircut made life easier, from exercise to gardening to work. It was the ambiguity that got to me—would she have cared if I had had cancer or would it have just been competition for her? Her intonation pointed toward the latter, but it was hard to believe this of one's own mother.

I stood at the top of the stairs with the blankets and towels. I kept at bay my realization that she would never see these rooms again and that now they would become, for me, empty shells littered with possessions. I noticed the hush in the upstairs hallway and looked at the pictures on the walls, pictures that would soon be gone. I imagined the dark squares they would leave behind them where no sun had reached for years, and the echoes that would resound from the curtainless storm windows and the thick plaster-and-brick walls. I began to sing. I sang nonsense. Cat-food commercials and childhood songs, the latter a habit that had been handed down from my mother, a way to stave off the onset of nerves. The need for noise overwhelmed me, but as I headed down the stairs, I grew quiet again. I saw that my mother had slumped down and lay on the floor, her body on the old wine-red Persian rug.

"No, Mother, no," I said, realizing as I did so that it was more useless than talking to a dog. A dog cocked her head. A dog gave you a soulful look. My mother was a passed-out bag of bones who reeked of shit.

"Why like this?" I asked. I stood over her body with my arms full of blankets and towels, and I began to weep. I whispered a prayer that no one would knock on the door, that Mrs. Castle would not think to check on us, though right about now Manny the handyboy might help me tote and haul.

I placed the towels on the bottom stair and took my grandfather's red-and-black Hudson Bay blanket, spreading it out on the floor beside her. It extended into the dining room. Then, so the wool would not scratch, I put a white Mexican wedding blanket down on top of that. I was not thinking sanely; I was wrapping fish or making spring rolls; I was thinking, *Super Giant Mother Burrito.*

I bent down, taking air in and neutralizing my spine—thank you, Stella, at World Gym—and put my arms up under my mother's armpits.

Her eyes snapped open.

"What on earth are you doing?"

I blinked. With our faces reversed to each other, I felt she could suck my eyes into her mouth. The rest of me, like the tail of a lizard or the end of a flat noodle, would swoop in and be gone in mere seconds. I kept my arms tense. Would she ever be powerless?

"Daniel!" she brayed. "Daniel!"

"Dad's not here, Mom," I said.

She looked up at me, her face dimmed and then reignited again, like a match flaring in the dark.

"I want that bowl," she said. "Now!"

To be that close to her. To be holding on to her and to see her brain open up like that, its scrambled insides, it was all I could do to keep to my task. As she spoke about things—Emily, the "pretty baby" (Emily had just turned thirty and had babies of her own); the kudzu near her father's cabin that had to be cut back with a scythe (the cabin was on land that was at the base of the Smokies and long out of our lives); and the stealing, conniving, not-to-be-trusted neighbors—I placed her body in the blankets and made an open-ended package with her talking head sticking out. Then I rested the towels on top of her chest and breathed slowly, counting to ten before I spoke.

"We are going on a sleigh ride," I said to her. And in my fists, I balled up the two free ends of the blanket, partially lifting her body off the floor. I heaved her over the carpet of the dining room, in through the kitchen, and out the side door.

"Toot! Toot!" she said. "Toot! Toot!" And then she grew silent and stared at the outside like a child in front of flickering Christmas lights. I wanted to ask her, *When was the last time you went into your backyard? When was the last time you smelled a flower or trimmed a shrub or just sat in the rusted white iron lawn chair?*

Grief was coming heavily now. Something about being outside, being in the fresh air, away from the acrid scent of her and the mothball smell of the closed-up house. My mother lay in her blanketed cocoon on the small raised side porch, which thankfully was at least partially shielded from the next-door neighbors by vine-covered latticework.

I went down the three stairs to the cinder-block path and walked around to the back of the porch, where as a child I had sat and kicked my legs over the edge and where now my mother lay as if on a shipping-and-receiving shelf. I was sweating, but I knew by the slant of the sun at my back that it would be less than an hour before light slipped below the houses that surrounded my mother's and left us alone in the last long night we would spend together.

I touched her treasured braid again. Some years ago her hair had passed out of its wiry stage and become soft. It had always been her crowning glory. Her brief life as a lingerie model before she met my father was one I'd envied growing up. Whatever else she was, she had been the most beautiful mother in the neighborhood, and watching her had taught me everything I knew about physical beauty. It was a bitter truth—my discovery— that daughters were not made in cookie-cutter patterns from the genes of their mothers alone. Random accidents of ancestry could blunt a nose or tip a forehead until beauty's delicate tracery gave way to an ordinary Jane.

Outside, with the air rushing over her, the fecal scent dissipated and I could think realistically again. I would not make it to the shed. What had I thought? The damage of dragging her down the three steps, of trying to heave her off the porch. And what would I fill the ancient bathtub with? Cold water from the backyard hose? The bathtub would be dirty and full of old lumber and broken bits of refuse that I would have to clean out. The last time I'd been in the shed, I'd noticed that my father's tool board, with all the ghost shapes of tools, had fallen off the wall and pitched forward against the tub. What had I been thinking?

"This is it, Mom," I said. "This is as far as we go."

She did not smile or say "bitch" or wail some final lament. I like to think, when I think about it, that by that time she was busy taking in the scent of her garden, feeling the late-afternoon sun on her face, and that somehow in the moments that had elapsed since she'd last spoken, she'd forgotten she'd ever had a child and that, for so many years now, she'd had to pretend she loved it.

I wish I could say that as my mother lay on the side porch and the wind began to pick up more and more so that the crows clinging on to the tops of the trees took flight, that she made it easy on me. That she pointedly listed all the sins she had committed during her long life.

She was eighty-eight. The lines on her face were now the cross-hatchings of fine old porcelain. Her eyes were closed. Her breathing ragged. I looked at the tops of the empty trees. There is no excuse to give, I know, so here is what I did: I took the towels with which I had meant to bathe her, and not thinking that near the latticework or by the back fence there might stand a witness, I smashed these downy towels into my mother's face. Once begun, I did not stop. She struggled, her blue-veined hands, with the rings she feared would be stolen if she ever took them off, grabbed at my arms. First her diamonds and then her rubies briefly flickered in the light. I pushed down harder. The towels shifted, and I saw her eyes. I held the towels for a long time, staring right at her, until I felt the tip of her nose snap and saw the muscles of her body go suddenly slack and knew that she had died.

T W O

My clues to my mother's life before me were not many. It took me a while to notice that almost all of them—the Steuben glass paperweights, the sterling silver picture frames, the Tiffany rattles that were sent a dozen strong before she miscarried her first, then second, child—were chipped or dented, cracked or blackened in various ways. Almost all of them had been or would be thrown either at a wall or at my father, who ducked with a reflexive agility that reminded me of Gene Kelly tripping up and down the sodden curbs in *Singin' in the Rain*. My father's grace had developed in proportion to my mother's violence, and I knew that in absorbing it and deflecting it in the way he did, he also saved her from seeing herself as she had become. Instead she saw the same reflections of herself that I pored over when I snuck downstairs after dark. Her precious still photography.

*　　*　　*

When my father met her, my mother was fresh from Knoxville, Tennessee, and made her living as a showroom model of underwear and support garments. She preferred to say, "I modeled slips." And these were the photos that we had so many of. Framed black and whites of my mother in better times, wearing black slips or white slips. "That one was eggshell," she might say from the corner of the living room, not having said anything to anyone all afternoon. I knew she was referring to a specific slip in a specific picture, and sensing this, I would choose the white slip I thought could be eggshell. If I got it wrong, the moment would burst — as fragile as a blow bubble glistening in the yard — and she would slump back into the chair. But if I chose right, and I would come to memorize them over time — there was the bone, the ecru, the nude, and my favorite, the rose-petal pink — I would bring the framed photograph to her. Hanging on to the thin cord of her smile, I pulled myself into the past with her, making myself small and still on the ottoman until she told me the story of the photography session or the man involved or the gifts that she had received as partial payment.

The rose-petal pink was my father.

"He was not even the photographer," she would say. "He was a junior water inspector in a borrowed suit with a pocket square, but I didn't know that then."

These were the years of my earliest childhood, when my mother was still powerful, before she collected what she considered the unforgivable flaws of age. Two years short of her fiftieth birthday, she began covering all her mirrors with heavy cloths, and when, as a teenager, I suggested we remove the mirrors completely, she objected. They remained there as she grew infirm. Her shadowy, silent indictments.

But in the photos of the rose-petal-pink slip, she was still worthy of her own love, and it was this love for herself that I tried to take warmth from. What I knew, I think, without wanting to admit it, was that the photos were like the historical documents of our town. They proved that long ago, there had been a more hopeful time. Her smile was easy then, not forced, and the fear that could turn to bitterness had not tainted her eyes.

"He was the photographer's friend," she said. "He was having a big day in the city, and the suit was part of his friend's lie."

I knew not to ask, "What lie, Mom?" Because that took her to a bad place where her marriage was just the long, arduous playing out of an afternoon con between schoolboy friends. Instead I asked, "Who was the shoot for?"

"The original John Wanamaker's," she said. Her face glowed like an old-fashioned streetlamp lit from the inside. Everything else in the room disappeared as if into a dark fog. I did not realize then that there was no place in these memories for the company of a child.

As my mother drifted into the past, where she was happiest, I appointed myself the past's faithful guardian. If her feet looked cold, I covered them. If the light left the room too dark, I quietly crept over and turned on a bookshelf lamp that would cast only a small circle of light — not too big — just enough to keep her voice from becoming a scary shapeless echo in the dark. Outside, in the street in front of our house, the workmen who had been hired to install the stained-glass windows in the new Greek Orthodox church — green because for some reason this color of glass was cheaper than most — might walk by and make a noise too loud to ignore. When this happened, I would meet the drowsy blank stare that came over my mother with ushering words meant to slip her back to the dream-past.

"Five girls showed up, not eight," I'd say.

Or "His last name, Knightly, was irresistible."

When I look back, I think how silly I must have sounded, parroting the phrases of my mother's lovesick girlhood, but what was most precious about our house back then was that no matter how wrongheaded everything might be, inside it, we could distill ourselves to being a normal man, woman, and child. No one had to see my father put on an apron and do overtime work after he got home, or watch me cajole my mother, trying to get her to eat.

"I didn't know he wasn't in the fashion industry until after he'd kissed me," she'd say.

"But what about the kiss?"

It was always here that she teetered. The kiss and the weeks immediately following it must have been wonderful, but she could not forgive my father once he'd brought her to Phoenixville.

"New York City," she'd say, looking down dejectedly between her splayed feet on the floor. "I never even got there."

It was my mother's disappointments that were enumerated in our household and that I saw before me every day as if they were posted on our fridge—a static list that my presence could not assuage.

I must have petted my mother's head for a long time. Eventually I saw the blue light of a television go on across the street. When my parents had first moved to Phoenixville, this neighborhood had been a thriving one, full of young families. Now the squat 1940s houses on quarter-acre lots were often rented out to couples down on their luck. My mother said you could tell who the renters were because they let the houses rot, but in my mind it was these very people that kept the street from turning into a place where the isolated elderly were slowly dying.

As darkness descended, so did the cold. I looked down at the length of my mother's body, wrapped in double blankets, and knew she would never feel the uncertainties that come with the fluctuation of air or light again.

"Over now," I said to her. "It's over."

And for the first time, the air was empty around me. For the first time, it was not full of hatchets and blame or unworthiness-as-oxygen.

As I breathed in this blank-space world—where my mother ended at the border of her own flesh—I heard the phone ring in the kitchen. I slipped off the back of the porch and walked back past the latticework. On the next-door neighbor's empty porch, I could see the local tomcat grooming himself. Growing up, Sarah called such cats "orange marmalades." I saw the old metal lid cocked at an angle on top of the neighbor's neatly tucked and rolled paper trash bag and made a mental note to take my mother's trash out. My whole life, she would instruct me about the proper way to fold a bag. "Paper bags, wax bags, are like your sheets. Hospital corners improve them."

The phone rang again and again. I walked up the three wooden steps to the door. My mother's feet extended out over the top stair. She had insisted that the answering machines I brought her did not work. "She's afraid of them," Natalie said. "My father thinks the ATM will eat his arm."

I smelled something as I shoved my mother's body just far enough aside to squeeze back into the house. It was the smell of lighter fluid and charcoal mingling in the air. By this time the ring of the phone was a hammer pounding from inside my skull, or a voice calling me from outside a nightmare.

The first thing I saw when I entered the kitchen was the step-stool chair beneath the wall-mounted phone. The red vinyl was cracked and taped thirty-five years ago, more than a decade after it served as my first high chair. Seeing it in the kitchen was like seeing a lion left standing, ignored. It leaped out at me, roaring with the voice of the phone above it, propelling me back to my father placing me there. I saw the slash of my young father's smile and my mother's wobbly wrist bringing peaches and bananas— all pureed by hand—up to my lips. How hard she had tried and how she must have hated it from the start.

I grabbed the phone as if it were a life raft.

"Hello?"

"Do you need help?"

The voice was old, feeble, but I was no less startled than if it had been coming from just outside the door.

"What?"

"You've been out on that porch a long time."

I would recall this later as the first moment where I began to be frightened, where I realized that by the standards of the out-side world, what I'd done knew no justification.

"Mrs. Leverton?"

"Are you two all right, Helen? Is Clair in need?"

"My mother's fine," I said.

"I can call my grandson," she said. "He'll be glad to help."

"My mother wanted to go into the yard," I said.

From where I stood, I could see through the small window over the kitchen sink and across the backyard. I remember my mother arduously training a vine to grow so that it masked a view of our house from the Levertons' upstairs bedroom. "That man will stare right into your private places," my mother would say, hanging her front half out my bedroom window, which was di-rectly over the kitchen, threading the vines and risking life and limb to make sure Mr. Leverton never caught a peek. Both the vine and Mr. Leverton were long dead now.

"Is Clair still out there?" Mrs. Leverton asked. "It's awfully cold."

This gave me an idea.

"She's waving at you," I said.

"The Blameless One," my mother had called her. "Butter wouldn't melt in her mouth and stupid as the day is long."

But there was silence on the other end.

"Helen," Mrs. Leverton said slowly, "are you sure you're all right?"

"Excuse me?"

"Your mother would never wave at me. We both know that."

Not so stupid, apparently.

"But that's pleasant of you to say."

I had to get my mother's body in. It was as simple as that.

"Can't you see her?" I risked.

"I'm in my kitchen now," Mrs. Leverton said. "It's five o'clock, and I always start making supper at five o'clock."

Mrs. Leverton was the champ. At ninety-six, she was the oldest fully functioning member of the neighborhood. My mother had been nothing in comparison to her. When it got down to it, the final competition among women seemed just as inane and grace-less as all those in between. Who grew breasts first, who scored the popular boy, who married well, who had the better home. In my mother's and Mrs. Leverton's life, it came down to who would be the oldest when she died. I felt like saying, *Congratulations, Mrs. Leverton, you've won!*

"You amaze me, Mrs. Leverton," I said.

"Thank you, Helen." Is it possible to *hear* preening?

"I will encourage my mother to come in," I said. "But she does what she likes."

"Yes. I know," she said. She had always been careful with her words. "Stop by anytime and give Clair my best." Her best, I did not point out, was as improbable as my mother's wave.

I hung the phone back on the upright cradle. Like my mother, Mrs. Leverton probably still insisted that phones were most efficient when they were connected by cords. I knew that she had been weakening in the previous year, but she had informed my mother that she still did exercises daily and quizzed herself on state capitals and ex-presidents.

"Unbelievable," I said to myself, and I heard the damp echo of it bounce off the green-and-gold linoleum. I wanted to rush out and tell my mother about the phone call, but when I looked her way through the screen door, I saw the marmalade tom standing on her chest and playing, like a kitten, with the ribbon of her braid.

Inside me, the child who had protected her mother ran to the screen door to shoo the marmalade tom from the porch, and yet, as I watched the huge scarred cat that my mother had taken to calling "Bad Boy" fall on her chest with his full weight and bat her braid with the ribbon attached to it with his front paws, I found myself unable to move.

Finally, after all these years, my mother's life was snuffed out, and I had been the one to do it — in the same way I might snuff out the guttering wick of an all but extinguished candle. Within a few minutes, as she struggled for breath, my lifelong dream had come true.

The marmalade tom played with the ribbon in her hair until he freed it, and it went sailing up into the air and landed on her face. It was then, the red ribbon on her cheek, the cat claw reaching out to grab it, that I shoved my fist in my mouth to cover my scream.

THREE

I sat on the floor of the kitchen. My mother's body lay positioned outside the door. I felt like turning on the bug light above her but didn't. *Look upon this,* I imagined saying to the neighbors. *This is where it all ends up.*

But I didn't really believe that. I believed, as my mother always had, that there was *them* and there was *us*. "Them" were the happy, normal people, and "us" were the totally fucked.

I remembered throwing water in her face when I was sixteen. I remembered not talking to her and seeing her dismantled, as she had never been, by trying to learn the language of apology. Watching her do that — admit that she was wrong — was one of the most helpless moments in my life. I had wanted to save her with a rush of talk about high-school chemistry and my recently failed algebra exam. To fill the silent moments while she toed the edges of the carpet with her foot as I sat in my bedroom chair and restrained myself.

Suddenly I spied, through the thick hedge that bordered my

mother's yard, Carl Fletcher coming outside with a plate of steak. As his own screen door banged and he plodded down the three wooden stairs to his lawn, a beer in one hand, a portable radio tuned to WIP sports in the other, I pictured a circle of tiki torches and throbbing white people in loincloths raising the remains of my mother high on a special catalog-ordered all-weather funeral pyre.

"I like the man next door," my mother had said when Carl Fletcher moved in six years ago. "He's pathetic, which means he keeps to himself."

Now he was on the other side of the latticework, in a yard that had been empty only moments before.

If Hilda Castle had called one day later, Sarah would have been visiting for the weekend, and she would have helped me carry my mother up the stairs to the bath. But more likely, Sarah would have made phone calls. The simple phone calls that any sane person would have made. I could not imagine my youngest standing above her soiled grandmother in the wing chair and saying, "Mother, let's kill her. That's the only choice."

On my hands and knees, I crawled over to the screen door and looked out over my mother's body and through the hedge into the adjacent backyard. Mr. Donnellson, who had lived in the house until his family put him in hospice care, had asked my mother to marry him a dozen years ago. "There's no one left," he said. "Let's be companions, Clair."

He had seen her getting her newspaper and shown up a few minutes later with a bouquet of mauve-colored tulips. "From bulbs his wife planted!" my mother repeatedly pointed out. I remember being charmed by his offer, so charmed I had been tempted to rush over to his house after he'd been spurned to see if, perhaps with only a shift in generation, his offer might hold.

When he died, my mother gloated in triumph. "I would have had to wipe up his drool for five years and then bury him," she said. On the day of his funeral, she had blamed her watery eyes on the onions she was cutting up with her ancient hand-sharpened paring knife.

Peter Donnellson's house had been sold as is by his three daughters, and my mother had braced herself for a teardown. Despite what was obvious—that the area had been going downhill for years—she fretted over the emergence of a Phoenixville nouveau riche. She worried for the roots of her giant maple trees that extended over into Mr. Donnellson's yard. She worried for the noise and for what she imagined would be the sound of children screaming almost every hour of the day. She had me research soundproofing schemes and considered replacing the windows on that side of the house with cinder blocks. "That will fix their wagon," she said, and I went, as I often did, to fill the electric kettle with water and listen to its soothing hum.

But Carl Fletcher moved in alone and didn't change anything. He had a job with the phone company and went to work out in the field early each morning. He came home at the same time every day but Friday. On the weekends he sat in his yard and drank beer. He had the paper with him and a book and always, always, the portable radio that he kept tuned to sports or talk. Occasionally his daughter, Madeline, whom my mother called the "circus freak" because of her tattoos, would visit. My mother complained about the noise of her motorcycle and "all of that flesh spread out in the yard," but she had never spoken to Carl Fletcher, and he had never bothered to introduce himself. What I knew of my mother's neighbors at this point was all second-hand, distributed, along with frozen soups or potted jams, by Mrs. Castle when we crossed paths.

As Mr. Fletcher turned his steaks over, I could hear the sizzle of the fat dripping into the fire over the noise of the game. From my kneeling position, one I refused to adopt anymore at Westmore—too hard on the knees—I crawled outside and knelt again at the edge of my mother's body. I thought of a man I'd read about who felt so devout he dragged a replica of Jesus's cross from one end of Berlin to the other, wearing only some sort of Gandhi-like diaper and traveling on his quickly bloodied knees.

The small scratch on my mother's cheek had congealed. Her eyes had purpled in halos around their sockets. I remembered turning her in bed and adjusting strips of sheepskin under her to stave off the inevitable bedsores during the lengthy convalescence that followed the surgery for her colon cancer.

Mr. Fletcher placed the steaks on a plate, took his meat and his radio, and went back inside. He was the sort of man who could be counted on, I realized, never to look up. I saw the coals still orange in his grill.

I would have had to yell "Fire!" for anyone but Mrs. Leverton or Mr. Forrest, who lived down the road, to pay attention. In the years after the final death throes of Phoenixville Steel, the streets nearby had become increasingly desolate. Properties often sat vacant, and from the spare bedroom where my grandfather's guns had once been kept, I had watched the demolition of a beautiful Victorian two streets away. Once the conical roof fell in, there was nothing to see but ancient dust floating up and out above the house's less prosperous neighbors.

I had tried to get my mother to move into a retirement home, but she would not budge, and part of me admired her for it. There was an ever-diminishing network of the originals now: Mrs. Leverton behind her, Mr. Forrest five houses down, and the long-suffering widow of Mr. Tolliver.

The one my mother had once considered her friend was Mr. Forrest. He lived at the end of the circle and didn't have any family at all. He had a house the same size as my parents', and his rooms were filled with books. When I drove by his house,

I often thought of the afternoons he and my mother had spent together, starting cocktails at five in anticipation of my father's joining them by six. I would answer the door, and Mr. Forrest would hand me a paper bag. Inside would be cured olives or fresh cheeses or French bread, and within thirty minutes of his arrival, I would tuck myself into a corner at the top of the stairs and listen to her laughter fill the house.

I leaned my body over my mother's, took the towel I had used to suffocate her, and covered her face with it. Then I made the sign of the cross. "You are so *not* Catholic!" Natalie said to me growing up, as I tried to imitate her. My cross remained a sort of flailing *X* marks the spot.

"I'm sorry, Mom," I whispered. "I'm so sorry."

I crawled back inside to retrieve the felt-covered brick that we had used forever to prop open the door. I thought of Manny, bringing in a month's supply of staples from the big-box store. I had been standing in the living room, and ever so briefly, when I turned to be introduced to him, his eyes had traveled to my chest. Later, my mother admonished me for wearing such tight clothes.

"It's a turtleneck," I said.

She had burst out laughing. "I guess you're right. The boy's a perv," she said. I remember wondering where she'd learned the word, if it had been something Manny had taught her. I'd known that, sometimes, when he'd had nowhere to go, he would bring movies over to watch with her. My mother had seen *The Godfather* more times than I could count.

I stood and put my hands on either side of my lower back to arch backward in what Natalie called my "construction-worker stretch." I was aware that I would have to pace myself as I did while modeling. That what I had done and what I was about to do would take the kind of physical stamina that a thousand dance classes might not have prepared me for.

I walked back onto the stoop and towered over her. If Mrs. Leverton was watching, back upstairs with her husband's binoculars, how would she account for what she saw? If she told her son, would he think that his mother was finally slipping? I smiled down at my mother. She would have loved that, loved that in reporting the way I handled her dead body, Mrs. Leverton might finally be knocked off her high horse and into the land of the elderly insane.

I nudged my mother's body with the edge of my jazz flats. Then there was nothing left but cursing and exertion.

"Fuck," I said repeatedly, regulating it like breathing, as I tightened my stomach to prepare for the lift. I grabbed my mother's body by the blankets, making sure to grip her up under her shoulders so she wouldn't slip. I kept cursing as I reentered the kitchen, dragging her after me. In one final tug, I got her whole body past the lip of the doorway and then lowered myself slowly down on the floor, with her between my legs. "In," I said, and kicked the brick out of the way. The door closed a little bit on its hinge, and then, with my foot, I helped it the rest of the way. As the door clicked shut with that whispering mustache seal of black rubber along its bottom edge, I became aware of my mother's death rattle. The long, slow rasp releasing from her chest.

At my own house that morning, I had methodically dusted the clear-glass globes and painted wooden herons I'd strung from invisible thread over the bedroom window. Now, in my mind, the spread wings of these birds fluttered like a warning. I would be a different person when I saw them next.

I looked at the clock over the kitchen doorway. It was after six. Somehow more than an hour had passed since I'd spoken to Mrs. Leverton.

I stopped for a second, holding on to my mother's body, and imagined Emily and her husband, John, climbing the stairs with their children, John taking Jeanine, who, at four, was the heavier of the two, and Emily cradling the two-year-old Leo. I thought of the sometimes successful Christmas presents I'd sent over the years: the pink and blue PJs with boots were a hit; the hard-knocking marbles-on-string game was judged age-inappropriate.

I stood up with the thought of Leo in his crib to bolster me, but then came its companion memory of my mother, her arms outstretched to hold him, allowing him to fall.

After positioning her body closer to the stove, I turned to run the water in the sink as cold as it would come. Again and again I took water in my hands and brought it up to my face, never splashing, exactly, but pressing my cheeks into the shallow puddles that remained in my palms. On hot nights, my ex-husband, Jake, had taken ice cubes and run them along my shoulder and back, curving them onto my stomach and up to my nipples until goose bumps covered my limbs.

I unwrapped the blankets from my mother's body. First the red and rough Hudson Bay and then the softer white Mexican wedding cotton. I walked around her body, pulling each corner taut. The downy towel remained on her face.

Leo did not bounce, as my mother confessed she thought he might, but his fall was broken by the edge of a dining room chair. Though he will have a scar on his forehead to mark the moment for the rest of his life, that chair may have saved him. Otherwise it would have been the much harder floor. My mother's face that day was surprised and hurt. Emily had blamed her, wrapped the bawling Leo in a blue fleece blanket, and called her horrible names. I stood between them and then followed Emily down the steep walkway to my car. I did not glance back to see if my mother was watching us from her door.

"Never again," Emily said. "I'm tired of making excuses for her."

"Of course," I said. "Yes," I said. "I know the way," I said, and got in the driver's side of my car. I drove more competently that day than I ever have, all the way to Paoli Hospital, going at top speed along winding roads.

I took my mother's skirt and flipped it up to reveal her calves and knees, her fleshy thighs. The scent of her earlier mishap flooded me.

"The legs go last," my mother said once. We sat in front of the television, watching Lucille Ball. Ball's hair, by then, was so red and false it looked more like Bozo's blood sample than Bozo's wig. She wore a specially tailored tuxedo jacket that created a largish hourglass shape and went down low in the back, but her legs, fishnet clad and decked out in high heels, went on and on.

I remembered calling home once from Wisconsin. Emily must have been almost four. My father answered the phone, and immediately I heard it.

"What's wrong, Daddy?"

"Nothing to get upset about."

"You sound strange. What is it?"

"I fell," he said.

I could hear the grandfather clock in their living room — its deep choral chimes.

"Are you lying down?"

"I've got that old quilt on top of me, and your mother is doing her best. Here she is."

I heard the receiver being fumbled, and I entered the anxious no-man's-land over the wire while my mother came to get the phone.

"He's fine," she said immediately. "He's just drugged up."

"Can I talk to him again?"

"He's a horrid conversationalist right now," she said.

I asked my mother what exactly had happened.

"He tripped on the stairs. Tony Forrest came over and took him to the doctor. It's his hip and those damn varicose veins. Tony says Edna St. Vincent Millay killed herself that way."

"With varicose veins?"

"No, stairs. She fell down them."

"Can I speak to him?"

"You should call later in the week. He's resting now."

I felt the distance of miles then. I tried to picture my father under the memory quilt, sleeping, as my mother bustled about the house, making meals out of dry cereal flakes and canned corn.

I was sweating in the closed-up house but too afraid to open a window. Too afraid another death rattle might escape my mother's lungs and seep into the air and wake the women who, like my mother, lived alone and feared such things. The nighttime intruder who comes and kills you. The dutiful daughter who suddenly finds her hand on top of a towel on top of your face, smashing that face in, something inside her hammering over and over again with a child's vendetta finally fulfilled.

I turned on the tap in the kitchen sink again. I waited for the water to heat. I saw the dishes from the early morning washed and put in the dish rack by Mrs. Castle and wondered what made her keep coming to a house like my mother's to help an old woman as the days, then years, passed by.

The Castles had moved to the neighborhood when I was ten. Mrs. Castle became known as the handiest wife while her husband was considered the handsomest man. When the two of them would visit our house to take away the rocking horses for the church fair, my mother and father would sit in the living room with them, each of my parents happily distracted—my father with Mrs. Castle and my mother with Mr. Castle, or Alistair, as she called him, the last syllable when she pronounced it sounding wistful, as if his name were a synonym for regret.

I suddenly knew what I would do. I would clean my mother as I had intended to, but this time without the possibility of protest, without her eyes clicking open like an ancient baby doll's, the starburst blue glass an instant indictment. I did not care anymore about the watery mess it might make on the floor. The critic was dead. Carpe diem!

I leaned down to my right and opened the old metal cabinet. Inside were enough saved-from-the-grocery plastic containers, with their bowed companion tops, to store the hearts and lungs of every citizen along Phoenixville Pike. But I was searching for something else. Something very specific in my memory. I burrowed in and tossed the plastic containers to the side and out the front until, in the very back, where no one had been in years, I found the saved-from-the-hospital sick bowl I was looking for.

It was a pale aqua-green, the color of the surgeon's scrubs. Seeing it again sent shivers down my spine. "He almost died" was always the last line of the story told. It had taken me years to wonder why, if the story was about my father, my mother always ended up as the main character.

I filled the small container with near scalding water and squeezed in a little dish soap. If my mother was greasy, this soap promised to lift it right off her! I shut the water off, took the dish sponge and dish towel, and knelt to my task.

I would start at the bottom and work my way up.

I peeled off my mother's blue men's orthopedic anti-embolism socks and balled them up, resisting an urge to lob them over her body and through the small back hallway that led into the living room. With aim and enough upper-body strength, I could have landed them among the balls of yarn in the basket beside her wing chair. Instead, I placed them to the side, to be dealt with later.

There were her toes, delicate when exposed. I had seen them intimately now for years. Mrs. Castle couldn't be asked to trim her toenails, and so, once a month on a Sunday, I arrived for the tasks of ancillary body maintenance, cleaning and trimming the places my mother had ceased being able to reach. Attending to her feet gave us a peculiar way to revisit the past, a repositioning in which I, by being silent, disappeared from the room, my whole body acting merely as her own hand had once acted. I painted her toenails a coral color from Revlon that, if not an exact match for the one she had applied once a week for forty years, was so close it drew no comment or objection.

I started with her feet by taking the dish towel and dipping it in the scalding water, wringing it out, and wrapping first one foot and then the other. Like a pedicurist, I worked one foot while the other was moistening. With the dish sponge — soft or rough side, depending — I scrubbed and buffed. On my mother's legs I saw the veins I knew lived beneath my own skin and that had recently begun to peek out behind my knees and shins.

"You have murdered your mother, true, but we find her exceptionally clean!" I saw it being sung as if in a musical, where witches held up apples and swung on ropes by their necks.

"It's a hard day, Helen," my mother would say.

"It will be okay, sweetheart," my father would say.

On the day my father died, I had arrived at the house to the sight of my mother cradling his head in her lap at the bottom of the stairs. In the weeks that followed, she talked over and over again about his varicose veins and how much pain they had caused him. How he was stiff in the mornings and often stumbled or tripped over the smallest wrinkle in the carpet. She repeated stories of his clumsiness over the phone to the grocer, who still delivered food to her, and to Joe, my father's barber, whom she had called in a deluded moment after she'd called me. Joe had shown up shortly after I had, worried that my mother might be all alone. He had stood in the front doorway, his mouth open, unable to speak. When our eyes met, he lifted his hand up and accurately made the sign of the cross before turning to leave. Was it from respect or fear that Joe had never commented on the open cleft at the back of my father's head or the arc of blood against the wall?

Slowly I worked my way up to my mother's knees. "They smile at me," Mr. Donnellson whispered to me once, delighted to catch a rare glimpse of my mother in shorts.

A few moments later, I was wiping the shit from my mother's rubbery thighs when I thought of the night my father nailed, straight into a wall upstairs, a list of hastily written rules:

Keep the Upstairs Linen Closet Locked
Do Not Leave Matches in the House
Monitor Booze

It took me a moment, as I thought of the tussles my father and mother frequently had—her in her nightgown and my father still dressed in his workday clothes—to realize that someone was pounding on the front door. I froze. I listened to the brass knocker sound against its base.

I made no noise. I could feel the soapy water seep from the sponge and roll down my arm from wrist to elbow. The small splash of a drop back into the old sick bowl was like a bomb exploding in an open field.

The knocker sounded again. This time there was a rhythm to it, like a friendly, half-familiar song.

In the silence that followed, I was aware of my muscles as I sometimes was when modeling. To hold a pose for a long time, the body had to work its way into stillness — it couldn't be frozen suddenly and kept that way. I tried, as I sensed the person standing on the other side of the door, to imagine myself at Westmore, on top of the art studio's carpeted platforms. My toes burrowed into the mottled brown shag while my elbows, long since inured to carpet burns, supported me.

Again the knocker sounded. Again the happy tune. It was "shave and a haircut, two bits," but this time it was followed by an insistent bang, bang, bang.

I realized whoever it was had been giving my mother time to get to the door between knocks one and two, and even between knocks two and three. It was late, after all. She was an old woman. I stared down at her. She could be sleeping with her gown pushed up around her hips.

"Mrs. Knightly?"

It was Mrs. Castle.

"Mrs. Knightly, it's Hilda Castle. Are you in there?"

Where else would she be? I thought with annoyance. *She's lying on her kitchen floor. Go away!*

Then I heard a rattling on the front window in the living room. The noise of her heavy platinum wedding band against the glass. I had asked her once why she continued wearing it after her divorce. "It reminds me not to remarry," she said.

Only when I heard her voice — a loud whisper — did I realize she had pushed the window open from the outside.

"Helen," she whispered loudly. "Helen, can you hear me?"

Bitch! I immediately thought in solidarity with my mother. What right had she to lift the window sash?

"I know you're here," she whispered. "I see your car."

How very Lord Peter Wimsey of you, I thought.

But my muscles relaxed as I heard the window closing. A few seconds later, I heard Mrs. Castle regain the concrete pathway. I looked at my mother's feet and legs.

"What did you have to give away to her?" I asked. I wasn't thinking of possessions but of the privacy that had always been so precious to my mother. That she had exchanged for the security of Mrs. Castle's daily visit.

I knew that Mrs. Castle would be back in the morning. I knew it as surely as her whispers had caught at my ankles like ropes.

It was obvious that I needed help. I got up slowly and stepped over my mother's body to the phone. I breathed in and closed my eyes. I could see, projected, a reel of film in which the sped-up figures of neighbors and police all clambered into the house. There would be so many of them that they would get stuck in the doors and windows, their limbs jutting out in bent, awkward poses like a group of Martha Graham dancers, only squished together by doorjamb and window sash, and dressed in uniforms or perma-creased tweeds.

I have never liked the phone. Ten years ago, during a misguided fit of self-improvement, I pasted smiley-face stickers on the phone in my bedroom and on the one in the kitchen. Then I typed out two labels and taped them to the handsets. "It's an opportunity, not an attack," they read.

The last address I had for Jake was at a college in Bern, Switzerland, but that had been a temporary teaching post at least three years ago. The easiest way to find Jake was to follow his former students, his acolytes, his day laborers, his worshippers. I knew it might take hours, but I also knew Jake was my only hope.

A body changed rapidly even in the span of a cool October evening, and I could not dispose of my mother by myself.

I hovered near the phone for what seemed like thirty minutes before I picked it up. Knightlys never called for help, and Corbins, my mother's blood, would rather use forks to stab out their throats. We dealt with things in private. We cut off our fingers and feet—our hands, our legs, and our lives—but we did not, no matter what, ask for help. Need was like a weed, a virus, a mold. Once you admitted to it, it spread and ruled.

As I lifted the receiver, I could feel myself as a little girl again, walking into the snow and disappearing, lying down in a giant snowdrift and listening to my mother and father calling for me—liking the sensation as I began to freeze.

FOUR

I was eighteen and in my freshman year of college when I met Jake. He was twenty-seven and the teacher of my art history class.

He could pinpoint the moment, he said, when his heart started helplessly charting a course to my groin.

He had been lecturing on Caravaggio and the idea of lost work when he turned from the board and saw me fumbling with my new glasses. I handled their gold-wire rims like I might a praying mantis, they seemed so strange and delicate to me.

"That night, I dreamed about you. I came into my bedroom, and you were sitting up, reading, with your gold-wire glasses on and all that long black hair. When I reached out for you in the dream, you disappeared."

"I'm sorry," I said, squeezed tightly beside him in the twin bed of my dorm room.

"Then this dog, whom I named Tank and whom my parents wouldn't let me keep, replaced you."

"Woof!" I said.

But I did not know about his dreams until after I'd first posed for him.

I remember the pink wool dress I wore and how soft the mohair felt against my skin. I had dressed up in my best outfit only to go to a room in the art building that smelled of burning coils from an old space heater, and take it off again. Eventually, my camisole and half-slip ended up in Jake's hands as he helped me dress so we could return to my dorm and undress yet again. His fingers, wide like spatulas, were capable of incredible delicacy, but when he held out the satin camisole and slip, they seemed strangely alien to me — the chewed ends of his fingernails, blackened with charcoal and paint, looked harsh against the lace trim I had coveted in Marshall Field's. This was the image I often connected with the loss of my virginity.

When it was time to paint Emily's first bedroom, Jake remembered the donkey that his grandfather had painted on the wall of his own childhood room. Riding on the donkey was a swarthy-looking man with crude features, and strapped over the animal's back was a large double basket that held flowers. What Jake remembered was the fact that, despite the bit in its mouth, the donkey seemed to be smiling, its eye closed in a sort of wakeful sleep.

While Emily lay curled inside me, occasionally kicking, he made the initial steps for the painting — sketching on the walls with charcoal. We had yet to get married and refused to admit that we both secretly worried to do so might be a mistake.

"They say that large, colorful shapes are best," I instructed Jake. "They stimulate the infant brain but don't overtax it."

Jake had dragged our mattress to the middle of the floor so I could lie there and expound such theories while he drew. He had become obsessed with the size of my belly—how Emily announced her presence, inch by inch.

"Total power," he said when he put his hand against me. "And it isn't even here yet. Sometimes I think it's mocking us."

"It is," I said matter-of-factly. "Rounded edges are soothing to baby," I read aloud from a book Mr. Forrest had sent.

"Why are we suddenly following rules?" Jake asked.

"Okay," I said, throwing the book on the floor, where it slid a few feet and then stopped. "Jagged edges make baby happy."

"That's the spirit."

"Knives and guns and depictions of brutality lead baby into the land of nod."

Jake came over to the mattress and joined me.

"Lizzie Borden is a favorite cartoon character for baby. Why not make baby happy and draw her covered in blood?"

"Keep going," he said.

"Pad baby's walls, if needed. Chintz is always nice. And nails. Lots of them."

"I want to fuck you," Jake said.

"Draw."

After we married, in that brief time when I pretended I liked to cook, I would cut the white fat off a slippery chicken breast and spread the flesh out flat on the broiler pan, only to imagine holding my mother's heart. Then I would stare out the window of the house we rented in Madison and see the cars lined up at the traffic light, leading away from campus like humming corpuscles lined up in an artery. It was all I could do to get my mind back and slide the broiler into the oven, knowing that one of the cars on its way to temporary faculty housing contained my husband and that he was coming home.

I was always careful to wash the knife and the cutting board and to hold my hands underwater until they ached red from the heat, so fearful was I of poisoning Jake or of accidentally touching the rim of Emily's baby bottle or blue applesauce bowl.

After I was sure I had washed every utensil and dried it, and the smells of whatever spices I'd culled from the full professor's wife who took pity on us had begun to fill the kitchen, I would have my reward and go into Emily's room. There, I would sit and wait for my new family to come alive when Jake walked in. Emily would be in her crib, facedown in the dead man's pose she most preferred, her diaper peeking up in back like a badly made paper hat. It was in that silence that I relaxed the most, in the short interval between baby sleeping and husband arriving, when I had finished, to the best of my ability, the wifely tasks. School itself seemed far away by then, the diploma I hadn't earned something I would never care about.

I dialed the phone with my back to my mother's body. For some reason I felt disloyal to her. I worried, if I were to turn, that her corpse would be sitting up and raging at me while pulling her skirt back down.

I had read in the paper that Avery Banks, one of the last of Jake's graduate assistants at U–Mad, was now an associate professor of sculpture at Tyler in Philadelphia. I racked my brain for the town the article had said he and his wife bought a house in. He had two children—daughters, I remembered—but in order to find him, I was going to have to engage in random-patterned directory-assistance hell. I called information three times. Finally, in Germantown, there was a listing.

"Is this Avery Banks?" I said when a voice greeted me.

"Who may I say is calling?"

"Helen Knightly," I said. I took my finger and lightly touched the numbers on the phone's base, counting inside my head to calm myself.

"I don't know a Helen Knightly," he said.

"So this *is* Avery then?"

He was silent.

"You knew me as Helen Trevor, Jake Trevor's wife."

"Helen?"

"Yes."

"Helen, it's so good to hear from you. How are you?"

"I need to eat," I said. In the hours since I had come over to my mother's and killed her, I hadn't eaten anything.

"Are you all right, Helen?" he asked. I imagined him standing by his phone with a ski mask on. Avery had favored full-body coverage when he went out in the cold with Jake.

"Something's gone wrong," I said. I could feel my desire to collapse, to blurt out to someone what I had done, where I was, what lay behind me on the floor. "Hold on a minute, Avery."

I turned sharply around, set the receiver on the taped-up high chair, and walked to my mother's body. I was relieved to find that she didn't move. Not even a twitch. I walked back to the phone and turned on the overhead light before picking the receiver back up. Mrs. Leverton would be sleeping now. I needed the chastening effect of the light switched on. As the fluorescent halo buzzed to life above my mother's head, I breathed in deeply and took control. I did not want him to hear so much as a quaver in my voice.

"I need to get in touch with Jake," I said.

"I haven't talked to him in a while," he said. "I do have a number for him, if you like."

"I'll take it."

Avery told me the number, and methodically, I repeated it back. I did not recognize the area code.

"Thank you. I really appreciate it," I said.

"I hope you don't mind my saying this, Helen," he said, "but it wasn't your fault Jake didn't get tenure. I've always worried you might have blamed yourself."

I thought of Avery standing in our living room in Madison. How he and Jake packed boxes and carried them silently out to Avery's Ford. I saw Avery going toward the white pickup, carrying the hand-me-down bassinet.

"Sarah, our youngest, is singing jazz at a nightclub in New York," I lied. "She's quite accomplished at what she does."

"That's great."

There was a silence on the line that neither of us filled.

"Thank you again, Avery."

"Be well," he said. I heard the beep of his phone as he hung up.

I closed my eyes and kept the phone to my ear until a recorded voice came on, informing me that the phone was off the hook. I saw myself in Wisconsin, walking out from behind the scrim of trees that surrounded Jake's ice dragon. All the full professors from the college had gathered to see it before the thaw set in, even the dean. I had ruined it by inadvertently breaking the transparent spine along its back. Later that night, the fight that unraveled us began. Suddenly, I could not imagine calling him.

Using my fingers, I felt along the wall to switch off the buzzing halo. I knelt once more to my task, and with the dripping sponge in hand, I hovered at the edge of my mother's underwear.

I peeled down her old-fashioned panties. They came away in my hands, the elastic shot through on both legs. I had grown used to the smell of her by now, a sort of fecal-mothball combo, with a sprinkle here and there of talc.

In order to remove her underpants, I ripped them open, and her body jiggled just a bit. I thought of the bronze statues that artists cast to resemble people doing everyday things. A bronze golfer to meet you on the green. A bronze couple to share a bench with you in a city park. Two bronze children playing leapfrog in a field. It had become a cottage industry. *Middle-Aged Woman Ripping Underpants off Dead Mother.* It seemed perfect to me. One could commission it for a schoolyard, where students ran from the building after working all morning with numbers and words. They could climb on the two of us at recess or drown flies in the dew that pooled in my mother's eyes.

And there it was, the hole that had given birth to me. The cleft that had compelled the mystery of my father's love for forty years.

This was not the first time I'd been face-to-face with my mother's genitalia. In the last decade, I had become my mother's official enema-giver. She would lie down, in a position not dissimilar to the one she now held, and after massaging her thighs and reassuring her that it would not hurt, I would open her legs. Working quickly, I would execute the doctor's orders and then descend the stairs alone, walking like a robot to the refrigerator, where I scarfed down leftover cubes of lime Jell-O and stared out the window into the backyard.

I placed the sponge back in the aqua-green sick bowl and rose from the floor. I drained the old water out and refilled it with fresh hot water, squirting in more soap. Then I took the kitchen scissors down from the magnetized knife rack above the sink and knelt again to my work.

The green night-light above the stove and the light of the moon coming through the window were my only companions. With the scissors, I sliced my mother's skirt from hem to waist. I laid it open on either side of her. I began, ever so gently, to bathe her hips and belly, her thighs and the virtually hairless cleft. I dipped the cloth and sponge repeatedly into the scalding soapy water and stopped over and over again to change it, wishing for the bathtub in the work shed, for a place we could lie together, as if I were a child again and she was stepping in behind me in the tub.

Finally, when I had removed all evidence of her accident and retrieved a fresh sponge from where they were kept above the fridge, I unbuttoned my mother's loose cotton shirt. I sliced away the straps of her old putty-colored bra. I squeezed out clean water from the sponge onto her breastbone.

Without the bra supporting it, my mother's remaining breast had fallen so far to the side that her nipple almost grazed the floor. Her mastectomy scar, once a dark slash, was now barely a wrinkled whisper of flesh. "I know you suffered," I said, and after kissing the fingertips of my hand, I traced them along her scar.

I must have been a teenager. It was still years before my father's death. Years before she called me over to feel the hard mass just beneath her armpit. I was standing in the doorway, watching them.

"You know how hard it is for me," my mother said to my father, tears streaming down her face. "Only *you* know."

She had unbuttoned her shirt and held it open to him. "Clair!" he gasped. She had rubbed a bloody wound in the center of her chest. I always thought of it as an adult's version of chicken, which was a game we played at school. Another kid would rub his nail across the inside of your wrist two hundred times. If you couldn't bear it after the benign rubbing turned into a ribbon of blood, you yelled, "Chicken!" and were known by the name.

"Get your mother a warm towel," my father said to me, and I bowed my head down. Getting the key to the linen closet from its secret place, I retrieved a fresh towel and ran the water in the bathroom until it grew warm.

The scar from what Jake had called her "martyr's stigmata," I would neither bathe nor touch.

I lifted her arms and cleaned the hairless armpits. I swept the sponge over the cap of her shoulders as I lowered her arms back down. I took my free hand and placed it under the drifting solitary bosom. What once was part of the glory she carried was now a lonely sack with the weight of feathers packed in the droopy corner of an old pillow. A surge of lust shot through me as I held it, as pure as an infant's appetite.

The rose trellis that climbed up the back of our house was lush with vines and flowers by the time I was six or seven. The trellis surrounded both of the small windows in my bedroom, and so at the height of spring, my mother had to keep the flowers and shoots artfully trimmed. It was an operation I loved watching and so, I grew to realize, had my father. The two of them came into my bedroom. She was holding a basket with the handle looped over her arm. Her clippers and work gloves were tucked inside.

"Time for a little high-wire gardening," my father said, and the two of them approached the first window, which was over an empty twin bed next to mine. I lay on the soft maw of my mattress and watched my father watching my mother as the window took the top half of her body. It cut off her head, her hands, her arms, and her shoulders until, at its most extreme, when she was leaning backward, resting her hips against the window ledge, my father held on to her in a way I knew even then to be sexual. Sometimes he slid his hand up along her thigh. Once or twice I thought I heard a smile in her voice along with her admonishment.

Outside, there was a scuffle in the trees and then a cat's low growling. Bad Boy was facing down another cat at the edge of our property.

I stood again and walked to the kitchen sink to dump and

replace the water. I thought of the uncared-for bodies that lay strewn in the streets and fields of Rwanda or Afghanistan. I thought of the thousands of sons and daughters who would like to be in the position I was in. To have known exactly when their mothers died, and then to be alone with their bodies before the world rushed in.

I listened to the cats' intermittent noises in the trees near the work shed. When I was growing up, there had been a hoot owl that came around every year and sat in the oak out back. My father would stand in the yard, holding me piggyback style, and hoot back at it. If it grew late and we stayed in the yard, my mother would join us, with lemonade for me and a neat scotch for the two of them.

I turned, resigned to finish quickly now, when the phone rang. I dropped the bowl, and the hot soapy water splashed out across the floor.

"Hello?" I said softly, as if the house were sleeping.

"You're there!"

"Jake," I said, "how did you know?"

"I couldn't get you at your house, and I still have your mother's number in my address book. How are you?"

I looked at my mother's body. It seemed almost to glow in the darkened kitchen. "Good?" I said.

"Avery just called me. He said something might be wrong."

"And you called here?"

"It seemed the place to start," he said. "What's wrong, Helen? Is it the girls?"

"My mother's dead," I said.

There was silence on his end. He had been my champion against her for the entire eight years of our relationship.

"Oh, Helen, I'm so sorry. When?"

I found I couldn't speak. I made a gulping sound instead.

"I know how much she meant to you. Where are you?"

"We're in the kitchen."

"Who is?"

"Mother and me."

"Oh, Jesus! You need to call someone, Helen. What happened? You need to hang up the phone and dial nine one one. Are you sure she's dead?"

"Very," I said.

"Then call nine one one and tell them that."

I wanted to get off the phone and enter the nowhere state I'd just been in, where no one knew anything and my mother and I were alone together. There was no easy way to say what came next.

"I killed her, Jake."

The silence was long enough that I had to repeat it.

"I killed my mother."

"Describe to me what you mean," he said. "Go slowly, and tell me everything."

I told Jake about Mrs. Castle's calling, about the Pigeon Forge bowl, about my mother's accident. When I said "she had an accident," he stopped me, his voice hopeful, and asked, "What kind of accident, Helen?"

"She lost control of her bowels."

"Oh, God. Before or afterward?" he said.

"And then she called Mrs. Castle a bitch and raved about how people were stealing things from her."

"Are they, Helen?" he asked, his voice leading discreetly into an adjoining room where sanity might dwell.

"No," I said. "She's lying here right in front of me on the floor. I broke her nose."

"You hit her?" I could tell I was shocking him. It made me feel good.

"No, I pressed too hard."

"Helen, are you crazy? Do you hear what you're saying to me?"

"She was dying anyway. She's been sitting up, dying, for the past year. Is it better that she should go to a hospice, babbling, and die in a pool of her own waste? At least I care. At least I'm bathing her."

"You're what?"

"I'm in the kitchen, bathing her."

"Just a minute, Helen. Don't go anywhere."

I could hear the sound of Jake's dogs. Emily had told me that every time she and the children visited, Jeanine spent the next week barking like a dog.

"Helen, listen to me."

"Yes."

"I want you to cover your mother's body and stay in the house until I can get there, okay? I'll get someone to look after the dogs and call you from the airport."

"Mrs. Castle will come in the morning."

"Does she have a key?"

"I don't think so," I said. "There was an incident a few months ago when someone broke in who'd been doing chores here. We got the locks changed, and I think Mrs. Castle never got a new key."

"Helen?"

"Yes."

"You have to listen to me now."

"Okay," I said.

"You can't tell anyone else about this, and you can't go anywhere. You have to stay in the house with your mother until I get there."

"I'm not deaf, Jake."

"You just killed your mother, Helen."

His dogs were whimpering in the background.

"What time is it where you are?" I asked.

"Early enough to get a flight out tonight."

"Where?"

"Santa Barbara. I'm doing a commission piece here."

"For who?"

"It's on private property. I haven't met the people. Helen?"

"Yes."

"What's the temperature there?"

"I don't know. I have all the windows closed."

"Is the corpse still...pliable?"

"What?"

"I'm sorry. I mean has your mother stiffened up yet? How long ago did you...Excuse me." For a moment I thought Jake had hung up the phone, but the jangling noise of the dogs' collars reassured me.

"When did she die?"

"Just before dark."

"And what time is it there?"

I looked up at the clock. "Six forty-five."

"Helen, I have another call. I have to take this. I'll call you back."

I heard the line go dead. I wanted to laugh.

"The art hustle never stops," I said, turning to my mother. For the briefest moment, I expected a response.

I waited by the phone while I stared at her. My mother's face must have been wet under the towel, and this disturbed me. I dropped to my knees and crawled over to her. Without looking, because I was not ready to see her face, I removed the towel in one swift flick of my wrist. I heard her yelling. I heard her calling my name.

I jumped up and walked quickly from the room, through the tiny back hall, and into the living room, where my day had started for a second time, a million years ago.

What had I been doing before Mrs. Castle called? I had gone shopping at the greenmarket in town. I had bought string beans from the elderly Armenian couple who sold only three things out of the back of a small pickup truck. I had gone to my dance class.

I saw the brass ash bin next to the fireplace and went to stand above it. If only I could vomit.

I knew then that my idea of counting on anyone in this was bullshit. What could Jake do, sitting in a rich man's house three thousand miles away? He had taken another call while I stood in the kitchen with my dead mother! "You got yourself into this mess, now get yourself out of it." When exactly had that become my philosophy?

Jake had been asking me questions about temperature and hours and stiffness, and obviously this was all about rot. He'd done enough ice sculptures in the cold capitals of the world to know things I wouldn't have thought of. Couldn't have thought of. Briefly I tried to recall the plot of a movie I'd seen with Natalie last fall. It hinged on whether the death was murder or manslaughter. I could remember the actress's face, her dewy beauty as she broke down on the stand—past that, I couldn't recall a thing.

My mother had been dead too long to cover it up easily, and I had, fatal tell, broken her nose. Now, out of the kitchen and away from her, I saw more clearly the trouble I was in.

I had never been able to do Jake's meditation exercises. I'd sit on the little round black pillow and try to om-out while my feet and hands went into prickly pins and needles. Inside my head, strange figures walked in and out as if my brain were a heavily frequented coffee shop.

I stood on my mother's porch and planted my feet. I could feel the straw from the mat through the soft, wet leather of my jazz flats. I thought of the old Victorian house imploding. I breathed in and out ten times, counting very slowly. I made the exhalation noises I usually ridiculed in yoga class. What I was going to do next could not be misinterpreted. What I was going to do next left me no way back.

It was dark; the cicadas were thrumming in the trees. I could hear the trucks shifting miles away on the ridge of the highway. I knew that, no matter what, I would not be able to stay in the house tonight. I could not wait the hours it would take for Jake to arrive. Besides, as the minutes ticked by, he did not, I noted, call me back.

As I breathed and counted with my eyes wide open, I stared into the house and saw the front hall, the stairs that led up to the three small bedrooms, and the thick padded carpeting that Natalie's son had installed to break a fall.

"We have to make sure the same thing doesn't happen to you that happened to your husband," Hamish had rather witlessly said. He knew the version of events that Natalie had told him—that my father had died when he fell down the hardwood stairs. I had stood by quietly that day, nodding my head, unable to look in my mother's direction.

They would have brought my mother's body out of this house on a gurney, I thought. They would have carried her almost vertically down the steep front stairs. She would have been another lonely old lady who died in her home. How sad. How helpless. How very very high she would rate on people's sympathy curve.

But that was not going to happen. I would make sure of it.

I walked inside. I resisted pausing in the living room to march in place. My muscles were stiff from the time on the kitchen floor, but, posing at Westmore, I had known and recovered from worse. I went upstairs and retrieved a simple white sheet. Then, two at a time, I descended the stairs.

Being careful not to glance at my mother's face, I stood at her feet, briefly bent down to close her legs, and then played the game that first Emily, and then Sarah, had begged me for when I tucked them in at night. A game my father had made up for me.

We called it "waft." I would stand at the end of their beds, with their top sheet balled up in my hands, and then shoot it out over their bodies, allowing it to slowly waft down over them. It was a game that, if given the choice, Sarah in particular never wanted to call an end to. "I love the feel of air escaping all around me," she had told me once.

For my mother, it was a one-time waft, and I did it so the queen-size sheet covered her face. It stuck to her damp body in an almost ghostly way. Hurriedly I repackaged her in the Mexican wedding blanket and the Hudson Bay as if she were a gift I was returning to the store.

I stood and walked into the small back hallway and opened the basement door. Then, holding her under her armpits, I dragged her headfirst to the top of the stairs.

I walked a few steps down in almost pitch-black darkness and flailed my hand along the wall until I found the light switch. The bare bulb at the bottom of the stairs came on. I walked down the rest of the way. These stairs, when I was little, were a dare for neighborhood children and me. Past the first three stairs, both walls fell away, and never, no matter how much one was needed over the years, was a guardrail installed. Hamish had even volunteered to fabricate one out of old pipes after laying down the carpet upstairs. "These stairs are the real death trap," he'd whispered to me when I'd brought him to the basement so he could choose among my grandfather's old guns as payment.

But what had always made the dare of descending into the dark basement worth it was the supersize brown refrigerator at the bottom of the stairs. This was where my mother kept tins of brandy balls and stores of Hershey's bars. Mason jars of pecans and almonds, Christmas boxes of peanut brittle left uneaten, and hideous sherry-soaked fruitcakes given to us each holiday season.

The Levertons gave everyone a box of After Eight mints. Mrs. Donnellson, before she died, would bring my mother a ham.

The ham, like all meats, went in a separate place—the long, low meat freezer that hummed to the right of the stairs, on top of which my mother sorted laundry or stacked magazines she wanted to keep. During my father's life, there was always a shifting parade of objects on top of the meat freezer. He had hoped she'd take up arts and crafts, so there were baskets filled with green foam blocks and giant discarded jug-wine bottles that, if she found the time, might make beautiful terrariums. Acorns, horse chestnuts, boxes of goggle eyes, and distinctly shaped twigs. River rocks polished in my father's workshop. Odd bits of driftwood he'd collected. And a pristine economy-size Elmer's that ruled over it all.

The gun had been my mother's idea.

"What does he want with a gun?" I whispered to her while Hamish was washing up. "Why not cash?"

"He's a grown man," my mother said. "Emily just gave birth to a child."

But by the time I could trace my mother's thought process and figure out that this was my mother's way of pointing out that both Hamish and Emily were adults, the insanity train had left the station and I was in the basement, showing Hamish the rack of guns.

We stood in front of the meat freezer as he took up each rifle and held it in his hands, testing the weight of it.

"I know nothing about guns, except that they're cool," he said.

I was no help. I watched him lean each rifle out of the wooden rack and hold it inexpertly by its stock as if it were a particularly thick-stemmed weed he had pulled from the ground. Hamish, like Natalie, provided the perfect light contrast to my darkness. Until she began to sprout enough gray hair that she chose to color hers what I thought of as an alien shade of red, Natalie had been the blonde to my brunette. When I stood by her son, I saw the same brown eyes his mother had, heard the same easy laugh.

"Why doesn't she sell these things?" Hamish asked. "She could make a mint."

I could barely hear him. He had taken the only pistol out of a felt Crown Royal bag and, holding it, had spread his legs wide as if it were something he'd seen cowboys do. As he aimed at a point on the opposite wall and put his finger to the trigger, I screamed and grabbed the barrel with my hand.

He held on, and we collided. Hamish took my right shoulder in his hand.

"What? You look so upset. What is it?"

I came very close to saying something. Words I had not spoken to anyone but Jake.

"My father taught me not to point a gun at anyone."

"I was pointing it at that lamp shade!"

He set the pistol down behind him on the meat freezer. He cupped my cheek as if I were the child and he the parent. "It's all right," he said. "No one's hurt."

I was shaking. He turned to slip the pistol back inside the purple bag, then cinched the gold braid closed at the top.

"I'll take this one," he said.

With Hamish's help, I put the rifles, which were much more valuable, back in their mounts. The pistol sat in its bag on a stack of starched linen napkins I had folded and left on top of the meat freezer. I remembered turning around and seeing it, imagining the dulled platinum barrel, the scarred brown grip, and thinking of my father lifting it, loading it, raising it to his head.

*   *   *

I positioned my mother's body so that, standing three steps down into the basement, I could grab her around the shoulders and, walking blind and feeling for each stair with my foot, could use my body to keep her from tumbling into the no-man's-land below.

I breathed in and tried to make my muscles strong, not rigid. I pulled my mother's upper body out over the edge of the stairs and walked down one stair and then another. Her weight against me increased with each step. I smelled the lilac scent of her hair through the sheets. I felt my eyes watering but would not blink. Down two, three, four, five. Her bundled feet thumping their arrival.

My mother's cocoon was unraveling. No hospital corners here. Her feet, first cleaned, were poking out of the sheets at the half-way point on the stairs. Her toes seemed blue to me in a way they hadn't before, and I wondered if that was the light of the base-ment playing tricks on me. I took another step. Another. I knew, because I had counted them dozens of times as a child, that there were exactly sixteen steps. I saw the meat freezer humming to my left. On top of it was a stack of *Sunset* magazines, hoarded hand-me-downs from Mrs. Castle, who had relatives on the West Coast. Also left, from the previous Christmas, were the prop gift boxes lined up in rows in their sun-faded finery of ribbons and bows. I imagined Mrs. Castle taking them down the stairs for her, or perhaps it had even been me. My mother may have indeed instructed me to bring them down and put them in the giant plastic bags that she kept them in eleven months of the year. I would have failed to do that for some reason. I would have taken the time the task was supposed to occupy and sat in the old wicker-and-iron lounge chair near the washer and dryer, calculating exactly how many minutes I could let go by before I should reasonably appear upstairs to keep my mother company.

Until she was eighty-six, my mother persisted in using the basement. It was the idea of her becoming disoriented or lacking the energy to climb back out that inspired me to buy her a cell phone. Until then, my mother would descend the first three stairs one at a time, bracing her hands against the wall and preparing herself to go unassisted. Then, setting her jaw, she would pivot and continue down sideways, stair by stair. It could take her thirty minutes to get to the bottom, and by the time she reached the basement floor, she might have forgotten what she'd come for.

But just as Natalie's father thought the ATM would eat his arm, when I'd placed the no-frills phone in my mother's hand on her eighty-sixth birthday, she'd looked from it to me and said, "You're giving me a grenade?"

"It's a phone, Mother," I said. "You can carry it with you everywhere you go."

"Why would I want to do that?"

"So you can always get in touch with me."

She was sitting in her wing chair. I had made her favorite drink, a manhattan, and ruined, she said, her recipe for cheese straws. "I don't know how you do it, Helen." Delicately, she spit a half-chewed cheese straw into her cocktail napkin. "You have a gift."

On top of the old mahogany dresser, beside the brown refrigerator, I saw the cell phone, where it had been for the last two years. She'd left it there the morning after her eighty-sixth birthday, which was also the last time she'd been in the basement. I'd seen it at least once a week for the last two years. In the irrational way

I'd always experienced her rejection, I'd ended up thinking that in order to avoid talking to me, she'd renounced an entire floor of her home.

Despite my going slowly, my mother's body swung out in an arc as the stairwell fell away halfway down. I watched the sheets unravel as her suddenly exposed lower half twisted backward onto the gritty cement floor. I held on despite the sounds—like Bubble Wrap being popped all at once—and rushed backward to the bottom, pulling her with me.

It was then that I heard the phone ringing in the kitchen.

I dragged her body free of the stairs and over to the meat freezer. I laid her lengthwise by the freezer's side, then hurriedly did my best to cover her again. The sheets were twisted beneath her. No matter what I did, after folding and draping, her marbling knees were exposed. She lay there, silent and broken, and I thought of the horror that had finally come with control.

When I was a teenager, I thought every kid spent sweaty summer afternoons in their bedrooms, daydreaming of cutting their mother up into little pieces and mailing them to parts unknown. I did this both prone upstairs and gymnastically about the house. As I agreed to take out the trash, I cut off her head. As I weeded the yard, I plucked out her eyes, her tongue. While dusting the shelves, I multiplied and divided her body parts. I was willing to allow that other kids might stop short of this, that they might not, as I did, work out all the details, but I could not imagine that they did not explore this territory.

"If you want to hate me, I encourage it!" I would say to Emily.

"Yes, Mom," she'd say. At six, she was already in possession of a nickname based on her greater reasonableness, her steely patience. "The Little Senator," Natalie had dubbed her for her practical negotiations in the world of the sandbox, where Hamish, though her peer in age, was prone to tantrums and would often sit and cry.

I grabbed at the prop boxes on the meat freezer and threw them in groups and singly into various corners of the basement, to keep temptation at bay. Even growing up, I'd known that the boxes inside the faded wrapping paper and frequently refreshed bows would not hold what I wanted most. They would leak from their seams or be smashed if the postman happened to fall on a slippery patch when delivering my mother's shin to a printing plant in Mackinaw, Michigan, or her foot to a trout farm outside Portland. Always, in my daydreams, I kept for myself her thick red hair.

I carefully placed the *Sunset* magazines on the edge of a nearby stair. Inside the meat freezer were the lean meat patties that my mother ate on her resumption of the Scarsdale diet five years ago, and two ancient hams from Mrs. Donnellson. I knew this without looking.

I turned the key in the meat freezer's lock and opened it. There it was, an almost-empty ice cavity for one.

Jake had asked me questions concerning lividity, stiffness, what signs there might be of how she had died, but I was done with that. I had now not only broken her nose but managed to mangle her body postmortem. There was no reason why I shouldn't fulfill my childhood dreams.

"At what point did you give up?" I said out loud, my voice, as I said it, startling me. In the corner opposite was the metal cabinet, full of my father's old suits. Tattersall; summer seersucker; flannel; dark, itchy wool tweed. I remembered the day I'd come down to fold the laundry several years ago, and opened up the cabinet. When I crawled inside, I was a child again, my upper body encased in his old suit coats. I had taken the tweed, with its suede elbow patches, and rubbed it along my cheek.

The cool air coming up from the meat freezer felt good against my face. I saw the amber bottles set on the windowsill above the washer to keep belly-crawling burglars out. I saw the purple glass bottles on the ledge of its mate.

I had never thought of how one cut up a body, only of the freedom to be had postsevering. The grisly reality of the sawing and the butchering had never preoccupied me. It was the instant flash, the twitched nose of *Bewitched,* the magic of going from having my mother to not having her that held me in its thrall. More than butchering her, if I could have chosen it, I would have changed her body from solid to liquid to gas. I wanted her to evaporate like water. Rising up out of my life and leaving everything else intact.

"If you aren't careful," my mother would say, "you'll fall in." At eleven, twelve, thirteen, I would be in the kitchen, leaning over, looking into the refrigerator for what I could eat. I perused the food with such care only when I thought it was safe. At other times I tried to act as if food didn't matter to me, as if it were too much of a bother. "Oh! There! That's food? Hmmm." But with my head in the refrigerator, I was the perfect prey, and as she listed my flaws—the ballooning ass, the "near matronly" thighs, the swinging arms I'd eventually have, like "a dimpled flesh bat," if I went on in my way—I would look at the tiny light in the refrigerator and wonder, *Could I move in there? Could I hide behind the cottage-cheese container and the orange juice made from concentrate?* It would be quiet inside the refrigerator once my mother closed the door. I could disappear in there.

I was staring into the meat freezer, at the millions of ice crystals built up along its sides and covering the two hams and lean patties in a shimmering mink of ice, and then I wasn't. Out of the corner of my eye, I saw the blue Pigeon Forge bowl.

"Mrs. Castle, will you take that downstairs?" I could hear my mother saying. "Maybe bring something else up."

I walked over to the card table and picked up the bowl. Nearby, hanging from a hook on the wall, I found a heavy rusted pair of shearing scissors. I turned the bowl upside down on the table and brought the handle of the scissors down hard, like a hammer. The blue-glazed shards scuttled off the table and across the floor.

I could not cut my mother up, so I walked over to her body and bent down near her head. I hovered over her briefly, then unwrapped the blankets around her face. There were her eyes, staring up at me, milky and blue. With the scissors poised in my right hand, I dug out her silver braid and sheared it off at the root.

FIVE

While my mother lay on the floor only a few feet away, I opened the old brown refrigerator and sat on the bottom step of the stairs with its light shining on me.

I grabbed blindly at the metal tins, not looking at the age-old and carefully punched-out labels. I ripped off their worn lids and sent them crashing to the concrete floor like spinning cymbals. Then, and only then, when faced with the used and reused wax paper, did I slow down and lift that first layer lightly away from what lay beneath. Here were brandy balls from my Tennessee grandmother's recipe. Or pecan meringues that smelled of dark-brown sugar. Baking together was something we did until the end, even though, for the sake of my figure and my mother's health, I routinely had to cycle through the freezer and dispose of what we'd made, pretending to my mother that I was giving the contents of the tins to the neighbors whom she still confusedly remembered living in the area.

I held a meringue and crumbled it in my hand. I watched the

light-tan dust and minced nuts fall to the ground. Always the admonition to use a plate, not to gobble like a turkey, to measure the heft and weight and imagine it applied to my waist.

The first time I had made myself sick as a child—purposely sick—was the year I turned eight. My weapon of choice was fudge. I had gone into the kitchen and methodically, like a soldier taking bullets in the gut, eaten a whole baking sheet of butterscotch fudge. I was ill for two days, and she was furious, but it had made my father laugh. He had come home and hung up his jacket on the coatrack inside the door; placed his hat, on which he often changed the small clipped feather that was tucked inside the band, on the front table; and turned toward the dining room.

"What are you doing there all alone?" he asked.

I had been forced to sit at the table, though all I wanted to do was lie down and moan.

"She's being punished," my mother had said, as she walked briskly over to him and took his briefcase from his hand. "I made butterscotch fudge, and she ate it all."

A particular intimacy of my father's came when he removed his glasses. The metal-and-plastic frames bit into his nose on either side, and he would take them off when he walked in the house. For thirty minutes he was as blind as a bat, but he didn't need accuracy, as this was the half hour before dinner reserved for a drink.

He had done this that day, as usual, but he had also laughed, as he usually did not, and it had come from someplace deep inside him. During this, he had grabbed my mother and kissed her hard on the cheek and then leaned down and kissed me on the forehead through my wispy bangs.

Working at the Pickering Water Treatment Plant, he measured water levels and analyzed the content of the local reservoirs. He traveled to surrounding cities and all the way to Erie to do the same.

"It's a little like you sat down and decided to eat a baking sheet full of sediment," he said. "Anyone would be ill from that."

I had asked him to stay at the table with me, to talk about water, about how each droplet under a microscope differed from another. His eyes were unfocused without his glasses, and I wondered how blind he was and what he saw when he looked at me.

I walked up the basement stairs and into the kitchen, the braid swinging from my fist. I pulled open the drawer near the phone, which held refolded tinfoil and salvaged twist ties, and found a gallon-size Ziploc freezer bag. I tucked the braid inside, sealed it, and scanned the kitchen. My mother's clothes lay balled up in moist clumps along the floor.

When I was three years old, I had come into the kitchen and found my mother sitting on the floor, with her legs jutting out in front of her. I could see her underwear, which I had never seen before. She was staring at a white spill of flour at her feet.

"Mom made a boo-boo," I said.

She stood up and grabbed the five-pound sack of flour from the counter, hugging it to her chest. She scooped her hand into it and let the contents fall from her fingers like snow.

I shrieked in delight and ran to her. She responded by moving away just as I reached out for her. She threw more flour from the sack, this time in wide arcs across the kitchen. I chased her in spinning circles, around and around, shrieking louder and gulping back my own laughter.

The chase went on until I stumbled and fell. I looked up at her for a moment. She stood near my high chair, laughing. I noticed the flour on her forehead and chin, and how it coated the invisible hairs on her forearms. I wanted her to come to me to pick me up, and so I wailed at the top of my lungs.

*   *   *

My purse sat upright on the dining room table. I tucked the Ziploc bag, with its silver prize, inside the center compartment and, as if I might forget something, looked all around me, doing a 360-degree turn. I jumped when I saw Mr. Fletcher in a lit-up window, staring back at me, until I realized I had not turned on a light in the dining room and that he was staring not at me but at a computer terminal, which, as he searched the Internet or played the same Byzantine games that Emily's husband liked, lit his face in flashes of blue and green.

When I reached my car and looked back up the brick path to the front door, the light dusting of white powder on my chest and legs—the sugar from the pecan meringues, the flour from the Mexican wedding wafers—was the only thing that marked me as having been in my mother's basement.

I wanted to weep, but instead I thought of where I could go. I had to relax. No one knew except Jake. What felt like other people's knowing—the call to Avery, the questioning from Mrs. Leverton, the whispering of my name by Mrs. Castle—wasn't. And no one would go into the house without me there.

I sat in my ancient Saab with the windows rolled up and placed my purse on the passenger seat, resisting the impulse to strap it in like a child. I put the key in the ignition and started the car. Slowly I pulled away, hunching over the steering wheel as if the streets were dense with fog.

Mrs. Leverton's house was dark except for the timer lights her son had installed. The clock on the dashboard read 8:17. Time for old women to be tucked in. But apparently not old men. As I drove by Mr. Forrest's house, I could see him reading in his front room. All his lights were on. He had never believed in blinds.

At least in the old days, he had always had dogs. *There he is,* I thought to myself, *an old man vulnerable to bullies and thieves.*

I was sixteen that day in Mr. Forrest's house, when I'd first seen color plates of women in various states of undress.

"They call them muses, Helen," he had said as he watched me turn the pages of an outsize book called simply *The Female Nude.* "They are women who inspire great things." I had thought of the pictures that stood throughout our house. Pictures of my mother in outmoded support garments or diaphanous peekaboo gowns, smiling winsomely into the camera.

The thirty-minute drive between my mother's house and my own had always been an excuse for talk. Some people talk to themselves in front of their mirrors at home, psyching themselves up to ask for a raise or undertake a self-improvement project. I had always talked to myself most inside the car on the back roads that led from Phoenixville to my suburban faux colonial in Frazer. The halfway point, mentally, if not physically, was Pickering Creek and the small one-lane bridge that crossed it.

The night I killed my mother, I sang to myself in a low hum in an effort to create a sort of white noise in between me and what I had done. Every so often I would say, "You're okay, you're okay, you're okay," as I pressed more tightly on the wheel to feel the squeeze of blood that pulsed at the ends of my fingertips.

At Pickering, I waited on the Phoenixville side for a beaten-up Toyota to pass by, and as I crept over the bridge, my car lurched up briefly on the patched road. My headlights seemed to catch something moving in the limestone ruins on the other side. It looked like a man, lit up and dancing over the dark rock, and I shivered in my clothes.

On the other side of Pickering, the trees were thinner and denser, and struggled during the day to get any sun through the crowded canopy above. A decade ago, excavation crews became a common sight here, and I would drive by to see one hundred birch saplings having been mown to the ground. I hated to say that Natalie's house, which was halfway between my mother's and my own, was one of the McMansions that had been carved out of these woods. It shouted up out of the forest, with mock storybook turrets and a front door fifteen feet tall.

Natalie and the now thirty-year-old Hamish had lived inside this gingerbread palace for eight years, ever since Natalie successfully sued the manufacturer that supplied the tires to her husband's truck. He had been idling on Pickering Bridge in a stare-down with another car and had revved his engine. His front tire exploded, breaking the axle and ejecting him through the windshield, and he hit his head on the old fieldstone bridge that had lain in ruins for more than a century. He died instantly.

Through the scrim of young white-barked trees that had grown back since the developers came and went, I saw Hamish lying in the driveway, one of his many cars ratcheted up, with a bright cage light hanging from the front fender. I slowed down and brought my car to a halt. Without a thought for what I would say when I saw her, I swung my car off the empty road and drove up the length of Natalie's driveway. I seemed to be doing almost explicitly what Jake had told me not to, but I couldn't stop myself.

As my headlights mingled with the glow from the broken car, Hamish rolled himself out on his mechanic's dolly and motioned for me to switch them off.

I turned off the ignition and got out. My first steps were wobbly on the gravel drive.

Hamish ducked toward me, flipping his hair to the side of his face.

"Mom's out," he said.

I had never stopped thinking of Hamish as the boy who played with Emily in the sandbox in the community park at the end of my street. "Hamish is going nowhere—fast," Natalie said in the years after Hamish Sr.'s death. She seemed happy about it. As if she'd lost one Hamish, but this Hamish was sure to stick around.

"Out where?"

"She's on a date," Hamish said, and smiled. His teeth were as white as stadium lights. Natalie had told me that he bleached them every six months.

I didn't know which was stranger, that I found myself in the driveway of my oldest friend after killing my mother or that Natalie had gone on a date without telling me.

"I just remembered I wasn't supposed to say anything," he said. "Don't tell her, Helen. I don't want to get her mad at me."

"No worries," I said—two ridiculous words that I had picked up from an Australian-born administrator at Westmore. It applied to everything. "The kiln has exploded." "No worries." "I'm canceling Thursday's Life Drawing class." "No worries." "I've murdered my mother, and she's rotting as we speak."

"Seriously, Hell," Hamish said. He had picked up the nickname habit at Valley Forge Military Academy, where Hamish Sr. had forced him to go to develop moral fiber.

"I'm not feeling too well, Hamish," I said. "I'm going to sit down."

I opened up my car door again and positioned myself sideways with my feet on the gravel. I bent from the waist and propped my body up with my elbows on my knees.

Hamish squatted down beside me. "Are you okay?" he asked. "Should I call Mom?"

The light from the hanging lantern came beneath my open car door to illuminate what met the ground. I saw Hamish's shoes in the dust and my own thoroughly filthy jazz flats. I edged them off with my toes while Hamish watched. I thought of the day in the basement when he had cupped my cheek.

"Will you lie on top of me?" I asked.

"What?"

I looked up at him, at his beautiful prematurely creased face, the freckles that peppered his nose and cheeks from too much time in the sun, his blazing white teeth.

"You trust me, right?" I said.

"Sure."

I did not stop to wonder what I looked like. I stood up, and so did he. I opened the door to the back and crawled in across the bench seat.

"Get in," I said.

I thought of my mother on the cold cement floor. I lay on my back with my feet hanging out over the drive. Hamish crawled in but sat on the edge of the seat with the open door behind him.

"I'm not sure what this is," he said.

"I'm cold," I said. "I just want to feel your body on top of me."

I wanted to fuck him.

I closed my eyes and waited. A moment later, I could feel Hamish gingerly—too gingerly—place his body over me. He was bracing himself against the backseat and still resting most of his weight on the floor.

"I don't know what you want," he said.

"I want all of you on me," I said, opening my eyes.

"Hell," he said. "I'm . . ." He glanced down his body instead of finishing the sentence.

"Just put your full weight on me," I said. "It's fine."

And then, within a moment, his body—all, what was it, 185, 190 pounds?—was laid out on top of me and pressing down. I felt his erection against me, the tops of my feet jostling the middle of his shins, his face to my right, his ear a seashell tunnel beside mine. I thought of the phone in my mother's kitchen. How many times had it rung before stopping?

I brought my right hand up and ran it along his side until I found the edge of his T-shirt, then slipped my hand up under it and onto his bare skin. He grunted beside me, an animal waiting to be touched. Sarah had had a crush on Hamish, growing up.

"We can do anything," I said.

It was as if I'd turned a key. He raised his head. His eyes looked dreamy and distant in a way I'd never seen the eyes of my best friend's son.

"Sure, baby," he whispered, and I tried not to hear the tone in his voice. A tone I was aware he adopted with the women I'd seen riding on the back of his motorcycle. They wore ludicrous shorts while wrapped around Hamish's Kevlar-encased torso and legs. I tried to picture myself clinging on to him. He had more than once invited me to do so, but I had always declined. "He has the hots for you," Natalie had said once, and the two of us had laughed together as we drove off to some sort of pitiless exercise class while Hamish peeled off in the opposite direction on his Japanese death machine.

His lips were pendulous, ridiculous, young. I reached my arm up and pulled his head down to kiss them. I was beginning to feel his weight, his bones against my bones. I would have wished it could be different than this, that I could have fucked my best friend's son without having to be made aware of it. I tunneled into it, firmly now, as I realized thinking was not going to get me anywhere. Morality was just a security blanket that didn't exist. All of it, what I had done and what I was doing, was not leading me perilously toward the edge of a cliff. I had already jumped.

I tugged upward at Hamish's shirt, and taking his weight away from me for a moment, he peeled it off over his head. He was beautiful, his chest muscular and divoted, but his beauty was as much about youth and a life still ahead of him as anything else. I felt a stab of regret.

I turned my eyes away from his face and unbuttoned my pants. As he rushed to help, he bumped his head on the inside of the passenger-side door. It made a horrible hollow sound. I thought of Mrs. Leverton hitting the ground outside her house six months ago. How she had called through the bushes to my mother to get help. How the enemies had fleetingly bonded. They were desperate to be able to continue living on their own in their own houses.

Mrs. Leverton thought I was a degenerate, a failure as a wife who modeled nude for a living, but in one solid sense she was envious of my mother. Mrs. Leverton had a son who wanted to do everything for her, but "everything" was an assisted-living facility attached to a nursing home with a pricey hospice program. "Everything" was paving the road to her death with his money. He would line her way to the grave with gold when all she really wanted was to be allowed to die in her own home.

"Jesus," Hamish said. He rubbed the back of his head and left my pants to fester around my ankles, the immediacy dangerously threatened once again.

I bit my lip. I writhed. "Fuck me," I said, and hoped that no one's God was watching.

This brought him back. He stared at me. "Wow," he said. With a final tug, he threw my pants onto the gravel drive. I winced when he ripped off my underpants. They were not high waisted or gauzy or old like handmade paper, but his stripping me cut too closely to what I'd just done to my mother. I propelled myself up and grabbed for Hamish's penis, which had poked above the waistband of his briefs.

As soon as I had my hand on it, I tugged him forward and down. He moaned in pleasure as I spread my legs and wrapped myself around him. "Oh fuck, oh fuck, oh fuck!" he wailed. I lay there in disbelief. He had ejaculated on my stomach. My fingers, sticky and enraged, squeezed. "Ow," he said, and placed a hand on my wrist. "Let go."

He moved around, flattening one of my knees painfully with his ass, until he was sitting on the seat behind my legs with his own legs bent up in a tent above them. I smelled the fetid smells of the backseat, where the crisp scent of my greenmarket groceries mingled with the danker smell of my ancient gym bag.

"Shit, I'm sorry," he said. "This is intense."

I lay there. Suddenly I was beside my mother in the basement. Mrs. Leverton was coming down the stairs with After Eight mints spread out in a decorative circle on an old enamel tray. The phone was ringing in the kitchen, and Manny was upstairs dropping condoms like so much rain.

"Will you take me to Limerick?" I said, as if I were asking to be voluntarily committed to an asylum just over the hill. I would not look at him. Did not want to see his face. Instead I looked at the square-cornered tear in the back of the passenger seat and tried to recall how it had gotten there.

Hamish was kind, even if motivated by an unnecessary shame. "Do you want to wash up?"

"I'll stay here," I said.

I could feel him wanting to say something but resisting. "I'll bring you a towel," he said, and I nodded my head at him, both to say yes to the towel and to make him, for the moment, go away.

I lay in the backseat and listened to the night noises surrounding me, thought of fucking Jake in Madison in the VW Bug. Avery would come and sit for the girls, and we would go to a dark spot at the edge of the U–Mad campus and leave the AM radio playing low while we made love.

I wanted to be looking up at the sky, but instead I was looking up at the waffled roof of my Saab. The cool night air rushed in the open door at my feet, and I shivered, drawing myself up and turning over to lie in a fetal position and stare at the back of the front passenger seat, where my mother's braid lay tucked inside my purse.

I had once read one of Sarah's true-crime books that she'd left at the house. It was a book about a serial killer named Arthur Shawcross, and the most vivid thing in it, for me, was the portrait of a woman whom he had obviously meant to kill but who was too smart for him. She was old for a prostitute and still doing speedballs and getting high. She'd gotten high for three days straight after Shawcross tried to strangle her while raping her in his car. He was a man who picked up a prostitute, drove to a deserted spot, and killed her after he was unable to perform. She had known how to talk to him, known how to brace herself so that his hands, enclosed around her neck, could not produce the leverage needed to crush her windpipe. And she had known that her survival was connected intimately with his ability to ejaculate. It had taken hours, or so she said, and it was arduous, but he was grateful enough that he didn't kill her and instead drove her back to the spot where he'd picked her up.

"How can you read such things?" I asked Sarah over the phone, brandishing, as if she could see me, the consumed-in-one-night book.

"It's real," Sarah had said. "There's no bullshit."

Hamish returned, smelling of Calvin Klein's Obsession for Men, which it embarrassed me to know. He ducked in the backseat and held out a small blue hand towel. I looked at it in horror, but I did not reach for it.

"That's okay," I said. "I'm good."

Again a quizzical look came across his face, but instead of asking me a question, he broke into a smile.

"You like having it on you," he said.

"Hamish," I said, sitting up and scrambling out of the car to find my pants and underwear, "your job is not to make me throw up."

"Harsh," he said.

"What I mean is that I'm still your mother's friend, and your seduction lines are calibrated for women half my age."

"If that," he said.

"Touché," I said, and zipped up my pants while slipping on my flats.

"You've got to admit this isn't our usual way of relating."

"We'll take my car," I said. "I'll drive. You go around the side."

"Sweet. Mom always makes me drive."

I sat down behind the wheel and whisked my purse off the passenger seat, tucking it by my side. I pictured an eight-year-old Hamish running to my car with a wild smile on his face. He had been smitten with Emily from the first time they'd met when they were two. I looked out the window at the full-grown man whom I had almost just fucked and who was now walking around to the passenger door. I didn't know who I was anymore or what I was capable of.

He swooped in and kissed me on the cheek.

"Buckle up," I said, my spine stiff against the soft and mealy seat.

I backed out of the driveway, the gravel crunching under my tires. It was Leo's baby carrier that had torn the hole in the back of the passenger seat. I had struggled to get it inside the car on the day my mother dropped him, trying to show Emily I could take care of it while she stood on the sidewalk, clasping Leo to her chest and shouting, "It doesn't matter, Mother! Leave it! Leave it!" until I shoved the carrier in and slammed the door. Inside the car, I turned and saw a spot of blood seep through Leo's blue baby bonnet. When I'd called to tell my parents I was pregnant for the second time, my mother had yawned extravagantly and said, "Aren't you bored yet?"

"Who is Natalie out with?" I asked as I swung the car onto the road and started off.

"Shit," Hamish said. "Don't make me tell you."

But I didn't want to talk about what had happened between us. "Okay, can we talk about your father instead? Are you ever happy that he died?"

"Man, what's with you? I'm sorry about back there, but chill out, okay? I want to make you happy."

"Sorry, I just came from my mother's house."

"Oh."

It was roundly known that my mother and I had problems with each other, that I attended her by duty, but now I had done something stupid, I knew. I had given Hamish knowledge of my previous whereabouts. I was a lousy criminal, and he was a lousy lay. We were perfect together.

"It's good with my mom," Hamish said. "We get along, and living together works for us. It was harder with Dad."

"You don't have to," I said, feeling guilty now.

"I'll tell you if you want."

I remembered Hamish as a toddler then, how he would allow Emily to boss him around and how, over time, she took advantage of this in a way I didn't like. He was that same boy now. He would tell me what I wanted to know in the same way he would endlessly give his toys to my small daughter or bring her, on demand, bucket after bucket of sand for building Barbie castles. Natalie and I had pretended only briefly that the two of them would grow up to be married. At a certain point we both realized that neither of us knew the first thing about what made a good marriage.

"You know your father and I didn't get along," I said.

We had driven out of the McMansions-set-in-birches section and were passing through the long no-man's-land of one-story warehouses and shabby '50s-era community halls.

"That's not unusual for you," Hamish said, looking straight ahead.

"What?"

"If you call 'mostly ignoring me' getting along," he said.

"I've never ignored you," I said.

"I know what you think of me."

"Which is?"

"That I'm lazy. That I'm a drain on my mom. Stuff like that."

I was silent. Everything he said was true. I pulled off Phoenixville Pike and onto Moorehall Road. I was taking the long way round.

"I'm a real bitch, huh?" I said.

Hamish laughed. "You know what? You kind of can be."

I slowed the car down and scanned the lot of Mabry's Grill for Natalie's car.

"He picked her up in a Toyota four-by-four," Hamish said.

I cleared my throat and put my turn indicator on for Yellow Springs.

"My dad was horrible in a lot of ways," Hamish said. "I don't miss the screaming between them and between me and him. He hated me."

It was the moment to say "No, he didn't" or "I'm sure that's not true," but I wouldn't. Hamish may have needed a tantric-sex tutorial, but his sense of the truth was exact.

"My mom's glad," Hamish said. "Though she wouldn't say it to me. His great dream was to move back to Scotland someday."

"How can she stand to live so near the bridge?" I asked.

"I'll tell you what I think," Hamish said. "I think it's because she wants to be there in case his spirit rises out of Pickering Creek so she can bash it over the head."

"That's how I feel about my mother," I said.

"I know," Hamish said, and reached out to touch my hair.

How long would it take Jake to get to Pennsylvania? The flight was at least five hours, maybe more. He was coming from Santa Barbara, not Los Angeles or San Francisco. There was too much I didn't know. I wanted to tell Hamish this: that the very same afternoon Jake had met my mother, he'd turned to me and said, "Why didn't you tell me she was nuts?" And how it had been like a curtain parting for the first time onto a larger world, the beginning of the great divide between Jake's and my mother's love. The force that, if I had let it, would have ripped me apart.

"She met him on the Internet—Mom's date," Hamish said. "He's a contractor from Downingtown."

"What?"

"She was afraid you'd judge her. I think she wants to get married again."

We passed the gravel yards and one or two low-lying buildings that, for as long as I'd lived in the valley, I'd never seen anyone enter or leave. These buildings sported two large *V*s on their corrugated windowless outsides and were protected by electrified fencing.

"Remember?" I said, nodding toward the steel buildings.

"I just wanted to get in because they were keeping us out," Hamish said. "I wasn't going to steal anything."

"A Toyota four-by-four, huh?"

"Helen, judge? Helen never judges. She loves everything!"

"Bitch?" I asked.

"Grade A."

"Who would want less?" I said, laughing.

"That's why Dad sent me to Valley Forge," he said after a

moment had passed. And my heart saw Hamish in his most difficult years. How he had tried to make his father happy and repeatedly failed, how when the three of them came to dinner at my house, he had made a point of sitting at the very edge of his chair, "like real soldiers do," and how he'd beamed as he passed the lamb chops to Emily. "You're not a real soldier," his father had said, heaping mint jelly on his plate as an awkward silence descended on the table.

On the other side of Vanguard Industries was the remnant of a town established in the years before the Revolutionary War, with additions being made sporadically after that until the end of the 1800s. Only seven buildings remained, and these were all on one side of the road. Those on the opposite side had been washed away in the same storm that revealed the great mother lode of gravel that comprised Lapling Quarry.

Everything in the small town was closed as Hamish and I cruised past. The still-functioning general store, with an attached tavern that served only Schlitz, had shut down at eight p.m. Through the windows, I saw the low lights on over the bar, and Nick Stolfuz—my age and the only son of the owner—mopping up.

At the corner of the boarded-up Ironsmith Inn, I hung a sharp right with the skill that came from years of retracing the same near invisible shortcuts.

It was on a drive with Natalie that I discovered the view of the Limerick nuclear plant. It was during a long, humid afternoon in the early '80s, when I was visiting my parents with Emily in tow. Sarah had stayed in Madison with Jake.

Every time I came home to Pennsylvania from Wisconsin, I would call Natalie, and we would go for long drives during which neither one of us would talk. It was our way of being alone without being alone, and it provided a justifiable excuse, to my mother, to Jake, to Natalie's husband, to get away for a little while from the emotional hotbeds that were so benignly labeled "domesticity."

We would purposely set off to get lost together. We would dead-end on old farm roads that hadn't been used for years or find ourselves in isolated churchless graveyards, our feet sinking into the gaps of air left by the only frequent visitors—the moles. Once lost and outside the car, wandering, we would easily separate, trusting that we would find each other again. If I looked for her, I might come up behind a long-dead chestnut tree and hear her crying. In those moments, I would feel the cords of my upbringing pulling me back. I had not been raised to hug or to comfort or to become part of someone else's family. I had been raised to keep a distance.

As I drove by the chicken coops and dark backyards and then hit the old keystone tunnel that separated the partial town from the rangy farmland and incipient suburban development on the other side, I noticed that Hamish had fallen asleep. His head nodded on the stem of his neck, and I saw no reason to disturb him. Judging Natalie as my mother had judged me was, I felt like telling her son, just my ass-backward way of showing love. I'd spent my life trying to translate that language, and now I realized I had come to speak it fluently. When was it that you realized the thread woven through your DNA carried the relationship deformities of your blood relatives as much as it did their diabetes or bone density?

Over the past ten years, Hamish had been brought in for various jobs around my mother's house. After anything Hamish did, from installing a sprinkler system that kept the hedges and ivy watered along the curb to once wedging himself into the smallest crawl space to rescue a feral cat, my mother had rewarded him with food. I would arrive in the afternoon to see how things had gone and find him sitting at the dining table, surrounded by the tins of cookies that were my mother's contraband.

Once, when my mother had gone back into the kitchen to, grudgingly, I felt, bring me a cup for tea, Hamish had seen the expression on my face.

"She told me you used to have problems with your weight."

He held out the tin of fudge, which, as my mother aged and I assisted at the helm, had become grainy with sugar.

"No, thank you, Hamish," I said.

"More for me!" He placed an entire square of fudge in his mouth, then winked at me.

I remembered taking the girls to various toddler parties held on the other side of the keystone tunnel. I would stand in the kitchen with the mothers, wondering what demonic communal mind created games like bouncing up and down on balloons until each child broke theirs, fell on the floor, and then ran to an appointed place to be showered with candy. Once, I had been beckoned in the middle of the night by the clipped voice of another mother. Emily had wet the bed at a slumber party. When I arrived to pick her up, she was sitting alone in the hallway on a rubber dog mat with jam in her hair. And while Emily pissed, Sarah hit. She kicked. She called the other children Fat Assholes, Big Babies, and her favorite, Jerk Bastards. The two of them reminded me of polarized Scottie magnets.

I looked over at Hamish and found myself wondering about a man who chose never to leave home. This choice seemed an unwise one to me, and yet, ultimately, it had been the one I too had made.

The car took the familiar loft of the final hill, and we rose up above the houses where Sarah had acquired a scar on her forehead from the deep digging nails of Peter Harper, and Emily had her first kiss on the brown plaid couch of a high-school saxophone player. I turned off the headlights and cruised, in the dark, over to the side of the road, then shut the engine off. Hamish's head jerked back against the seat. His eyes flickered open, then closed again.

Since they were first built, the Limerick nuclear towers, lit up in the distance, had become an ominous presence. So much encased power. The large white udders cut off and opening out like craters.

I sat in the car with the sleeping Hamish and looked out over the rolling farmland and past the treetops backlit by the lights surrounding the towers. Natalie and I had talked of taking a field trip to the plant to see how close we could get, but the plan never came to anything. It seemed we had silently and mutually agreed that this distant image was best, that the reality of the thing could not help but be disappointing. We had always called this view the "future that was no future."

When I'd found out I was pregnant with Emily, I had called my father at his office. I had been to the student health center in Madison and taken a blood test. The nurse who called with the results recommended that I sign up to receive counseling on birth control. I sat in a circle of other girls, some of whom were pregnant and others who had had a close call, and found myself the only one smiling. I wanted it—her, him, whoever was inside me who was one part Jake and one part me.

"Not everyone wants a child so young," my father said. "I *am* happy, Helen. Is Jake?"

Jake sat at our rickety dining table, silently offering me support.

"Yes."

"Girl or boy?" he had asked me. "Which would you prefer?"

"It doesn't matter, Dad. I thought about it, but I don't care either way."

"Then I'll selfishly say I'd love a granddaughter. It would be like having a little Helen to visit us."

Next came the call to my mother. When I rang the house, I could hear KYW in the background. It was an all-news station she listened to throughout the day. Bulletins of murders and fires and peculiar deaths.

"Well, are you proud of yourself?" she asked.

"What?"

"You're throwing your life away, you know that? Pissing it down your leg."

I stared at Jake.

"Mom?"

"What?"

"I'm going to have a child."

"There are no awards given out," she said.

Something about the expression on my face made Jake stand and take the phone from my hand.

"Mrs. Knightly," he said, "isn't it wonderful news? I'm incredibly happy at the prospect of being a dad."

I took his seat at the table and looked up at him, marveling. Though I had entered the confused state my mother often put me in, I sensed that if I watched his face and listened to his voice, I would come back to the new world that Jake and I had made. A world my mother didn't rule.

Nearly eight years later, it had also been my father whom I sought out at the local Catholic church. I was in town, but I didn't tell my mother this when I called. I didn't want to see her until I'd spoken to him.

A man he worked with had told my father about the rising cost of maintenance at St. Paul's Parish, and my father had suggested the vestry consider keeping sheep. With all the ancient headstones jutting up and out in uneven rows, the sheep could keep the grass down better than any mower, and their munching was exact, my father said. "No clippers needed." He had even volunteered, though he had no connection with the church, to come and tend them when he could.

The girls and I approached him from the parish parking lot. I carried Sarah in my arms, though in Madison I had told her that, at four, she had grown much too old for Mommy to carry her around. Emily, however, smiled for the first time since I'd packed the two of them and three suitcases in the Bug.

"Granddaddy!" she yelled. As we reached the churchyard wall, Sarah slid down my side to the ground. My father turned and dropped his rake at the sight of us. Emily scrambled over the wall by using the horse-mount steps while I lifted Sarah up and over to join her.

After they had been introduced to the sheep, Sally and Edith and Phyllis, and my father had shown them how he cared for them — cleaned out their wooden shelter, filled bowls with food and water — and talked to Emily about a bully she was frightened of, the girls were content to play among the graves.

My father and I walked.

"I see it in your face," he said quietly as we crossed out of the churchyard and entered the newer section, where mowers, not sheep, were responsible for the maintenance of the flat markers.

"We're getting a divorce," I said.

Without speaking, the two of us sat down on a white marble bench donated by a family who had lost three of its members in a car crash.

We were silent for a moment, and I began to cry.

"I always think of how much life there is in the graveyard," my father said. "Flowers and grass grow better here than they do anywhere else."

I leaned my head into his shoulder. I had discovered a level of affection with Jake and knew I would miss it. I sensed my father's discomfort almost immediately. He pivoted ever so slightly, and I sat straight up.

"Have you seen your mother?" he asked.

"I couldn't bear to," I said. "I called from a pay phone, and she told me where you were."

"Will you move back home?"

"I'd like to be near you," I said, "but I think the girls need..."

"Of course," he said. "Of course."

I could see his mind working as I had hoped it might. I thought of the small glass-backed clock that sat on his dresser, how as a child I had watched it in fascination to see the brass gears moving inside the four beveled panes.

"Mr. Forrest has a friend, a real estate agent," he said. "There's a new development in the area near where your mother and I once looked. Nice two-stories, not split-levels."

"But..."

"It will be my gift." He patted my hand.

I stood and straightened my skirt. The ride from Wisconsin had been long and hot. Guiltily I watched his back as he moved closer to the churchyard and his grandchildren. I did not want to be like my mother. I did not want to depend on him.

S I X

I don't remember when Hamish finally roused. I had spent the intervening time staring into the dark, toward the Limerick nuclear towers, and thinking of my father.

In the night, at a nonparticular hour, the lights at Limerick begin to flash green, then red—the one color answering the call of the other. It was always a message Natalie and I imagined as an SOS, as if inhabitants were trapped inside the molten core and, under cover of darkness, were communicating with an unknown other on the outside.

When Hamish reached out for me, I had almost forgotten it all. How and why I had ended up where I was.

"I used to believe I had a female twin in the world somewhere," he said.

I stared blankly at him, but then the weight of his palm on my thigh jostled me back from where I'd been.

"That wasn't bullshit," he said. "I don't use that as a line."

I kissed Hamish slowly, as if they were true, those dreams of childhood—that we were adopted, that we had fallen whole from the sky, that our parents were not our parents but hologram projections that proved there was another world to be escaped into.

As the light blinked on and off in the distance outside the car, Hamish leaned into me. I felt his weight and breath and resilience. He reached over to my side of the driver's seat and pulled up the lever until my seat shot back. Neither of us spoke. We grappled with the awkwardness of the stick shift and steering wheel, but our persistence was united and thorough. I knew there was no way I was leaving that spot on the hill until Hamish and I were satisfied in our separate vacuums. It was sex of determination and will, sex of mountain climbing and straining and checking a goal off on a list made only moments before. The passion came from a limited supply of air and time and an obvious illicitness.

When we reached a place we both sought—two feverish patients chasing an itch—I was halfway into the backseat with my head at an almost right angle. Hamish had used his arms to keep his full weight off me, and looking forward, I could see only the warm, moist margin between our abdomens as his head moved upward toward the roof of the car. I closed my eyes and met the slamming of his hips. I would not leave the car or the moment. I would chase the animal that had wanted to murder my mother since my earliest age. Until today, I realized, it had been an innocent urge I carried inside me like a spleen, optional but always present, in some way part of the whole.

Between Hamish's collarbone and his left biceps, there was a tattoo I had never noticed. I thought tattoos were highly stupid—a way, like ordering an upside-down Frappuccino, that people lacking direction claimed identity in the world. I stared at it now as a wave of nausea and hilarity rose in my gut. It was a circular tattoo, very suburban-mall "oriental" in look and no doubt inked at Thad's Parlor next to the auto-body shop. You could pick out in the minimal blue the tail of a dragon, and if you followed it, you swiftly arrived at the head, biting that tail.

"Jesus, Hell," Hamish breathed beside me. "Fuck."

"Thank you, Hamish," I said.

"You're most awesomely welcome."

"I should get home," I said.

Hamish moved to glance at his watch and sat up. I thought only then of Natalie. I pictured her out on her date with the contractor from Downingtown. I remembered her quoting, when we were girls, from an Emily Dickinson poem. "Because I could not stop for Death—/ He kindly stopped for me." She had been en pointe in her despised toe shoes, and at the end of each line, she spun in a circle until, dizzy and slightly drunk from the brandy we had stolen from her mother, she fell into my arms on her bed.

"Death?" she queried, looking up at me.

"Nice to meet you, sister," I said in a warbling baritone.

In the scattered moments after dropping Hamish off, I didn't know whether to congratulate myself or break out the ice packs. It had been two decades plus since I'd had sex in a car with a man who hadn't yet reached an age when he coughed or spit or groaned when he woke up. We had agreed, vaguely, to see each other again, and his eyes had focused on me with what I can only call a Vaseline-on-the-lens acuity. He saw sex and experience. Through my own clouded perceptions, I saw, when I looked his way, the last vestiges of grace.

It was deep night. Clouds covered the moon, and in my neighborhood, unlike Natalie's, outdoor lighting had not become a competitive sport of motion sensors and solar-powered path spotlights. There was the occasional faux carriage lamp, and the Mulovitches at the end of the block kept a bare bulb on over their front door that was bright enough to interrogate their pot-head son by, but my lawn and the lawns surrounding it were pitch-black.

My father and Mr. Forrest had found a home for me in the very neighborhood where my father had once looked when I was a teenager. On move-in day, he had driven the three of us over in his car and snapped photos as the Realtor handed me the key. When I walked inside, I was able to ignore the walls that needed to be painted and the floors that needed to be cleaned because my father had come the day before and had had delivered two beds for the girls and a mattress and dresser for me.

Barefoot, I left my car and walked onto the lawn. The grass was cool but dry against my feet, the heavy dew still hours away. All in all, it was early. Somewhere, Westmore students vomited in the shrubs at the edges of half-acre lots in which kegs sat on back porches. Teenage girls passed out in places they shouldn't, and Sarah would be, if I knew her, just starting her night out in the East Village. It took me a moment to remember her current boyfriend's name, but as I reached up to touch the branch of the dogwood tree, I remembered its fill-in-the-blank quality. Joe or Bob or Tim. A one-syllable, easily replaceable name. Like Jake.

I walked to the center of my front lawn and lay down, spread-eagled. I looked up at the stars. How did I end up in a place where doing such a thing marked you for crazy, while my neighbors dressed concrete ducks in bonnets at Easter and in striped stocking caps at Christmas but were considered sane?

I let my shoes and purse fall from my hands. Only a few stars were out. The earth was cold beneath me. "There are children starving in China," my mother had frequently said to me when I gorged on food.

"That doesn't mean I'm not hungry," I whispered now. I thought of her face when I had brought Jake from Wisconsin to meet them. He had been the first, and last, direct challenge to her power. She had welcomed him with a floor show so extreme that it was almost painful to watch. She forced herself to smile and bow and scrape as if he were the lord of the manor and she merely a lowly thing. Why hadn't I seen the truth? She had a steely resolve that surpassed anything Jake and I might build. Our swizzle-stick empire was so fragile in the end. "The only thing you've ever loved is your mother!" he had yelled at me. I had refused this truth, brought my hands up as if to stop a blow.

I knew where my mother was. She was not in the heavenly skies but in her basement, stone-cold dead. I had her braid in my purse to prove it. I forced myself to stare at the sky — unblinking. If she was there, I couldn't make her out. She could be a dark star behind a cloudy mass, like the tiny tumor that finally comes to kill, but I did not see her, no matter how hard I looked.

I turned onto my side. The final leavings of Hamish drained out of me. I felt spent and oddly whole and ready to sleep. I thought of the platform I was scheduled to mount later that day and the pose I was meant to strike. I was in the fourth week of sitting for Tanner Haku's Life Drawing class. I had, until the day before, been working out in front of the mirror with small weights and doing yoga even more diligently in order to keep my muscles teeming just below my skin. I knew that was what Haku wanted, and I knew adapting to the teacher's wishes was the linchpin of life modeling. Not just striking the pose but under-standing what amount of physicality he or she wanted you most to bring. Natalie was having her usual cream-cheese-and-bagels semester, as the instructor she was perpetually assigned to was a faux Lucian Freud. He wanted rolls of fat and body hair and a good patch of scarred or rash-strewn skin.

"Slump!" he would command.

Modeling had been something I'd talked her into. She had been reluctant at first, self-conscious of her body, but it had led to a part-time job in the bursar's office, and now she balanced the two.

I pushed myself up off the ground and stood, gathering my shoes and purse and finding my keys with the trusty flashlight attached. This, like the cell phone, had been another mother-inspired gift. I had often approached the mall like a sergeant arming a battalion. Mother and I would have cell phones. Mother and I would have flashlight key chains. Mother and I would have new stainless-steel teakettles, down-filled pillows, Scotchgarded all-canvas slipcovers. If. Then. If we shared *X,* then all would be ready and steady and right. When I inserted the key in the lock of my door, I saw my own epitaph: SHE LIVED SOMEBODY ELSE'S LIFE.

Years ago, when I began to feel overwhelmed by having to care for my mother, I started to dispose of small items throughout my house. Perhaps that's why I wouldn't have blamed Mrs. Castle if she had stolen the Pigeon Forge bowl. In some sense, after all she'd done, I'd more than once felt like opening my mother's jewelry box and saying, "Help yourself." Unfortunately, young Manny of the condom had already done that, a fact I had successfully kept hidden from everyone.

I took my coat off and let it drop to the flagstone floor instead of hanging it up. In contrast to my mother's house, I always kept at least one window open, even as it grew cooler. I liked the feeling of air constantly coming in to refresh the rooms. I walked to the shelf in the living room, and between the Virginia Woolf and the Vivian Gornick (I file my authors on a first-name basis), I spied tonight's item: a weeping Buddha made of wood. A gift from Emily.

As if I am committing a crime, I will take an item—a paperweight, a dried-flower arrangement, a small cameo brooch of my great-great-grandmother's—and "accidentally" dispose of it on trash day. I've done this on a whim, never planned. I'll see something resting on a shelf and feel the need to grab a piece of newspaper or an old rag and cloak it, like a magic trick. Then I'll walk rapidly to the curb and dump it into the sole pristine can of labeled waste waiting to be forked up by the garbage truck. A lightness overtakes me. One less stone weighing me down.

I looked at the weeping Buddha, the size of a fist and carved of gnarled wood. It would be the first item of my own that I disposed of—a gift from my child. But as I reached out to grab it, I thought of Manny.

I touched the Buddha with my fingers but let it remain on its stand.

I walked upstairs to my bedroom, trying not to think of Manny having sex in one of the rooms of my mother's house while, most likely, she was downstairs, sitting in her chair in the living room. What did I owe him besides the tips I had given him above and beyond what my mother had paid him?

I turned on the bedside lamp. What had I been reading before this day began? Emily had sent me a new translation of the *Tao Te Ching.* The slim volume itself was comforting to hold, but when I opened the pages and tried to read, it was as if all language had turned to Xs. I was not a fish or a door or a reed and never would be. I was a fetid human creature à la Lucian Freud.

Over my dresser I had hung an early drawing Jake had done of me. He'd based it on a photograph Edward Weston took of Charis Wilson before she became his wife. I sat the wrong way on one of our metal-and-vinyl kitchen chairs from the house we shared in Wisconsin. I wore my childhood Brownie beanie, which Jake drew to resemble Wilson's sporty beret, and a bra and short slip. When I spread my legs, I made the slip come up to the tops of my thighs. Though you could see nothing through the slip, which drifted down to act as a veil, the invitation was there. With that drawing, I went from being a bright student in the classrooms of my professors to being a pinup in the faculty gallery attached to the university library.

I crawled into my bed and pulled the blankets over me. I remained fully dressed in my soiled clothes. I thought of the nightly rituals of beauty that I had learned growing up. How adult I felt the first time my mother applied moisturizer to my feet. After this came socks and then old-fashioned lace-up ankle weights. "Otherwise," my mother said, "you'd rip the socks off in the middle of the night and ruin the effect." As I drifted off to sleep, I remembered one of so many countless phone calls from Mrs. Castle over the last few years. She had arrived to find my mother wearing dainty Danish-green cotton gloves, over which she'd fastened a pair of aluminum handcuffs. She had informed Mrs. Castle that she had misplaced the key. Did I happen to remember where it was?

SEVEN

I was eight when my father had an accident in his workshop and was rushed by ambulance to the hospital. He did not come home for three months, and I was not allowed to see him. My mother said he would be gone for exactly ninety days and was visiting friends and family in Ohio. When I asked who, or why we couldn't join him, she hushed. Mr. Forrest's visits grew more frequent, and the Donnellsons and Levertons brought us meat loafs and casseroles, which I often found on the stoop after school.

I would let myself in and sit at the dining room table, reading. I allowed myself just enough light via the dimmer switch on the chandelier so that when darkness fell, the house did not go black. My mother came down from her bedroom in the early evening, and we made dinner together. I had decided, after my father had been gone a week, to hoard the casseroles. Instead we made peanut butter on Ritz crackers, or Swanson suppers, or my favorite: endless rounds of cinnamon toast. My mother would be wearing the gown she had slept in — white and diaphanous — and I would remain in my school clothes.

"Still eighty-two days," she would say. Or "Only seventy-three."

It became a shorthand with which we would greet each other. "Sixty-four." "Fifty-seven." "Twenty-five."

Over those ninety days, it did not matter what time I reached home. I would stop in front of Mr. Forrest's house on my way back from the bus stop and tap on the window to wake his sleeping dog. Tosh, a King Charles spaniel — "The only breed!" Mr. Forrest said — would come to where I stood and sadly paw the glass.

If I spotted a casserole on our doorstep, I would hurry it to the kitchen and wrap it in tinfoil to hide in the basement freezer. I was worried my father might never come home, and feeding us would become my responsibility.

When I had tried once to explain what was wrong with my mother, it felt hopeless.

"She doesn't do much," I'd said.

"It may seem like that to you, Helen," Miss Taft had said. She was my second-grade teacher, and my class was her first.

"She doesn't drive," I tried.

"Not everyone does."

"My father does. Mr. Forrest does."

"That's two," she said, and held up two fingers. She smiled at me, as if supplying me with whole numbers would solve everything.

"She used to go for walks," I said, "but she doesn't do that anymore."

"Raising a child takes all of one's energy," Miss Taft said.

I stared past her to the map of the world that hung over the blackboard. I knew when to shut up. My mother's problem was my fault.

Ninety days after my father left, he returned. My mother had put on a suit I'd never seen before and meticulously combed and coiffed her hair. It was the first time I realized that beneath her diaphanous gowns, she had been losing weight. I remembered then that I had never seen her eat more than one or two of the Ritz crackers she heaped with Skippy. She had also never said a thing about the hoarded casseroles.

My father walked in the door and smiled sheepishly at me. His hat had a crisp new feather in it, though he too had grown thinner. I went to hug him—something we did not do—and he held out a large plastic bag, inadvertently blocking my way.

"I brought these for you," he said.

He turned to envelop my mother. I saw her face as she came toward him. Her tears had already made inky troughs of mascara under her eyes.

"I'm so sorry, Clair," he said. "I'm home to take care of you now. I'm strong again."

Without even speaking, he lifted her up, cradling her easily and drawing her to him. In my head that day, I equated "I'm strong again" with only that—his physical ability to carry more weight. Inside the bag I held were plastic dishes in aqua-green. One was a pitcher and one was a tray and one was a kidney-bean shape, which I later learned had been his sick bowl.

In the weeks and months that followed, it became a riddle we played out.

"Why did you go away?"

"To get better."

"Better from what?"

"Better than I was."

"What was wrong with you?"

"I can't remember because it's gone!"

Quickly, I forgot too. I needed him. It was my mother who had the problems. My mother who was afraid. So afraid that nothing could make her unafraid. She felt safer in my father's arms. She felt safer in the house on Mulberry Lane. Or under blankets. Or with her feet tucked up beneath her and a hot-water bottle nestled in her lap.

My father would greet me in the morning when I came down for breakfast.

"It's a hard day, sweetheart," he would say.

This was our shorthand, and it never changed. On hard days, my mother stayed in bed with the blinds drawn until my father and I left the house. She knew why we had to leave, but still she thought our abandonment of her cruel. My father and I kept our voices low in the kitchen and wolfed down our food. When there were no crisp bills from his wallet for me to take to buy my lunch, I totted up money from the change jar in the kitchen, being careful not to let the sorting of coins make any noise.

At age eleven I confided in Natalie about the way my mother behaved, and held my breath when she said her mother was the same way. I had never been so happy. But my excitement drained away when I queried her further. Natalie's mother drank booze. That was enviable to me. The ease of being able to locate it in a bottle was like a dream.

It was on a hard day—

"Are you okay, Mom?"

"It's a hard day, Helen."

—that Billy Murdoch was hit by a car in front of the house.

I was in high school. My father had spent the night before away from home. "An overnight business trip to Scranton," he'd said. Everyone else on our short block seemed to be gone that afternoon. But, most important, it was a hard day.

On the afternoon Billy Murdoch got hit, my mother paced herself as she always did on a hard day, filling the hours with house chores to try and keep busy, to try and keep from sitting on the couch or at the kitchen table and giving in to it. It was as if, if she cleaned and washed and organized, she could keep her terror just enough at bay for her to breathe.

She told me later, in one of her bottomless whispers, when she was speaking from a place she lived in for months afterward, that she remembered hearing the sound—the sound of Billy's body being struck by the car. "Like a pumpkin being hit by a baseball bat," she said.

It was around two o'clock in the afternoon, and my mother had just come up out of the basement with a load of my father's socks and underwear. Something about the astringent smell of bleach always heartened her, and the basket felt warm against her chest.

Her usual routine was to place the basket on one end of the couch and snap, then fold, my father's boxer shorts, placing them in two stacks: plain white and thin blue stripes. His socks came next, matched and mated, with folded-over tops.

When my mother heard the sound, she did not rush to the window to check it out, as everyone else later agreed they would have. She stood at attention for a single second and then went about what she was doing. Everything she did after the sound was even more focused, even more robotic, until the next sound came.

It was the sound of a car peeling away, squealing down the block at high speed. Some entry was made then in her nervous system that something wasn't right outside. Despite all the empty chattering noise that filled her brain on a hard day, she dropped the two socks in her hand and walked, not ran, to the front door. Then she blacked out until she got to the edge of the curb. Her fear for the boy made her act, but like a dog trained not to go beyond the boundary of his own yard no matter what, she was brought up short by the mailbox.

He had been riding his bike, which had now landed on the edge of our lawn, its front wheel spinning slowly before it stopped.

My mother raised her hand to her chest and started to rub hard with the knuckles of her right hand into the soothing worry stone of her sternum.

His lower limbs jerked once, then twice.

She put her left hand on top of our mailbox to steady herself. She was six feet away from him.

"Billy?" she whispered.

The doctor said later that if mercy had been attending him, he would have been walking. That way, the car would have hit him head-on and lower to the ground. Whoosh, he would be plowed down—dead immediately.

I've always wondered what he must have thought during those final minutes as my mother stood so close to him. How could the world change so fast? Could he know, at eight, what death was? Cars came out of nowhere and hit you two houses down from where you had grown up, and a woman who had always seemed just a typical adult, in those rare moments you saw her in her yard, stood at the edge of the road but did not comfort you. Was this punishment for having stayed home sick from school? For having broken the rule of remaining in the house while your mother was gone?

I was sixteen. Natalie and I would put on Danskin unitards and make up dance routines in her parents' refurbished basement. We used her father's circular bar to propel us across the room, where we perfected a tumbling routine involving the long, low couch and the bearskin rug on the floor. Our dances were narrative and sweaty, and contained sit-ups and leg lifts that cropped up out of nowhere.

"He didn't wonder anything," Natalie tried to reassure me in the days to come.

By the time I got home, his body was gone, but I could still see the long stain that smeared the pavement like an exclamation mark. "His brains were smashed," Natalie said. "He wasn't thinking anything."

But I had listened to my mother sobbing in my father's arms. "He called me 'ma'am,'" my mother said over and over again. "He looked across at me and called me 'ma'am.'"

My father, who, if not exactly social, was roundly liked in the neighborhood for his hellos and his courtly manner when he ran into the neighbors at the local grocery, had tried to explain my mother's inability to walk into the road.

"Why didn't she call someone, then?" asked Mr. Tolliver, who lived around the corner and led his own wife on humiliating walks in which he forced her to pump her arms and raise her legs high like a one-woman marching band. "Mrs. Tolliver is a rounded woman," my mother said. "He shouldn't have married a rounded girl if he didn't want a rounded wife."

"Clair was frozen," my father explained. "Literally frozen to the spot. She *couldn't* help him."

As the men and women of the neighborhood drove home from work, they were stopped by police and told to park their cars and walk or, if it made more sense, to circle around in the opposite direction. But most of them parked their cars and got out, joining the crowd that stood on the Beckfords' lawn across the street.

They were angrier, it seemed, at my mother than at the faceless, nameless stranger who had mown Billy Murdoch down. It took every person who joined the group two or three times hearing the story before they understood how what my mother had done was possible. And it wasn't exactly that they understood. It was more like, by rote, it began to sink in. Clair Knightly, whose husband they all knew, had stood in her yard and watched a boy they all knew die. She did not help. She did not go to him. None of them asked what his parents would wonder for years: *Did Clair Knightly even speak to him? Did she say anything?*

The answer was that my mother both wept and sang.

She stood at the edge of her property and rubbed her chest furiously, back and forth with the sharp knuckles of her right hand. Her left hand flitted from her head down to her side.

"Billy," she said over and over again, as if naming him might pull him closer.

His head was on the road, and it was facing her. His eyes were open. She saw his mouth moving but couldn't get herself to stop repeating his name in order to hear what he had to say. By saying "Billy," she was keeping herself in the present, anchoring herself there by the mailbox. Instinctively she knew this was what she must do if she was going to try to help him.

When there was a break in her rhythm, she heard him.

"Ma'am?"

That was the moment she knew she wouldn't be able to do it. She didn't bother saying his name anymore. She stared at him. She stayed right where she was, kneading and rubbing her chest until, as she revealed to my father two days later, she had rubbed a bloody cavity from her throat to her breastbone.

The other thing the neighbors never found out was the song my mother sang him. It was a song that, whenever I heard it coming through the vent that led from her bedroom to the bathroom, put me on guard for the advent of a bad day. It was a rhyme she remembered from childhood, and she would sing it repeatedly, the words running together into a sort of chant.

Posies are bright, clear, and gay.
Daffodils sprout on the lawn in May.
Flowers and girls are often the same.
Rose, Violet, and Iris are names.

She would hum the next few lines, whose words, I assumed, she had forgotten long before. It soothed her, and I knew this, but when I went to her bedroom to ask if she needed anything, I would remain in the doorway until her lips stilled.

My mother sang and hummed this song to Billy Murdoch until a delivery truck drove up, heading for the Levertons', who, in celebration of their wedding anniversary, had already left the day before on a trip. The young man, in white coveralls and a ponytail, leaped out and in a flurry ran past my mother. He bolted up the stairs through our open door, found the phone on the side table in the family room just next to the couch piled with half-sorted boxers and socks, and called the hospital.

By the time the ambulance and the police arrived, Billy was almost gone, and everyone had questions for the incoherent woman singing an incoherent song.

After that, we kept the blinds drawn and pretended the trash on our lawn had fallen there by accident. I stayed away from school for six weeks. I would meet Natalie on a wooden bench in the park five blocks from our house.

"Not yet," she'd tell me, and hand me the assignments I'd missed. Even her parents preferred not to have me come over to her house anymore.

"I hate this," I said.

"Remember Anne Frank?" Natalie said once. "Pretend you're like her, and you can't go anywhere until you get the all clear."

"Anne Frank was exterminated!"

"Well, not that part," Natalie said.

I began to spend my time calculating. I was a junior. I had eighteen months to go until, somehow, I would get out.

I did not tell my mother this. At home, all roads revolved around her more than they had before. My father and I whispered our hellos in those first six months after Billy died, and when the doorbell rang, we scurried like mice into dark corners, hoping whoever it was would go away. A rock came through the front window once, and we hid this fact from my mother, claiming instead that it had been my father reaching back to turn the page of a newspaper and poking his elbow through the glass. "Can you believe that?" he said with his best variety-show voice. "I didn't know I was that strong!"

"Or that oblivious," my mother said, weakly playing her part of condemning him, though we all felt the lack of her sharp tongue. Judgment, her savior and guardian, had left her. Her perch at the window of the living room, from which she could watch Mrs. Tolliver marching by or call the next-door neighbor's child a slut, was cloaked in a heavy wool curtain that we ceased to open.

Shortly after Christmas of that year and three months after the accident, the Murdochs moved. A truck pulled up in the middle of the afternoon, and four men loaded all their possessions in a little less than three hours. Natalie and I were bike riding when we came over the hill and saw Mrs. Murdoch standing in the front yard with the dog, Billy's dog. She wore a short checked coat and a circle skirt in heavy gray flannel, a pattern from Simplicity that everyone seemed to have made that year. I remember braking a little as I took in the moving van and the boxes, Mr. Murdoch's back disappearing into the house, and then my eyes met Mrs. Murdoch's, and it was everything I could do to keep my balance. As it was, my front tire wobbled dangerously as I all but ceased to pedal.

Natalie came up beside me on her green Schwinn ten-speed. "Let's go," she said softly.

And we did. I put my feet on the pedals and moved past Mrs. Murdoch. Billy's dog, a Jack Russell named Max, strained against his leash, and I had to remind myself it was the wheels of the bike he hated, not me.

How can you apologize for the mother you love? The mother you, too, hate. The only thing I could hope was that Mrs. Murdoch would have plenty of people to love her in the future, plenty of people to console her and to listen to the story of how she lost her son. My mother would have only my father. Then she would have me.

EIGHT

The day the neighbors showed up in the yard, my father had told us he was in Erie, Pennsylvania, shaking up vials of poisonous silt and calculating the rate of sedimentary accretion in the local drinking water.

My mother was in the kitchen, and I had just come in through the side door. After Billy died, she stopped asking me where I'd been. I could have been sleeping with the boy she called the "horror," who lived down the road and had a tattoo in a time when such a thing was equal to the mark of Cain. She needed all her energy to stay upright.

At some point, after the buzzer on the stove had rung and I'd come out of the downstairs bathroom, having washed up, my mother and I both heard the same low sound together.

It was a gathering of men.

I can't say how I knew to be scared, but I was. I can say that I was immediately relieved my father was away. Far enough away that he would be gone for days still. And I've never known if this was exactly why the men chose that day to come.

In sixth grade I had studied a photo of a lynching in the South. It was a small black-and-white photo that had been mimeographed and distributed by our history teacher, who believed history made the most impact when it was illustrated. Parents throughout the district had complained when their children came home with photos of lynchings, or Auschwitz, or the head of an African warlord raised and dripping on a stick. But the teacher had been right, and the fascination I had had looking at those images now gripped me in the pit of my stomach as I stood with my mother while she held a vegetarian casserole in her hands.

The space between the stove and counter was a short one, but that day the noise outside was a lengthening agent she could not have predicted. We heard it, and the heat of the casserole burning through the dishcloth my mother held it with made her drop the Pyrex dish on the floor.

"You go," she said.

Panic filled her eyes.

"They want you," I said.

"But I can't. You know I can't."

And I did know.

I knew my mother's limitations because they formed the marrow of my bones. I realized then, as I had sensed for years but never named, that I was born in order to be her proxy in the world and to bring that world back home—whether that meant bright construction-paper creations from my first years in school or meeting the angry men out in the yard. I would do it all for her. That was our particular unspoken contract, how this child served this parent.

It had been warm out that day, and I'd changed into a pair of cutoffs upon my arrival home from school. My mother despised cutoffs, thought them cheap and unkempt for the same reasons I loved them, the mangy endless fringe that I could pick at with my nails. I had known I could wear them just as I had indulged in polishing my fingernails that spring. My mother was too weak, for the first time in my life, to make her judgment voluble.

As I tiptoed from the kitchen through the back hall and into the living room, I grabbed the quilt that hung over the side of the couch. I don't know what I thought I was going to do with it, but instinct told me to cover myself as best I could. I remember I wrapped it around my shoulders as if it were a giant beach towel.

One of the men saw me through a window, and the noise in the side yard flared louder. I was barefoot, and my hair, so thin my ears poked through, hung down on either side of my face. I wanted Natalie to be there. As if together we would be an army that could flank and conquer a crowd of men.

I walked through the small living room, and as I put my hand on the doorknob that led to the screened-in porch, I heard my mother risk two words from the kitchen, where she hid. "Stay safe," she said very quietly. I knew the effort this took was heroic for her. But something had happened in the time I had crossed the room and put on, as I later thought of it, my superhero cape. My mother, in that moment, had ceased to exist for me.

The first person I saw, when I came through the screened-in porch and out the door, calmed me. It was Mr. Forrest. He was with Tosh. He was standing off to the side of the cluster of fathers and husbands, and he made a point, when I glanced at him over the waist-high fence, of trying to smile. But it was a sick and worried attempt. Tosh, usually frenetic under the best of circumstances, was hidden behind Mr. Forrest's legs.

"Where's your mother?" one of the men asked. There were six of them, seven if I counted Mr. Forrest.

"She's inside," another one answered him, though he was staring at me. "She's always inside, right?"

This truth, stated so boldly out in the open air, was like a poison arrow coming out of nowhere. I felt a tightness in my chest and paused just long enough to take a breath.

"Can't you speak?" Mr. Tolliver asked. I hated him, and this hatred was unaided by my mother's judgments of how he marched his wife around our block. He kept a small piece of wood painted white and in the shape of a gravestone that said, HERE HE LIES, COLD AND HARD, THE LAST DOG WHO SHIT IN MY YARD! The rhyme was supposed to make it funny. I've always traced my disdain of what generous people call "lawn art" to the first time I read the words of that mock grave.

"Be kind," Mr. Forrest said, his voice coming forth in a higher register than usual. His collar was unbuttoned, but he still wore his necktie from work. I realized later that he must have run into the men while taking Tosh for a walk around the block.

The men grumbled. Most still wore what passed for work clothes—worn slacks and jackets, an occasional Windbreaker with the steel company's logo.

"Helen," Mr. Warner said, "we are here to talk to your mother."

Mr. Warner, whom my mother had nicknamed the "Blusterer," considered himself a spokesman for every occasion. He could hold court on any subject. He had once stood in our front yard, lecturing my father—who knew more about water treatment than anyone within miles—on the benefits of sewage silica plants in Liberia. "He's read an article," my father said when he finally peeled himself away as darkness came. "It's nice that the man's excited, but even I don't want to talk about sewage *that* much."

I stood on our side of the chain-link fence.

"Come talk to us, Helen," said a father I didn't recognize.

Why didn't I see the warning in Mr. Forrest's eyes before I lifted the friendship latch and walked out into the side yard? I must have been looking at the men near the hedge and not at him. Only after I turned and shut the gate behind me did I see his face. I could read fear like tarot cards.

"Where's your mother, Helen?" Mr. Warner asked.

"Helen," Mr. Forrest said, "you should go back inside."

I knew enough, or at least I thought I did, to advance from against the gate and move closer to Mr. Forrest. But as I did, he backed away.

"My mother is unavailable. What can I do for you?" I asked, using the most grown-up voice I had. I was anxious now. I stepped toward Mr. Forrest once more.

"I wish I could help, Helen," he said, his voice hollow. He knew what to fear, and I didn't. I was beginning to hover there, in the vicinity of the truth, but with my bare feet in the grass and my quilt for a cape, I could not yet imagine men like my father, who lived all around us, wanting to hurt me. The Murdochs had moved. It had been eight months since Billy's death. The end of my junior year was only a month away. But what I hid behind the most, the thing that made me blindest up until the minute it happened, was that I was a girl. In the world where I was raised, unlike the one in which I made sure to raise my daughters, girls did not get hit.

Mr. Warner advanced toward me and stopped.

"We have business with your mother, Helen, not you."

This, I now saw, had been simmering ever since the inquest. My mother was never officially held accountable in Billy's death because, according to the report of the medical examiner, his injuries that day had been traumatic enough that he would have died regardless of whether she had stepped into the road. It was the missing hit-and-run driver's fault, not hers. Perhaps she might have held him, as other women would, or rushed to call his family, or an ambulance, but none of these actions, the authorities concluded, would have saved Billy Murdoch's life. Officially, she was merely an innocent bystander.

When I looked behind me, Mr. Forrest was holding Tosh in his arms.

"Mr. Forrest?" I was balancing on the edge of something thin and perilous, and he was the only thing I had to trust.

"You can come with me, Helen. Why not do that?"

One or two of the men laughed when they heard this, and then we all watched Mr. Forrest walk quickly to the three flagstones set into the side of the yard that led to the sidewalk.

"Tony tends toward the hysterical," Mr. Warner said. "No one is going to hurt you."

But I was not relieved by this. If Mr. Warner was my only protector against the cluster of fathers and strangers, then I was in what kids at school called "deep shit." Mr. Warner knew the cuts and quarter cuts on every major meat. He could name them and tell you their qualities. Tender, stringy, chewy, or moist. Perhaps Mr. Warner would not be the one to do the actual quartering, but I could easily picture him pontificating over my corpse.

"Where's the bitch?" Mr. Tolliver said. His face was bright red—swollen with pride.

"Where's the *crazy* bitch?" said the father I didn't know. Their particular macho one-upmanship involved adjectives.

Phoenixville Steel, I knew, had fired Mr. Tolliver that winter. Men all over the area were losing their jobs. My father, whose own job was secure, took the news hard each time he heard it.

" 'Let go,' " he would say, and shake his head. "I hate that phrase, as if the man's an animal and he's being released into the wild."

Mr. Warner shot the men a sharp look.

I would find out soon enough that my mother, too afraid to watch, had locked herself in the downstairs bathroom and turned on the transistor radio.

"I don't know what to do, Mr. Warner," I said. He had sons. They were one, two, and three years older than I was and barely spoke to me except to grunt hello in the presence of adults.

"It really would be best if you went and asked your mother to come out. I don't want you to get hurt. *You* haven't done anything."

He said this with the compassionate care that a physician delivering a temporary reprieve might. But the news I heard was still bad. My mother, if not me, would be hurt.

"I can't do that, Mr. Warner," I said. "Why are you here?"

I knew why, of course, but I wanted to hear them say it.

"Bitch," Mr. Tolliver said.

I saw the line of distress cross Mr. Warner's face. This was not, at least, what *he* had intended. It was also not what two or three others had wanted. I could see them splitting up behind Mr. Warner. There was Mr. Tolliver and the man I didn't know, both of them wearing Phoenixville Steel softball jackets. And there were the others, like Mr. Forrest before them, who were beginning to edge closer to the corner of the yard, tripping into the front vegetable garden in which, since my earliest childhood, my father had planted and tended and snipped herbs for my mother.

It was this that finally pushed me to make a move. When Mr. Serrano, who was an accountant and had a young daughter, crushed my father's Italian parsley, I dropped the quilt from my shoulders and stepped forward.

"You'll kill it."

It was that word.

Mr. Tolliver's friend was suddenly to my right, but I was watching Mr. Serrano step carefully back from the border of the herb garden. Just as I exhaled, I felt the sting of a slap across my face.

I fell onto the grass, my own hand going up to my cheek. Mr. Warner was jumping past me to restrain the unknown father, whom Mr. Tolliver was patting on the back. I saw Mr. Serrano look down at me as he fled the yard. It was not my first awareness of the pity people had for me, pity like a vast sea that was impossible for me to cross.

The good men left with sincere apologies thrown over their shoulders, but not to me. They apologized to Mr. Warner. I was on the ground. I was a teenager. I didn't matter. Mr. Warner said, "No problem." He said, "Talk later." He said, "Take care."

He had stopped the man who'd slapped me from doing more, and so I supposed I should have been thanking Mr. Warner, but I wasn't. I was edging toward the quilt, which I'd dropped a few feet behind me. It seemed the only thing in the yard to offer protection.

Mr. Tolliver and his friend had appeared ready to storm the house and find my mother, but they were no match for the law Mr. Warner laid down, and, I imagine, a female teenager in cutoffs and T-shirt lying on the ground was probably scary to them. The sight of me begged a question neither had intended to pose. Mr. Warner told them to go sober up and get some food. "Go home to your wives," he said.

The spring evenings stayed light for a long time, but the day had just crested that point where darkness was inevitable and the sun had begun to descend into the line of fir trees that separated our yard from the Levertons'.

I had reached the quilt, and sitting up, I grasped it to my chest. I would not cry. I remember promising myself that, despite the sting in my cheek. What was oddest was that my father's crushed parsley seemed worse to me than the slap. It was one of the joys he brought into the house for my mother. When he did, clipping rosemary or marjoram or thyme, the scent would linger on his fingers, and he would run them through my mother's hair to make her smile.

"You can tell your father," Mr. Warner said, standing above me, "that it is the consensus of the neighborhood that your family should move."

"We have the right to stay," I said. I had chosen my side.

He stared at me a moment and then shook his head.

He left the yard, and I wrapped myself tighter in the quilt. It was a memory quilt that we'd bought at the Kutztown Fair. "See that?" the woman who sold it to my father said. "That's all handwork. No machines at all."

My father had bought it, sure that my mother would be impressed. She had been. She put it over the arm of the couch, and during aimless afternoons when Natalie was busy and I had to keep myself entertained, I would spread the quilt out over the sofa and make memories up for my family.

"This bright red patch symbolizes a slap on the cheek to Helen when she was sixteen," I whispered to myself that night in the yard. Already it worked. The slap fell into the hole that was my accumulating past, and I stood, walked inside to clean up the casserole from the floor, and heard the scratchy sound of a big-band radio station as I passed the bathroom door.

NINE

The night the men came to our yard, there were two adults within my reach: my mother, hiding in our downstairs bathroom, and Mr. Forrest down the street.

As I grabbed my jacket off the hook by the kitchen door, I spied one of the photographs of my mother from years ago. It was a small one, 4x6, and in it she wore a slip with an ornate lace bodice. The ecru one. It sat propped up among a grouping of knickknacks beside the red-velvet love seat, which to me was the most uncomfortable piece of furniture in existence.

"It encourages people to leave sooner," my mother would say when I complained.

"What people, Mom?" I'd respond.

I walked over to the photograph and paused. I wanted to hurt her, but she was always crumbling and crying, barking and biting, and to reach her seemed impossible to me. I lifted it and traced the outline of her body with my finger. I slipped the frame into my jacket pocket, and I left as quietly as possible through the front door. There was no way my mother could have heard me over the noise of the radio.

After twilight the streets seemed deserted. No one was outside on their lawns anymore. I thought briefly of what an aerial view of our neighborhood would look like with all the roofs sheared off. In how many houses would happy families be settling in for the night, watching TV with bright bowls of popcorn in their laps? In Natalie's house her mother would be slowly passing out, assisted by what she called "a little splash." Natalie would be up in her room, mooning over Hamish Delane, who had just moved to America with his family. Over and over again she'd drawn inscrutable lines on a page until she confided it was "Mrs. Natalie Delane."

To take the tops off all the houses and mingle our miseries was too simple a solution, I knew. Houses had windows with shades. Yards had gates and fences. There were carefully planned out sidewalks and roads, and these were the paths that, if you chose to go into someone else's reality, you had to be willing to walk. There were no shortcuts.

His door opened before I could ring the bell.

"I hoped I might see you," Mr. Forrest said. "Come in, come in. Let me take your coat."

"I brought you something," I said.

I reached into my jacket and pulled out the framed photograph.

Mr. Forrest took it from me. I stood in the hallway and looked around, past the porcelain umbrella stand and into the drawing room, which I had seen only from the outside, and into the dining room behind that, which was elevated by three wide wooden steps.

I had been fuming on my way over, and inside his house I could feel the heat of it on my cheeks.

"She's a beautiful woman, your mother," Mr. Forrest said, looking at the picture.

"Right."

"Let's sit down in the drawing room, shall we?"

It had taken me this long to notice that Mr. Forrest was being incredibly nice to me, even solicitous. I knew how extraordinary this was. Mr. Forrest had no use for almost anyone in the neighborhood other than my parents. He was never rude, but he was perfectly pleasant in a way that, I would realize as an adult, was the suburban equivalent of a stiff-arm.

He had been in our house multiple times over the years, but I had never stepped inside his home. Now I stood on the edge of a silk rug in front of his fireplace, uncertain what to say.

"Sit," he said. As I did, he whistled loudly, and bounding into the room came Tosh. "I know who you really came to see," he said, and smiled.

Tosh slowed to an obedient halt in front of Mr. Forrest and sat down on the floor beside him, facing me.

"I owe you a deep apology," Mr. Forrest said. "I shouldn't have run away. I've never felt exactly comfortable here. In that, I'm not unlike your mother."

I spied an oval tray near the mantel. It sat on a spindly cherry-wood table, and arrayed upon it were crystal bottles that refracted light. Mr. Forrest followed my eyes.

"Yes, you deserve a drink," he said nervously. "I know I'd like one. Come, Tosh." He led Tosh over to the white-slipcovered couch where I was sitting and patted the space beside me. Tosh jumped up and immediately leaned into my side. "That's a good boy," Mr. Forrest said.

While Mr. Forrest's back was to me, I hugged Tosh and held him to me, petting his floppy ears.

"Port is my choice for you," he said. "We can sip it and talk about disgusting people before putting them aside."

He handed me the bloodred liquid and went to sit opposite me on a gold velvet chair that made his knees jut up into the air in front of him.

He laughed at himself. "I never sit in this chair," he said. "It's called a slipper chair, and ladies used to have them in their boudoirs. It belonged to my great-grandmother."

"I see you through the window sometimes," I said.

"A dull thing to look at," he said.

I had my arm around Tosh and was scratching the space beneath his right ear. His mouth hung open in a panting smile, and occasionally he would tip his head back and look at me. I took a mouthful of the port and immediately wanted to spit it out.

"Sip," he said, seeing my face. "I did say that, didn't I?"

What felt like the longest minute in the world passed as I tousled Tosh's fur and swerved my head around the room.

"Helen, what happened after I left?"

"Forget it," I said, suddenly not wanting to talk about it, wishing instead that I could be alone with Tosh.

"I'm sorry, Helen," he said. "In general I leave the neighbors alone, and if I don't go flouncing over to their houses, they let me be."

"His friend hit me," I said.

Mr. Forrest put down his glass on the marble-topped table beside him. He looked as if he too had been hit. He inhaled.

"Helen, I'm going to teach you two very important words. Ready?"

"Yes," I said.

"And then I'm going to get you something else to drink because you obviously detest that."

I had held the port in my hand but could not bear even to pretend to sip.

"Here they are: 'fucking bastard.'"

"Fucking bastard," I repeated.

"Again."

"Fucking bastard," I said, more surely.

"With verve!"

"Fucking bastard!" I said, almost yelling.

I sat back into the couch, on the verge of laughing.

"There are millions of them. You can't beat them, believe me. You can only hope to find a way to live quietly among them. Sitting and reading in this window, with all my antiques and books... You wouldn't know it by looking at me, but I'm a revolutionary."

I wanted to ask him if he had a boyfriend, but my mother had scolded me never to pry.

"You know I'm a book collector," Mr. Forrest said. "Would you like to see some of my newest acquisitions?"

"What about my mother?" I asked. I pictured her curled around her transistor radio like a conical seashell.

"Her?" he said, and stood with his glass. "We both know she's not going anywhere."

He came over to retrieve my undrunk port. Tosh's tail beat against the back of the couch as he drew near.

"I hate her," I said.

"Do you really, Helen?" He held both our glasses and looked down at me.

"No."

"You will always be stronger than she is," he said. "You don't know that yet, but it's true."

"She let Billy Murdoch die," I said.

"That was her illness, Helen, not her."

I stared up at him, not wanting him to stop.

"It must be obvious to you that your mother is mentally ill," he said. He placed the glasses on the silver tray and turned back to me. "What does your father say about it?"

"Mentally ill." It was as if someone had just very gently placed a bomb in my lap. I didn't know how to dismantle it, but I knew no matter how scary it might be, there was a key inside it — a key to all the hard days and locked doors and crying jags.

"Haven't you ever heard those words?"

"Yes," I said meekly.

"Haven't you ever connected them with your mother?"

I had used the word "crazy" but never "mentally ill." "Crazy" didn't seem so bad. "Crazy" was a simple word like "shy" or "tired" or "sad."

Tosh jumped off the couch, sensing Mr. Forrest's desire to move. I stood.

"We'll look at books and make you a G&T," he said. "You don't owe your life to your mother, you know. Nor does your father, for that matter."

"You just said she was mentally ill."

"Your mother is a survivor. I'll no doubt send you home with a book or two that she wouldn't know about otherwise, and you'll return the photograph as a favor to me."

Tosh, Mr. Forrest, and I all went through the dining room and into the kitchen. After the two other rooms, the kitchen was a shock. It was all white and incredibly utilitarian. Nothing was out on the counters that would suggest he'd eaten or prepared anything to eat in months.

He opened his fridge while I leaned against the sink.

"You can give Tosh a treat," he said with his back to me. He found the bottles he wanted and opened the freezer. "They are in that white porcelain bunny jar by the sink."

While I fed an ecstatic Tosh treats that looked like miniature bunnies, Mr. Forrest made me a drink.

"Why are you friends with her?" I asked.

"Your mother is fascinating. She's incredibly witty and beautiful."

"And mean," I said.

"Regrettably you and your father see a good deal more of that than I ever will. We have books. We can keep on that level, and then I leave."

He handed me my drink. "Imagine, if you will, the demise of all the fucking bastards of the world," he said, and knocked his glass to mine.

"What about my mother?"

"Your mother is not a fucking bastard. Fucking bastards are simple by nature. Now drink up, because soon you'll be in a room where no liquids are allowed."

The G&T was better than the port, and cool. We drank as Mr. Forrest led me down a hall that ran off the kitchen.

"Somewhere in this hallway I turn into another person," he said. "But for your sake I'm going to try and remain tethered to reality."

We reached a doorway that was half glass, through which I could see small spotlights in the large room on the other side.

"Let's put our drinks down here. Are your hands clean?"

I placed my drink next to his on a built-in shelf.

"I think so," I said.

He reached up to a second shelf and brought down a wooden box. Inside there were several pairs of small white gloves made of cotton.

"Here, wear these."

I put on the gloves and stared at my hands. "I feel like Mickey Mouse," I said.

"Minnie," he corrected. "Are you ready?"

"Yes."

He turned to Tosh. "Sorry, boy."

He opened the door and flipped a switch to his right. In a circle all around the room, the spotlights were joined by small lamps that were connected to the upright beams of bookshelves. There were no windows in the entire room.

"I think of this as my city," Mr. Forrest said to me. "I shut the door, and the world falls away. I can be in here for hours, come out, and have no idea what time it is."

He brought me over to a long table. I couldn't resist running my hand along its shiny surface.

"It's from New Zealand," he said. "Made from an old railroad bridge. Heavy as hell and it cost me a fortune, but I love it."

He stooped over to the center of the table and drew toward him a large, flat box made of cardboard.

"These are archival boxes," he said. "I keep color plates in here and some letter prints, which arrived yesterday. They were horribly packaged in recycled freezer bags. The horror!"

He opened the box. The first letter I saw was an *H* under a cloudy sheet of what I took to be tracing paper.

"See, it's perfect that you came today. Though I admit I'm partial to the *S* in most medieval alphabets."

He picked up the *H* by swiftly lifting it in what he explained was its protective vellum, then opened it in front of me.

"See their faces?" he said. "Usually they are so stoic. But this artist challenged convention by making the characters within the letters have expressions. I didn't know it until I saw them in person, but I won't be able to sell these. At least not yet."

Mr. Forrest reminded me of a geeky kid I knew at school. He spent most of his time in the audiovisual room, tinkering with sound equipment. In the cafeteria, he had once spoken so excitedly about the qualities of static that everyone grew silent until David Cafferty, a jock who was missing his two front teeth from being kicked in the mouth during football practice, began the avalanche of laughter that buried him.

"How old are these?" I asked.

"Sixteenth century, but besides the faces, what makes them special is that they were drawn by a monk who'd taken a vow of silence. I like to think this was the only way he could communicate. Wait, you'll see."

Mr. Forrest quickly took each letter out of the box and arranged them down the length of the table in their folded vellum.

"It's a story," he said. "I haven't figured it all out yet, but from the lance one of the figures carries and the frequency of certain colors, I believe the monk was telling his own story."

I looked at the *H* in front of me. Two figures comprised the verticals. Across the horizontal, one figure was passing something to the other.

"Is this food?" I asked. I thought of my mother's ruined casserole.

"Good, Helen," Mr. Forrest said. "That would be grain. The plates tell the story of the harvest, which was very common, but they also tell this other story. There, now, we have them in order. Come follow the plates with me."

Mr. Forrest circled around the other side of the table and joined me at *A*.

"This is the figure to watch," he said, pointing at a male figure who had what looked like a bowl cut. "See how he's dressed in blue and gold?"

"Yes."

"He will be in almost all the letters. This was very unusual. These alphabets are largely decorative, and to draw too much attention to any repeating figure was not done."

"Here he is again," I said, pointing to the *C*.

We walked slowly down the length of the table together. I studied each letter and followed the blue-and-gold figure.

"I take it your father isn't home?"

"He's supposed to be in Erie."

"How is he these days?"

"If I could get my driver's license, I could at least do the grocery shopping."

I reached the *X* and leaned in close. On the slant that began on the left, there was a figure who could have been sleeping. On the slant that began farther right and crossed over the body of the sleeping figure was the blue-and-gold figure. He held only the handle of the lance. The rest was buried in the sleeping figure.

"He murdered someone!" I said.

"Bravo, Helen! Very good! It took me much longer to see."

The *Y* was the murderer imploring the Gods, his arms raised up and his head visible only from the pitched-back chin as he screamed. And the *Z* had no human figures in it at all, only a series of lances interconnected over and over again, and at the very end, an anvil.

"You make money this way?"

"Yes. I travel to different antiquarian book fairs, and I try and find things at estate sales. I always take a pair of gloves along. I've plundered just about every nook and cranny within a hundred miles."

"How much is this worth?"

"Do I see a burgeoning collector before me?"

He began to gather up the letters, starting with the *Z* and moving up toward the middle of the alphabet, where the box sat. He placed the latter half of the alphabet inside and then continued from the *M* up to the *A*.

"All I've got at this point are pictures of my mother in slips."

"Do you know what a muse is, Helen?"

"I guess."

"What?"

"Poets have them."

He placed the stacked letters inside the cardboard box and put the lid on it. "Other artists do too." He walked over to the shelves along the back wall and went immediately to a large white-spined book. He turned and brought it over to me, delivering the hefty volume into my hands.

"The Female Nude," I read.

Mr. Forrest pulled out a round-backed wooden chair. "Here, sit. Many artists have muses. Painters, photographers, writers. There is something very muselike about your mother."

I sat at the shiny wooden table and looked at page after page of nude women. Some lay on couches and some sat on chairs, some smiled demurely and others had no heads at all, just legs, breasts, and arms.

"My father works with sediment."

"That doesn't mean Clair can't inspire him."

"In what?"

"She keeps him going, Helen. If you can't see that, you're blind. They are interlocked—each sustains the other."

On the pages in front of me were two paintings of the same woman. *"The Clothed Maja,"* I read aloud. *"The Nude Maja."*

"Yes. Goya," Mr. Forrest said. "Aren't they wonderful?"

I looked at the two paintings side by side, then hurriedly closed the volume.

"Mr. Warner said everyone thinks we should move," I said. I saw the holes in the wood of the table now, where iron must have been driven through to secure the bridge's beams. They were filled with perfectly cut pegs made from a wood that was lighter in color.

"Do you want to move?"

"I don't know."

He was quiet for a moment, and then he offered me his hand.

"I think you should allow me to help you learn how to drive."

"In the Jag?"

"Are there other cars? I wasn't aware."

I flushed with happiness.

* * *

On my way home, I carried two things: the picture of my mother in her ecru slip, which I would replace, and an open invitation to come play with Tosh. But what preoccupied me most were visions of myself at the wheel of Mr. Forrest's car. I would wear a colorful scarf around my head and huge sunglasses, and, somehow, I would smoke.

It was dark out now, but there were no lights on downstairs at our house. Inside, I saw that the bathroom off the kitchen was empty and that the radio had been left, along with my mother's knitting, at the base of the stairs. I went up to my bedroom and took a pair of pajamas from the bottom dresser drawer.

I changed and went down the hall to brush my teeth. I thought of the nudes hidden in Mr. Forrest's house. He had forgotten to give me a book to take to my mother, and somehow this delighted me, as if I'd won a competition, as if his loyalty, however obliquely, had been transferred to me. In the bathroom I filled my pink plastic glass with water and brought it back to my room.

I could hear the snap of the metal blinds as I entered my bedroom.

"Where did you waltz off to?" my mother asked. She walked to the second window, directly over my bed, and snapped shut the blinds.

I did not respond. Instead I walked past her and sat down in an old chair I kept in the corner of my room. It was piled with half-dirty clothes, as it always was, but instead of moving them, I sat high on my mountain and looked over at her.

"Really, I was worried sick," she said.

I said nothing.

My mother began pacing back and forth on the braided rug.

"Look, Helen, you know it's hard for me," she said.

Nothing.

"There was no way I could face those men. I haven't even been out in the yard since, well, you know, since that boy fell in the road."

He was hit by a car! I screamed it, but only inside my head.

"Where were you?"

She looked at me, half accusing and half pleading. Her hands were shaking and reaching out about her to soothe some beast I couldn't see, some phantom self that haunted her day by day. Mr. Forrest's words were the only ones I heard: "mentally ill."

"I suppose you went to Natalie's. Don't think I can't smell booze when it passes by me. What did you tell that woman? Did you tell her your crazy mother was cowering in the bathroom? You won't get very far bad-mouthing me to the neighbors, getting drunk with Natalie and her bilious mother. I can't keep this house in order without help. Do you know where Natalie's mother comes from? Do you? The South, just like me, but she did one of those 'I'm moving north and losing my accent' maneuvers like the South is some sort of trash bin she's fleeing from. Believe me, if you think your little friend Natalie's mother is any better than me, you're crazy."

I saw myself as if outside my body. I rose from my chair as my mother continued speaking, though I could not hear her anymore. Her hands were waving about her ever more wildly, and all I wanted was for it all to stop. The pink plastic glass was in my hand, and then my hand was shooting forward, and only the water hitting my mother's face woke me to what I had done.

I wanted to tell her that I'd been hit; I wanted her to comfort me. I wanted to scream at her and rake my nails down her face. I wanted her to be sane. But instead she cowered, and I screamed, "Mr. Warner informed me that it is the consensus of the neighborhood that we should move!"

And then, just as promptly as I had stood up, I sat back down again on the lump of discarded clothes.

My mother did not make a move to dry her face. She smiled weakly at me and spoke very softly. "Mr. Warner would use a word like 'consensus.' He's a..."

I could fill in the words—an actual Mad Lib! "Pompous ass."

I could see that my mother was grateful for this, that I had greeted her back on the road she walked down. Water dripped off her nose and lips. Her face appeared glossy in the lamplight.

"One of the men hit me, Mom," I said.

The more words I spoke, the more I felt my resolve, my separation, my autonomy, leaking away from me. She would own me yet.

She half turned away from me and looked down.

"Helen," she said.

"Yes."

"It's just that..."

"Yes."

"It's just that I have... Well, you understand. You're my daughter. I don't fit in around here."

I noticed my mother was toeing the edge of the carpet. The movement was obsessive and seemed to match the rhythm of her shaking hands. Somewhere she was trying to retrieve the language of apology but was struggling.

"Why don't I brush your hair?" I said. "Like Dad does."

I stood, and my mother brought her hands up in front of her face. She looked at me from behind them.

"I want to," I said. "It will feel good, and then we'll both go to sleep and things will be better in the morning."

What I did not say was that I did not intend to speak to her again. That in the morning I would wake up and leave the house early so I wouldn't have to see her. That I would begin to squirrel food away so I could claim I wasn't hungry at dinnertime. That Mr. Forrest had given me a gift greater than any driving lessons or G&T. He had called my mother "mentally ill," and I, even if my father never did, was determined to see this as our truth.

The next few weeks were exhilarating. When my father came home, I told him what happened in the yard and that Mr. Forrest had offered to teach me to drive. I didn't need to mention that I wasn't speaking to my mother because it was with this news that she greeted him at the door. All I knew was that in not speaking to her, it felt as if I were storing nuts or bullets. I grew stronger every day.

Mr. Forrest would pull up in his Jaguar and honk the horn, and I would grab my jacket and fly down the stairs. Sometimes I would be aware of a shadowy presence in the living room, but it took exactly three giant steps from the bottom of the stairs until I was out the front door, and so I chose to believe that her presence was diminishing with my every escape from it. Outside was sunlight and the willow-green car with the jaguar leaping boundlessly in the air.

Once I was outside my house, Mr. Forrest and his car were only twenty concrete stairs away, but I was always too afraid to slide down the metal banister to get there faster. I had a vision of my head split open on the sidewalk, followed by a vision of my mother, unable to come down to where I'd fallen, unable to call an ambulance, or worse: pushing herself to the point where she stomped around in the brains and muck of me while gasping for air and gesticulating wildly.

When my father began to house-hunt in Frazer, Malvern, and Paoli, he went alone. He took Polaroids of the rooms and yards. He would bring them back to my mother, and in the dining room, they would spread out the photos, making a sort of montage of each house, separated from the others by the dark walnut of the dining table.

I would return from driving with Mr. Forrest, and the three of us would circle around the table, looking cautiously at what might become ours. It was through this experience that my father decided to equip me with a camera of my own.

"This way," he said, "you can take pictures of your schoolmates or a band recital and bring them home to your mother."

"I don't go to band recitals," I said.

"Right. Well, things you do do, then."

He smiled weakly, and I knew not to say anything. That somehow doing so would be disloyal in that all of it pointed to the fact that my mother might never again make it past our door.

But I did enjoy the house-shopping via photographs. At night, I could dream about bedrooms that floated in the sky next to a one-car garage in which sat a cherry-red Jaguar with real wood inlay on the dash.

I couldn't tell sometimes whether my mother was interrogating my father or the houses.

"Fancy wood paneling," she'd say, "but hideous green carpeting. What do you have to say to that?"

"It looks like grass," my father said.

"Filthy grass, at best."

And though it was my turn to speak, I held back.

When it was finally time for my mother to see the three houses that had passed muster, plans were put in place for nearly a week. My mother chose her outfit for the day and kept it laid out in the spare bedroom, where her father's rifles still had pride of place along one wall. I decided that I would find a silent way to show her my support even if I still refused to speak to her.

I was dieting stringently at the time, and a few mornings before the Saturday of the houses, I sliced up my carrots and celery for the day and stared at them. Using the orange circles of the carrots as notepads, I made my own dietetic version of the sugar hearts from Valentine's Day. "Good luck!" I wrote with a black felt-tip on one carrot disk. "Triumph!" I wrote on another. Then I got into it. "Fuck them!" I wrote. "Take good care." "Eat carrots!" "Tallyho!" "Avaunt!"

The next step was to hide them around the house in places she would find them. The toes of the shoes she'd put in the spare room with her outfit. Beneath the fluffy puff I had once coveted inside the powder on her dresser top. In her chipped and lipstick-stained teacup. As I crept about the house, going into and out of each room in search of places to hide these carrot notes, I forgot my hatred of my mother and opened to my love. It was, like a playground seesaw, so easy to pitch from one side to the other.

On the morning of the big day, my father asked me to leave the living area and remain in the kitchen with the swing door closed. By that time my mother had not left the house itself in nearly a year, and our yard in nearly five. The neighbors, knowing my father was spending his weekends house-hunting, had grown oddly quiet.

As my father hustled me into the kitchen and kissed me lightly on the forehead, his thoughts preoccupied with my mother, who was humming loudly upstairs in a wavering voice, I saw the blankets he had stacked on the dining room table and knew what they were for.

The morning had started with my father waking early and coming down to fix my mother breakfast on a tray. He had a volume knob on his love for my mother, and her weakness seemed to turn it up so loudly that the reverb shut me out.

The blankets were meant to calm her. They were heavy gray

movers' blankets. Felt on one side and quilted cotton on the other. My mother had last left the border of our yard when I was eleven. All the way to the local drugstore and back, she had never taken the blanket off her head. Instead, my father and I guided her to the aisle where they sold feminine supplies. No matter how torturous it was for her, she had wanted to be with me when I bought my first menstrual pads.

From my place in the kitchen, I saw her through the diamond-shaped window in the swing door. She was deathly pale and wearing the apricot linen suit that had lain out all week. On her feet were the pumps in which I'd placed the carrot slices. My father embraced her and then held her in his arms as he softly spoke words I couldn't understand but knew meant comfort. He rubbed her tensed back until she stepped out of his embrace and stood ramrod straight, her posture the stance of the model she'd once been. I saw that she had taken the time to apply what she thought of as outside makeup, not just the powder and gloss she usually wore but the whole nine yards, for no one to see but my father and the dark cloth — mascara, eyeliner, foundation, and red matte lipstick.

She's ready, I thought. *It's now or never.*

My father lifted the first gray blanket up and wrapped it around my mother's waist, pinning it loosely with safety pins. It fell to just below her feet and skimmed the ground. The next blanket was draped around her shoulders and pinned down the front. Up to this point, she still looked like a big kid playing some kind of monk dress-up. But it was the final blanket that had been the hardest one in the past. The blanket that went over her head.

When I had assisted my father, I could not help feeling that as we put this blanket over her, we were sending her to the gal-

lows. I had held the blanket up so I could still see her face—
"Are you all right, Mom?" "Yes." "Dad and I can get them." "I'm
going."—and then I had lowered the blanket and stared at the
wavy lines of the machine quilting, knowing my mother needed
the reassurance of this slow suffocation when she went out into
the world.

I saw my father lean in to kiss my mother before unfolding the
final blanket. It was in these moments, I knew, that my father
loved my mother most. When my mother was broken and helpless, when her hard shell was stripped away and her spite and
brittleness couldn't serve her. It was a sad dance of two people
who were starving to death in each other's arms. Their marriage
an X that forever joined murderer to victim.

My father draped the fateful hood over her head, and my
mother disappeared, replaced instead by a hollow vision of dark-
gray wool. They took the steps toward the door in a rush. I left
my spot in the kitchen and felt the cool morning air flood in from
outside.

Just as suddenly as my father swooped my mother up in his
arms, and as she moaned like an animal trapped in a snare, I
rushed forward into the dining room and then to the stoop in
time to see them disappear out the front door and down the
stairs.

My father had planned ahead. The Oldsmobile was facing the
opposite way of the other cars, with the passenger side nearest
the house and the car door open. I saw Mrs. Castle and her husband drive by. My father ignored them, when on another day he
would have waved. Mr. Donnellson was out mowing his grass
and looked up with pity toward my parents.

My mother did not struggle. She was suffering too much to

have the energy for that. The moans grew louder even though they were farther away. If I had not once helped encase my mother in blankets, I would not have believed it was she. It seemed instead like a movie one might see in which a woman was being kidnapped. My father, the criminal, would call home for a ransom that I had no choice but to deliver: here is my heart, here is everything I cherish, here is my mother for my mother.

My father got my mother inside the car and tucked the blankets in so he could close the door. The car door slammed, and he jogged around the front to the driver's side.

It will be better when we move, I thought, but just as quickly knew this for a lie.

My father glanced up. I waved from the stoop. Down the street I saw Mr. Warner standing in his yard with his middle son. Quickly, I turned to hide.

My parents didn't even make it inside the first house. The Realtor stood on the lawn and peered into the car as my father explained that he was sorry but that things just weren't going to work out. He was no longer interested in buying a house.

"She was very uppity," my mother said later. "Very curious about who I was. *My* shroud would have served her well!"

Mr. Forrest had come by to ask after the house-hunt. He sat on the sofa, his arm resting on the memory quilt. My father brought in a tray of cocktails, and I stayed on the Victorian love seat at the far end of the room.

Watching her construct her criticism of the Realtor from the borrowed observations of my father was incredible. She joked about the woman's hair and nails, and called her accent a "concoction of cornpone." And there I was, unable not to speak.

"What's cornpone, Mom?"

There was only the slightest pause.

My father handed her a scotch, and she sat back in her wing chair as if nothing unusual had happened in the last twenty years.

"Should you tell her or should I?" she asked Mr. Forrest.

"Ladies first," he said.

After serving Mr. Forrest, my father took his scotch and sat on the ottoman near my mother's wing chair. We all watched her. She still had on her apricot linen suit, and her thin legs were encased in skin-tinted panty hose and crossed at the knee.

"Cornpone is two things. It's a bread you can eat and it's folksy bullshit. She was the latter. All compliments and sweet until she saw your father wouldn't budge. Then her voice changed completely. Suddenly she was from Connecticut!"

Mr. Forrest laughed appreciatively and so did my father while she continued skewering the Realtor. I sat and watched the three of them from my perch on the hard red-velvet love seat, wondering if she'd read the carrot notes. I saw that inside the four walls of our house, my mother would remain the strongest woman in the world. She was impossible to beat.

After Mr. Forrest left, my father tucked my mother into bed, and I went into the backyard, where eventually he joined me.

"What a day, sweet pea," he said. I could smell the scotch on his breath.

"Mom's different, right?" I asked.

I couldn't see my father's face clearly in the dark, so I watched the tops of the fir trees, which were outlined by the blue night.

"I like to think that your mother is almost whole," he said. "So much in life is about almosts, not quites."

"Like the moon," I said.

There it hung, a thin slice still low in the sky.

"Right," he said. "The moon is whole all the time, but we can't always see it. What we see is an almost moon or a not-quite moon.

The rest is hiding just out of view, but there's only one moon, so we follow it in the sky. We plan our lives based on its rhythms and tides."

"Right."

I knew I was supposed to understand something from my father's explanation, but what I came away with was that, just as we were stuck with the moon, so too we were stuck with my mother. Wherever I'd travel, there she'd be.

TEN

The night I killed my mother, I slept only a short time, but I dreamed. I dreamed of snakes slithering into the orifices of my daughters and of not being able to help or even to scream. But I woke because of pebbles against the windowpane.

The sky outside the windows was a deep blue, and I knew who I would see down in the yard before I stood. It had been something he'd done when the girls were young and he'd forgotten his keys. He stole the small glazed decorative pebbles from our Wisconsin neighbor's flowerpots and pitched them against our bedroom window in the dark.

I walked to the window. I felt like it had been more years than I could count.

"Jake?"

"Let me in," he said. His voice was soft but strong and made me think of what my mother had said after I'd put him on the phone from Wisconsin. "It sounds like you're marrying an anchorman."

I had slept in my clothes. I didn't want to turn on a light or look in the mirror. Hanging above me were the clear-glass globes that now took on the cast of separate worlds. I imagined a mother and daughter in each of them. In one, the mother and daughter would be sharing an old-fashioned sled as they slid down a deep, downy bank of snow. In another, they drank hot cider and told each other stories in front of a fire. In the final globe, the daughter held her mother's head beneath the surface of the icy water, strangling her as she drowned.

I forced myself to stand in front of the mirror that hung over a beaux arts dresser Sarah and I had pulled from the wrecked Victorian in my mother's neighborhood. The mirror was even older, and its glass held small circular wear marks the color of ash.

I looked exactly as I had the day before, but there was something behind my eyes I couldn't name. It was not fear or even guilt. I shifted my body slightly so one of the mirror's wear marks—a black dot with a wavy black circle surrounding it—was positioned exactly in the center of my forehead. Bang-bang.

I had not seen Jake in almost three years, since shortly before Leo was born. He had touched my nose with his index finger and said, "A true button. I've never known anyone else with a button nose! Jeanine has it too."

"Yes," I said. "And your hazel eyes."

"I'm hoping this one gets your blue."

We had stood, looking at each other, until John came out of the bedroom where Emily was under strict orders to stay in bed.

"Am I interrupting something?" he asked.

"We were just fighting over who has more gray hairs," Jake said.

"That's easy," John said, with the humor of a pear. "Helen does."

My hair had begun to silver years ago, in my late thirties. I'd thought long and hard before coloring it. There was something sad to me about saying good-bye to my original color by dyeing it and keeping it dyed. In opting to wear it very short, I sometimes felt I resembled a stick woman in a black skullcap.

Jake was standing outside the back door, holding a brown leather backpack. I could see him through the half pane as I approached, tapping his fingers against the leather strap, a habit of his—finger tapping, foot wiggling, knuckle cracking—that had driven me mad by the end of our marriage. But it seemed reassuring somehow. He still had the same nervous energy he'd had so many years ago.

I unlatched the bolt and drew the door open toward me.

We stared at each other.

He had aged in a good way. The way wiry men who seem unconcerned with their appearance but who have deep habitual hygiene and exercise habits age. Stealthfully. At fifty-eight, he had salt-and-pepper hair but still appeared to be in fighting trim.

"I've been to the house," he said. "Why did you move her?"

I gasped. He stepped over the threshold and took the door away from my hands, shutting it firmly and bolting it.

"How?"

"You left the living room window in back unlocked. I didn't know if you were inside or not, so I climbed onto the grill and popped the screen. Helen," he said. He looked right at me, there in the tiny hallway. "What have you done?"

"I don't know. You were talking about rot, and I thought, *Freezer.*"

"You killed someone," he said, enunciating each word as if I couldn't understand. He looked angry enough to strike me.

I backed into the laundry room. He had never hit me. He was not the hitting type or even one to raise his voice. He reasoned. He analyzed. At worst, he stewed.

He had conditioned himself to going gloveless in the cold of Wisconsin years ago. I saw his ruined thumb and finger, where the nails had become permanently discolored.

"What did you think putting her in the freezer would achieve?"

"I don't know," I said. I could feel the shelf I kept the laundry supplies on gouging into my back. "I don't know."

He came forward, and I flinched. "Don't be afraid." He took one of my arms in his hand and pulled me away from the wall. A box of softener sheets fell to the floor. "Come here," he said.

And then he encased me. Encased me in a way the thirty-year-old Hamish never could. There was history and knowledge and even, as amazing as it was, compassion in this embrace. I thought of how he would talk about his work as ephemeral, and that all things were ephemeral when it came down to it, even relationships.

"I don't know what I'm going to do," I said. I let myself lean, for a moment, against his rough gray coat. "I should have called someone, but I didn't."

Ever so gently he removed the backpack from his shoulder and placed it on the dryer.

"You called me," he said.

I kept my head burrowed into his chest even though I could feel him wanting to pull back and look at me. I did not want to be looked at by anyone. I could not believe what I had done, but at the same time, inside me, like a kernel just beginning to grow, I felt justified. No one—not even Jake, who could conceive of it better than anyone—knew what my life with my mother had become.

"I couldn't do it anymore," I said. He put his hands on my

shoulders and forced me to look at him. I was crying in a hideous leaking sort of way. I had forgotten, as the years passed and our conversations were had only over the phone, me always in Pennsylvania and him in one city after another, how kind his face could be. I saw the gentleness that Emily had grown so close to. I saw the man Jeanine and Leo called "Big Dad," and whom, for obvious reasons, they preferred to me.

"Oh, Helen," he said. He put his hand to my cheek. "My poor Helen."

He kissed me on the top of my head and then held me against him, rocking me. We stayed that way for a long while. Long enough for the light outside to go from deep to light blue. Long enough for the first bird of dawn to be joined by a chorus. Only Jake could get away with saying such things to me.

When we pulled apart, he suggested coffee, and we moved down the long back hallway, on the wall of which I kept a map of the world that had once been my father's. Over the years, the countries at shoulder height had been rubbed raw by the accidental brushing of my winter coat whenever I left through the garage. I spied the just-spared Caracas out of my left eye.

My father had brought the map over two weeks before he shot himself. "Why now?" I'd asked him. He smiled as Emily came to greet him. Every man, even her grandfather, a secret disappointment to her in those first years away from Jake. "So that Emily and Sarah can learn their geography!" he'd said.

I turned on the lights in my kitchen. They were recessed and supposed to be better than old-fashioned overheads, but the slight broken-filament sound they always made as they heated up had never failed to disturb me. I went to the long counter and pulled the coffeemaker away from the wall. I wanted to talk about something besides my mother.

"Who are you working for in Santa Barbara?" I managed.

"Some computer guy," he said.

Jake came and stood close beside me, as if we were two line workers on a conveyor belt. He took the glass pot from my hands and turned on the faucets of the sink to rinse it out. I tossed the old grounds out and replaced the filter.

"He has homes in about a dozen places. Actually, Avery was the one who hooked me up. He's friends with this guy's acquisitions rep."

"Acquisitions rep?"

After handing me the pot, Jake turned and leaned against the counter. I spooned in the coffee, keeping my mind on the count.

"Are you sure you want to hear about this?"

I nodded my head.

"It's a whole new world. I do more and more private commissions. It beats the teaching. I like to say I burned out in Bern."

"So, you're a whore," I said.

"Now that's my Helen."

I smiled at him weakly. "Thank you."

"My flip-flop artist," he said. He took a cursory look around. It had been eight years since he'd stood in my kitchen. In a quick moment during a party, we had had a private toast to Sarah, who had graduated high school that day by the skin of her teeth.

I snapped in the filter and turned on the switch.

I did not look at him but at the counter, at the small golden flecks in the old linoleum. I had never been comfortable asking for help.

He walked over to the kitchen desk, where I paid bills and kept my own records, which was separate from the desk in the living room, where I kept my mother's, and hung his coat off the back of an old Mexican chair. The coffee gurgled into the pot behind me. I thought of how the roof light of our VW Bug had gone on the night we knew it was over. He was dropping the girls and me at home before going to hang out with a group of teachers. I saw his features briefly, sickly, sadly, and then he closed the door. I stood in front of our small house with Sarah in my arms and Emily holding my hand. "Good-bye, Daddy," she said. And then I said, "Good-bye," and so did Sarah. Our words like so many useless cans rattling at the back of the car.

We moved over to the glass-topped dining table, and he pulled out a chair.

"What do we do?" I asked.

"That's all I thought about on the way out," he said. I realized how tired he must be. In all the years of flying, he had never adjusted to it. Sarah had told me that when she'd asked him to describe his globe-trotting life, he'd responded with one word: "Lonely."

I did not sit but stayed standing, my arms crossed against my chest. I had four hours before I was due at Westmore at ten o'clock.

"Before I crawled in that window and saw her in the basement, I thought it would be simple. I somehow thought we'd just say that she had died, and you'd been so distraught you'd called me, and though I'd implored you to call an ambulance, you waited for me to come before you did. Now I'm not sure what to do. Having her down in the basement and nude, and you having left her there, makes it stranger."

On the tip of my tongue I found the name Manny, but I did not say it. Instead I turned and took down two mugs from the hooks underneath the cabinets. I poured the coffee into them as it continued brewing.

"Couldn't we say," I said, "that I found her that way? That she fell?"

As I placed his cup in front of him, he looked at me.

"What do you mean?"

I sat down and wrapped both hands around my mug. "I mean, we say what you said, that I was so upset I waited for you to arrive, but that instead of trying to explain how she ended up down there, we just say that that's how I found her."

"Nude with a broken nose in the basement?"

"Exactly."

I sipped my coffee. He reached his hand across the table and touched my forearm.

"You do realize what you've done, right?"

Weakly, I nodded my head.

"You really hated her, didn't you?"

"And loved."

"You could have taken off, done something else instead."

"What?"

"I don't know. Anything but this."

"She was my mother," I said.

Jake was silent.

"So what's wrong with my plan?"

"They'd treat it like a crime," Jake said. "They'd be much more likely to scrutinize things."

"So?"

"So," he said, "they'll figure it out, Helen. They'll put it together that you didn't just find her that way but that you put her there."

"And then what?"

"There'd be an investigation."

I drank my coffee and leaned back in my chair.

"Stonemill Farms," I murmured to myself, saying, as I often did, the name of my own development. It had always sounded like the name of a medieval jail to me.

He was wearing a blue sweater, which he peeled off over his head. Underneath I saw the kind of T-shirt only Jake would wear. Against a beige backdrop and underneath a picture of a stick-figure man lying in a hammock strung between two green trees, there was a short slogan: "Life is good." If there was a reason for our divorce, it was this in a nutshell. On this point, we had always disagreed. It was also, I guess, our reason for marrying.

"Do you ever draw nudes anymore?" I asked.

"My hands don't work that way these days. I'm working with sheet metal now."

"Should we make the phone call?" In my mind I had connected calling the police to finally taking a shower. I didn't care if what I said on my end of the line made sense anymore.

"Why did you bathe her?" Jake asked.

"I wanted to be alone with her," I said. The word "alone" rang in my head. Suddenly I looked at Jake and felt he was still thousands of miles away and that this would be true no matter how close he moved.

Through the closed windows leading out back, I could hear the neighbor's baby scream. It was a child whom I had never seen but whose screams were the unhappiest I'd ever heard. And long. They arced and warbled and started up again. It was as if the mother had given birth to an eight-pound ball of rage.

I finished the dregs of my coffee. "Another?"

He handed me his empty cup, and I took both mugs over to the counter to refill. We had always done that well together—drunk coffee. I would be his model, and he would sit and sketch me, and between the two of us, we could drink three pots of coffee in an afternoon.

"I think you should tell me how it happened. Exactly how."

I carried the cups back over to the table, setting his down but holding on to mine. "I think I should shower," I said. "I have to be at the college for a ten a.m. class."

Jake pushed back his chair and looked up at me.

"What's wrong with you? You're not going to Westmore. We have to figure this out and then call somebody."

"You call," I said.

"And say what, Helen? That you were tired and it seemed like a good day to murder someone?"

"Don't use that word," I said.

I walked out of the room. I thought of Hamish as I climbed the stairs. A day when he would want to kill his mother would never come.

Outside the upstairs front window, I could see the line of poplars that swayed in the breeze. Their remaining leaves were golden and peach, and fluttered on their stems. Years ago I had thought that getting away from my mother would be only a matter of time, that fleeing meant taking a car or an airplane, or filling out an application for the University of Wisconsin.

I could hear Jake stir in the kitchen. The creak of the floor under my faux-terra-cotta-tile linoleum. Would he stand at the sink and wash out the mugs? Would he watch the jays and the cardinals in their daily clamor for food underneath the crab apple tree? The views from my windows, whether leaf-turning poplars or birds at their feed, often felt like the farthest distances I'd ever traveled. I tried to imagine the Helen who had taken the wheel from her father that first Christmas vacation when he had driven all the way out in the Olds to get her. "I'll drive this leg," I'd said as we headed toward the interstate. "Our road trip," my father had called it in the years that followed, as it became increasingly clear we would never have another.

I went into the bedroom and quietly closed the door. In the bathroom, I turned on the shower to let the water heat. While standing on the rug in front of the sink, I realized that I was undressing in the way one would if her clothes were caked with winter grime or the remains of heavy yard work. I rolled my pants down carefully to the ground and slipped them over my socks, stepping gingerly out onto the rug, as if, by disturbing the trouser cuffs, the silt of a dead body might escape into the air. I

peeled off my socks. On my toenails, I wore my mother's color—
that muted coral I detested—which I had put on two weeks
before on a long afternoon during which we watched television
together. The sound of the PBS program about stock trading was
like a dentist's drill boring into me while my mother napped in
her red-and-white-flocked wing chair.

I was still, I knew, the woman Hamish had wanted to make
love to. Still the woman to whom girls at Westmore routinely
said, "When I'm old, I want to look as good as you," not realizing the insult. But whereas I felt my mother had possessed,
throughout her life, true beauty, I had always believed that I
lived on borrowed time. I knew that the same bones that made
my mother a domestic Garbo underpinned my more average
looks. My father, though delicate around the eyes, was also long-
jawed and bulbous-nosed, and so I had inherited just enough of
his qualities to blunt my mother's. I believed it galled her that a
painting of me existed in the Philadelphia Museum of Art. And I
had rushed to point out that it was only my body. "My face wasn't
interesting to Julia Fusk," I said, trying to please her when I saw
on her coffee table a monograph of the exhibit that Mr. Forrest
had brought.

The steam from the shower filled the bathroom. I thought of the
box of my mother's slips that I'd stolen from the basement some
years before. I had put them in tissue paper in the bottom of
a spare bureau in the walk-in closet. Sometimes, I would open
the drawer and stare down at the rose-petal pink. It was such
a simple thing, the satin piping on the bodice that became the
spaghetti straps that looped over her shoulders. The slight swish
and sway of the silk around the middle of her body. The tug of it
when it met her hips.

I could see the general outline of my body in the fogged-up

mirror. Having lost all shyness by having spent my career taking off my clothes in public, I enjoyed how demure the steam made me seem. Quickly, just before stepping in the shower, I leaned into the mirror and drew a smiley face. In the clear spots, I saw my reflection. "Ugly is as ugly does," my mother would say.

I heard Jake coming into the bedroom as I closed the frosted shower door. The idea of him being so close by after all these years both scared and delighted me.

At some point my father began sleeping in the spare room. Every morning he would wake up and make the bed perfectly as if no one had lain down there the night before, as if the empty bed waited for a never-invited guest. Even I believed this for a very long time until, like my mother, I began to lie awake at night and listen to the sounds of the house. When my grandfather's rifles were pulled off the rack, I could hear from my room the popping of the clasp that held the stocks. At least once every few months, I noted this distinctive sound, and in September of my senior year in high school, I decided to investigate.

It was unusually hot for September, and the humidity seemed only to increase after dark. The night noises coming through the open windows made my progress across the hall and past the top of the stairs go undetected. When I reached the spare room, I opened the door as quietly as I could.

"Go back to bed, Clair," my father said in irritation. He was looking down at the rifle, which lay across his lap in the deep blue of his terry-cloth robe.

"Dad?"

He looked up and came to standing immediately.

"It's you," he said.

The rifle dangled from his arm, its barrel pointing toward the ground. Behind him I saw the rumpled sheets of the bed. The pillow, I knew, he had brought in from the master bedroom. The case matched the sheets on my parents' bed. On the table was a tumbler of orange juice.

"What are you doing?" I asked.

"I'm cleaning them," he said.

"Cleaning them?"

"Guns are like everything else, honey. They need to be cleaned to keep them in working order."

"Since when do you care about guns?"

"Right."

"Dad?"

His eyes seemed far away. He would focus on me for a moment and then drift.

"Why don't you just bring your stuff in here? You're not fooling anyone."

"No, honey, that's silly. I come in here sometimes when I can't sleep. So I won't disturb your mother."

"Are you done with that?" I said, indicating the rifle with the thrust of my chin.

"I can rely on you not to tell your mother about this, can't I? Her father's guns are very precious to her, and I wouldn't want her knowing that I was fooling around with them."

"But you're cleaning them, you said."

"Right." He nodded his head in agreement with himself, but I was unconvinced.

I could not bring myself to move away from the door and go over to him. Seeing him in the soft clothes of pajamas and terry-cloth robe had always been strange for me. He was up and dressed before I was, and he changed into his pajamas only after I went to bed. On the rare occasions when I saw him like this, I didn't know how to classify him. He wasn't the father I knew but more of the caved-in man who had appeared on and off since I was eight years old.

He took the rifle and returned it to its rack, then shut the clasp that held the barrel.

"Someday I'm going to convince your mother to get rid of them."

He walked over toward the head of the bed, picked up the orange juice, and drank it down all at once.

"Let's put you to bed, okay?"

We walked out into the hallway and across to my side of the house.

I lay down on my twin bed. "How about a round of waft?" he asked.

And though this was a routine that we had abandoned years ago, I nodded my head. Anything to make my father stay longer in the room. Anything to make him focus back on me.

When I shut off the shower, I heard Jake talking in the bedroom. I grew very still, and in trying to eavesdrop, I thought of Mrs. Castle coming by the night before, how the water had seeped from the sponge and run down my arm until it hit my elbow, the drops falling from me back into the pan of soapy water.

"I don't know how long yet."

I reached for a downy white towel from the towel rack. I had bought half a dozen three years ago in a splurge at the mall. Three for me and three for my mother. I had thought that if we used all white towels, we would suddenly be sunnier individuals, bright and happy, desperately clean.

"Just use the Science Diet and wet food on the weekend. Grace likes the beef, and Milo the lamb and rice."

He was talking to his dog-sitter. Giving him the facts.

"Yes, you know I'll make it up to you, babe. This is old business, and I need to be here right now."

I saw myself wrapped in the deceitful towel. Old business.

I heard him say his good-byes and the beep of the phone being hung up. I had managed to keep myself in good shape, but nonetheless I could see that through the eyes of the world, not just Jake's, I was indeed old business. I had come to treat my body like a machine both for the sake of my job and for the sake of my sanity. This had paralleled the increased physical maintenance my mother required. Everything between us was best as regiment. Habits were comforting in a way that love wasn't. Mrs. Castle, I thought, was somewhat daunted to find that I kept my mother's cuticles in tip-top shape, or that I buffed her calluses while her warped feet lay on a tufted footstool, or that I still indulged her belief in cellulite creams at the age of eighty-eight.

"Fuck! Helen!" I heard Jake scream.

I opened the door. He held the braid. I had removed it from its Ziploc bag the night before, as if it might suffocate.

"What the . . . Why would you do such a thing?"

I looked at him. He seemed more horrified about this than he was that I had killed her.

"I wanted a memento," I said. "A keepsake."

"I can't . . . I mean. My God," he said. Realizing what was in his hand, he threw it back onto my unmade bed. "You slept with this?"

"I brushed and braided it every week. I loved it."

I felt humiliated, standing there in my towel, my hair wet and spiky. I thought of my mother pleading with me to make a concession in my no-makeup existence. "Just a spot of lipstick, please," she'd said, and in my bathroom cabinet I had the tubes of vivid color she'd encouraged me to buy: Honeydew Frost, Maximum Red, Mauve Mayberry.

"I have to get dressed," I said.

"What do we do with that? You can't keep it," Jake said. The braid lay in the jumble of my bedclothes.

"I know."

I stood in a towel on the small rug in front of my dresser. I felt, in front of him, as I never had—ugly. I wanted to call Hamish.

"I'll wait downstairs for you. Is there a phone down there? I looked for it but couldn't find one."

"That's the number my mother had."

"And this one's different?" he asked, indicating the small black phone on my desk.

"Yes, it was Sarah's idea. The phone downstairs is inside the liquor cabinet, under a pillow. Sarah calls it the Bat Phone." I had never had to stand in my own house, half nude, and explain myself before. Certainly not since I'd begun to do things like hide my phone. "And there's a slogan on it about opportunity, which you can feel free to ignore."

"You know I'm here to help you, right?"

"I do."

The moment he was out the door, I felt relief. I liked hiding in my own darkness. I liked it to the point that I'd neglected to realize it was what I'd been doing more and more. Crouching with my mother in her house and ignoring the raucous, wild, demanding world. Even Natalie and I now saw each other mostly at Westmore. We would drive to the nearby Burger King in the afternoons and drink the brown-colored water they called coffee, groaning as we got out of the car.

I walked to the phone and dialed her house, not thinking what I'd do if she picked up. But it was Hamish.

"Hello?"

I found myself unable to speak.

"Hello?"

I hung up. I wanted to drive out to Limerick in my car and fuck him again.

A moment later, the phone rang.

"It's called 'star sixty-nine,' " he said. "Who is this?"

"Helen."

He paused and then echoed my name back to me.

"Good morning, Hamish," I said.

"When can I see you again?" he asked.

To think, even if for the wrong reasons, the feeling was mutual made me smile as if I were half, as opposed to closer to twice, his age. I tucked my chin down but saw my painted toes and quickly looked up. Reminders were crowding in on me.

"Maybe tonight," I said.

"I'll count on it," he said brightly.

"I can't promise. I have a lot to get done, but maybe."

"I'll be home," he said, and hung up.

When Jake started leaving the studio we'd fashioned behind a drape in the living room and going out into the cold, I didn't question it. At first he went alone for an afternoon and hurried home in the pale-blue Bug, the car shaking up to the outside of our temporary-faculty-housing Quonset hut and sputtering to a sudden stop. We were not too far from town, and I could walk if I needed to run chores. Besides, I had Emily and then Sarah to attend to. He would return half frozen and amped up, talking about ice on leaves and the way an underground stream meandered at the base of a tree.

"And berries. These dark-red berries. If you crush them, they make this sort of thick viscous dye!"

Now I put down the phone and turned to where my mother's braid throbbed on the bed. Even I knew it was too damning to keep. I took my orange-handled shearing scissors from the pencil cup on the dresser and walked over to the bed.

In the bathroom, I leaned over the toilet, squatting down so no hair would fly away. I began to slowly slice the braid into bits small enough to flush.

For her colon surgery, they had had to shave what hair was

left from her pubic area. Tucking her in at night, I'd think how we had come full circle. "It's like handling a giant baby," I said to Natalie. "When she's too tired to fight, she just collapses onto me, as if we hadn't been battling each other for half a century."

Natalie listened to me and asked questions. Her parents were younger than mine by a decade and had moved into an assisted-living community on the edge of a perpetually flooded golf course. Her mother had stopped drinking and become the leader of the community's pep step class. *What will I tell Natalie?* I wondered.

At the thought of this, I nicked my finger with the scissors. Blood and hair floated on the surface of the water. When I was done with the braid, I stood and flushed the toilet, waiting for it to resettle and then flushing it again. I made a mental note to squirt in some Soft Scrub later to clean under the rim.

I remembered taking my mother to the doctor. The blankets, the towels, the constant cajoling, and how once she arrived and removed her wrappings, no one knew she was anything but just a little fearful and strange. She might moan and scratch, but when we hit the entrance door, she performed.

I was present at a rectal examination of my mother when, calling back to her long-held notions of hospitality, she tried to distract the young intern from what he was doing by telling him the story of the meticulous restoration of Jefferson's Monticello, which she had read about in *Smithsonian* magazine. I sat nearby in the visitor's chair, helpless. The intern, a West Indian, was too polite to continue the examination while my mother chattered on. The result was that our visit took a very long time.

When I stepped into the walk-in closet, I could hear Jake's voice coming up through the floorboards, but I couldn't make the words out. Denied the braid, I opened the bottom drawer of the dresser I kept in the closet and took out the rose-petal-pink slip.

I walked downstairs in my old black sweater and jeans. I had let the slip fall over my hips like a tunic. Since I made my living taking off my clothes, the ones I wore to and from Westmore were barely noticed. And it would be an outfit Sarah might like when she came.

Jake was standing in the kitchen, knocking back shots.

"Well, I've told Emily," he said.

"You what?"

"I didn't tell her the gruesome details," he said, "just that her grandmother's dead. I needed to talk to her. I was supposed to go up there at the beginning of next week."

"Oh," I said. I was aware of the shape of my mouth as I said it.

"She won't be coming out."

I thought of Leo slipping through my mother's fingers, tumbling down, and the sound of his soft skull against the edge of the chair. Emily had called me after she'd returned home. "I don't blame you, Mom, and it's not just Leo. I can't be around Grandma anymore."

"Good for her," I said, though I couldn't help but take it as rejection.

Jake began to tell me more. About Emily saying she was sorry for me and that she hoped this would mark a transitional period toward self-empowerment and other of the yin-and-yang-speak that I knew both she and Jake believed in. My eyes drifted over to the empty bird feeder hanging in the dogwood tree above the drained and barren birdbath. I watched it swing slightly in the breeze. It seemed to mock my lack of motherliness, a hollow plastic tube bereft of food.

Emily had been in love with being a mother since the moment her eldest, Jeanine, was conceived. I'd watched her pick her children up and bury her nose in the space between their heads and necks just to breathe in the scent of them.

"Why are *you* here?" I asked Jake. *"Really."*

Jake screwed the cap on the vodka bottle and walked it over to the antique liquor cabinet that my mother had passed on to me after my father's death.

"Because you are the mother of my children," he said. His back was to me. He placed the phone on top of the bottles and then grabbed the pillow from the sideboard and put it inside too. I didn't know if this made me feel less insane or more, Jake being so careful to replace things just the way they were.

"And," he said, turning, "I hated your mother for how she treated you."

"Thank you," I said.

"Where is her braid?"

"How much vodka did you have?" I asked.

"Enough. The braid?"

"I cut it up and flushed it down the toilet."

"Good."

"Did Emily know you were drinking?" I asked.

The first time I'd walked into Emily's house in Washington, it was a one-two punch. First, I noted that the entire house had wall-to-wall white carpeting and that I was not allowed to wear my shoes past the foyer, and second, when I asked for a drink, I was told that they kept no alcohol.

"She chose to believe me when I told her it was grief," said Jake.

"Lying?"

"You are having your usual effect on me."

"Which is?"

"Not good."

I smiled. Jake had pulled me in the direction of faith in the world, and I had pulled him toward a place where daggers awaited behind every smiling face. At some point we'd snapped apart like a doll made from nothing but opposable parts.

"What's next?" I asked.

"What's next?!"

"You seem to be in control," I said. "Let's do this your way."

"We call the police."

"I thought you didn't like that choice," I said.

"I didn't, but I think you're right. We say that you found your mother like that last night but waited until I arrived to call them. We should do it now. I've already been here half the morning."

"If we're doing this," I said, "I'd like to go back to the house and clean up."

"You're worried about housekeeping?"

"I want to see her again," I said. I winced at his expression of disbelief. It wasn't as if he were suggesting anything.

"Get your coat. I have a rental car, but you should probably drive."

Just as we were dressed and ready, Jake caught my hand and squeezed.

Outside on the concrete path leading to the driveway, I pictured driving Jake's car just beyond Hamish's house and having him meet me. It was a red Chrysler convertible and very low-tech, but without youth on my side and after perhaps being accused of murder, I could use it to distract him. A bauble.

I drove out the entrance of the subdivision. For a while Jake and I were silent. But when I hit Pickering Pike and started heading toward Phoenixville, I saw Jake begin to take notice of the area.

"God," he said, "it's like nothing has changed here. It feels frozen in time."

I was reviewing my mother's kitchen in my mind. The scattered plastic containers and the scissors on the floor might, I thought, be seen as elements in a failed robbery.

We drove by the VFW next to the lumberyard. "Wait until you see Natalie's house," I said. "She has three en suite bathrooms!"

"What will you tell her?"

"I'd like to be able to tell Natalie the truth," I said.

"You know you can't, Helen."

I didn't respond. I thought suddenly of the Edgar Allan Poe story in which someone was buried inside a wall, alive.

"I'm the only one, Helen. Me. No one else."

"Natalie knows how I felt about my mother."

"Maybe so, but this is different. You've gone beyond where most people go. This isn't something you share."

"Most people are idiots," I said.

We passed the old tire factory. When Sarah was four, she'd been certain Jake lived there.

"When you talk like that, it's hard to be in the car with you."

"Why?"

"Because it reminds me of how you could be all the time. Even when things were good, you turned bleak. You hated everything."

"Obviously it's my time to drive around in cars with men who feel the need to tell me the truth about myself," I said.

But he didn't ask whom I was referring to. Miles ticked by on the Playskool speedometer that had been made to look like a race car's controls. We passed Natalie's house. I chose not to point it out.

"The old bridge is still here," Jake said, his tone offering an olive branch. "I remember that when your father took us out for drives, it was always this spot that marked a change in him. He used to get all cheery, sort of. Remember? Like he was rousing the troops so that we would all hit the house united to have a good time. I didn't understand it at first."

"And then you did?"

"Last night, when I climbed in through that window, it all came back to me. That place was a prison."

"And you married an inmate," I said.

I clenched the steering wheel. I did not particularly like being in the car with Jake. Too much history, like too much truth, could prove a painful thing.

"How is Emily?" I asked.

"She's good," Jake said, smiling. "She's having no trouble adjusting to being thirty."

"She was thirty…" I said, and then Jake joined me, "…from the day she was born!"

We laughed in the tinny rent-a-car together.

"And John?"

"Well, I haven't exactly ever warmed to him, but he's good. He's responsible."

"I think he hates me," I said.

Jake cleared his throat.

"That would be a yes?"

"In general he disapproves of all of us. Sarah too."

"Poor Sarah."

"They divided us, Helen," he said. "Sarah chose you. You know that, don't you?"

I looked away from him.

"Shit!" Jake said. We had just hit the outskirts of Phoenixville.

"Beautiful, isn't it?"

"I had forgotten. I had completely forgotten."

"Not all of us grew up in the great Northwest, with a rock edifice for a dad and an undulating waterfall for a mother," I said. "Some of us pushed up through asphalt."

"Just think of what it must have been like for her," he said.

"Who?"

"Your mother. I mean, why would she even *want* to leave the house when outside there was . . . this?"

"I know this is going to make you laugh," I said, "but I've sort of grown fond of it over the years."

"Of this?"

An old bridge that bisected two parts of the town loomed up. Underneath was strewn a circle of trash. The barrel that had formerly held it was blackened from fire.

"Admittedly," I said, "it has seen better days, but it still has a downtown. They've even tried to revitalize it."

"Come meet Helen, your hostess from the Bureau of Touristry and Death."

"That's the Phoenixville spirit," I said.

We pulled up behind a car at a stoplight, but when the light went from red to green, the car didn't move.

"There's no one in it," Jake said.

I looked, and sure enough, without even having drifted over to the side of the road, the car had been left there, abandoned.

"That creeps me out," I said. "What should I do?"

"Pull around it," Jake said. "That's somebody else's mess to deal with."

We did.

"East Germany felt cheerier than this."

"Watch it," I said. It was as it had been back in childhood. I could call my mother names, but no other child could. I still worried for the declining businesses of the town, and I often frequented Old Joe's son for my haircuts.

"Sorry. I know it gets prettier where your mother's house is."

This was a concession for Jake, and I knew it. As newlyweds, making the long drive out from Madison with Emily, Jake had expected to see the sort of stately homes that came from his greatest exposure to the East, which was actually the South. He had seen *Gone With the Wind* on television and fallen in love with Vivien Leigh.

Besides the cluster of mansions that were built by the owners of the ironworks on the north side of town, Phoenixville was full of old brick tenements and leaning clapboard houses. Most of the supposed revitalization consisted of looming big-box stores on the former site of the steelworks or the old silk-and-button factories.

I took the neighborhood shortcut behind the railroad tracks, which led through the parking lot of the Orthodox church and onto Mulberry Lane.

"Wait," Jake said, leaning forward in his seat. "What's that?"

Then I saw them. The block was swamped with police cars and an ambulance.

"Hang back."

Accidentally, I pressed the gas with my foot still on the brake.

"Helen," he said, "do what I say."

It took all my energy to nod my head.

"Slowly, I want you to pull into one of the parking spaces."

The church parking lot was all but deserted on a Friday morning. I did as Jake told me to. When I was in the spot, Jake reached over and turned the ignition off.

"Fuck," I said. "Oh, fuck."

"Let's just sit here a minute."

"Sarah's number is under mine. What if they call her?"

"They disconnected her phone last week," Jake said. "She only has her cell."

Sarah had not told me this. I risked a look past Jake and through the passenger-side window. I could see Mrs. Castle standing on the front walkway, talking to a policeman. For a moment, I thought she looked over at the parking lot.

"We have to get out of here," I said.

"No, we don't," Jake said. "We need to figure out what we'll do next."

I thought of waking up as a child in the middle of the night. Sometimes my father would be sitting in the chair at the end of my bed, watching me in the dark. "Go back to sleep, honey," he'd say. And I would. I thought of Sarah. I knew that after a few bright spots early on, her life in New York had flatlined. I'd sworn that the last few times she'd visited, coins had gone missing from my change dish.

"I can't, Jake," I said. "I just have to tell them."

I saw two policemen come out the front door. They had white plastic bags tied over their shoes.

"What are they holding?" I asked.

"Paper bags."

"*Paper* bags?"

The two of us watched as they brought the bags over to where Mrs. Castle stood, clutching them in their hands.

"Did she make them lunch?"

"Helen," Jake said, his voice suddenly drained, "they're collecting evidence."

We sat stunned and silent for a moment, watching the men clip a slip of paper to the top of each bag and place it in a cardboard box.

"It isn't just about you anymore," he said. "I climbed up on the grill this morning. I went in through the window."

"I'll tell them the truth," I said. "That I dragged you into this."

"And why didn't I call them myself?"

I didn't know what to say, so I said what I had always thought. "Because you're too good for me."

Jake looked right at me. "That isn't going to help. Do you understand? My fingerprints are on the window, in the basement, and on the stairwell. I didn't call them when I should have after I first talked to you."

I nodded my head. "I'm sorry."

We both sat back in our seats.

"Try to breathe," he said, and for the first time the only thought in my head after an instruction like that wasn't *Fuck you.* I breathed.

On instinct, when we heard a siren coming down the road, we sank lower in our seats. It was an ambulance.

"Why another one?"

"Another what?" Jake said.

"Ambulance?"

"The one at your mother's is the coroner," he said.

We both peered over the edge of the door.

"It's pulling into Mrs. Leverton's driveway," I said. I was gleeful. Elated. As if this would cancel out the sight of police cars outside my mother's house. As if Mrs. Castle could be standing in our yard, describing how she preferred to toast the bread for sandwiches first before she cut off the crusts. How cream cheese and chives, though admittedly an acquired taste, had always been her favorite lunch.

"Is Emily's number there?" Jake asked.

"What?"

"You said Sarah's number was over the phone. Is Emily's?"

"Not after Leo. Emily asked me to take it down."

"She had a way with kids, your mother."

"I killed her, Jake."

"I know," he said.

"They'll find out, won't they?"

"Probably. Yes."

"How long?"

"I don't know. Soon."

"I wish I had died along with her." I had not expected to say this or even feel it, but there it was. He did not respond, and I wondered suddenly if I was speaking out loud or only inside my head. I would not get to see my mother again. I would not get to brush her hair or paint her nails.

"Poison and medicine are often the same thing, given in different proportions," I said. "I read that in a pamphlet while I was waiting for my mother at the doctor's."

I did not tell him that I thought it applied to love. I wanted to touch him, but I worried he might pull back.

"Eventually she got better at leaving the house. I could get her to her doctors' appointments by using a bath towel. It took her forty years, but she graduated from blankets to bath towels," I said.

Jake was thinking, and I was staring straight ahead at the low cement retaining wall that bordered the parking lot.

It always took me a moment to recognize him without his dog. He had lost the last of five King Charles spaniels two years before and decided he was too old to risk another one. "Dogs don't understand us leaving them," he'd once said when we'd met on the sidewalk outside my mother's house.

"There's Mr. Forrest," I said. I indicated the dapper old man standing on the hill over the retaining wall.

"Yes, her only friend," Jake said.

In the distance, I could see Mrs. Leverton being loaded into the ambulance. A paramedic was holding up a drip of some sort, and I could see Mrs. Leverton's head above the sheet. Almost simultaneously, a smoky gray Mercedes pulled up, and her rich son got out. Mr. Forrest watched it all from the hill in front of me. He was wearing stiff corduroy pants with a crease and a gray flannel suit jacket, under which appeared to be a conglomeration of sweaters and turtlenecks to keep him warm in the unpredictable fall air. A cashmere muffler, because he believed deeply in cashmere, was tied tightly around his neck. He was at least seventy-five, I knew. He had stopped coming by to see my mother shortly after my father's suicide.

"I think we should leave," Jake said.

I was staring at Mr. Forrest. As if he knew, he turned his head in our direction. His glasses were the same as they'd always been — thick tortoiseshell squares — and he would have had to see me through the slightly tinted glass of the front windshield of a car I did not own. I looked directly back at him and swallowed hard.

"Did you hear me?" said Jake. "I want you to back out and leave the way we came. The shortcut."

It was among the subtlest things I'd ever seen, Mr. Forrest's nod of his head in my direction.

"Okay," I said. I turned the key in the ignition. After carefully backing out, I drove away.

I did not tell Jake about Mr. Forrest. I was beginning to feel a certain inevitability building, but at the same time I didn't want to peer too far into the distance.

"You'll go to Westmore," Jake said, "and I'll call Sarah."

"And tell her what?"

"Nothing, Helen. I don't know!" he said.

I drove along the railroad tracks on the access road all the way out of town. It was as if we were fugitives. I hated it. Absolutely hated that even my mother's corpse could still exact such control. Seeing a bank of gravel just ahead, I drove into it. The wheels spun beneath us and then stopped.

"What the fuck are you doing?"

I put my head against the steering wheel. Numb.

"I should go back."

"The hell you will."

"What?" I said. I had never seen Jake so angry. "I'll go back. I'll tell them what I did. You'll be free and clear."

Tears rolled down my face, and I turned to get out. He leaned over me and held the door shut.

"It isn't always just about you and your mother."

"I know," I blubbered.

"And it would be nice for our daughters not to find out that their mother killed their grandmother, and then their father popped through the window like some demented jack-in-the-box!"

A train rounded the bend. The engineer honked loudly, seeing our car so close to the tracks, and then the car shook and shuddered as the train barreled past. I screamed. I screamed the whole time it took to pass us.

When it was quiet again, I stared miserably at the empty tracks. My eyes felt the size of pinpricks.

"I'll drive," Jake said.

I was wobbly when I stood, and Jake made it around to the driver's side before I could take a step.

He placed his hands on my shoulders. "I'm sorry if that was too much," he said. "I'm thinking about the girls, understand?"

I nodded my head. But it didn't sound entirely right to me. It was not so much the girls as it was his entire life. His dogs. His career. Someone he had called "babe" on the phone.

"Your mother ruined so much," he said. "I don't know what we're going to do, but we need to be functional. You're not in your mother's house anymore. You're out in the world."

I nodded again.

He hugged me to him, and I let myself hang limp in his arms. I thought of the warble of Sarah's voice on the CD she'd made me. Of the dreams she somehow kept alive in a way I couldn't imagine doing. She would come with me over to my mother's house and describe Manhattan as if it were so much glittering cake. Meanwhile her phone had been disconnected and she routinely took back as much food from my house as she could fit among the vintage clothes in her duffel bag.

"Manny," I mumbled into Jake's shoulder.

He loosened our embrace. "What?"

"Manny."

"Who is Manny?"

I went cold somewhere inside myself. My heart slipped in my chest like a chip of ice.

"He used to run errands for my mother or fix little things around the house. Things Mrs. Castle and I weren't up to."

"So?"

"About six months ago, I found a used condom in my old room."

"I don't understand," Jake said.

"And my mother's jewelry box had been broken into."

"He had sex in your old room? With who?"

"I don't know. We got the locks changed. Mrs. Castle knows about it and so does the congregation of the church. I never reported the jewelry missing."

"Why are you telling me this?" Jake asked.

I looked at him but didn't know what to say—what would be good enough.

"Oh, God." He turned and walked away from me.

I stood by the car. I had not thought of Manny in any real way since the night before. I remembered placing my hand over the weeping Buddha but could not remember whether I had thrown it away or whether it still sat discreetly on my shelf.

When Jake walked back toward me, his face was ashen.

"We will get in the car," he said. "We will not speak. I am taking you to Westmore. When you are contacted, you'll act surprised. Don't act devastated. By the time the police get to you, they'll know you wouldn't be. Go numb or something."

"But I *would* be devastated," I said. "I *am* devastated."

"Get in the car."

I walked around and got in on the passenger's side. Jake turned on the ignition and carefully backed up in the gravel until we met the road again.

"I'll handle the girls. I don't know what I'm going to say to them. After I drop you off, I'm going to call Avery and arrange a lunch later in the week. That way I'll be able to bolster the idea that I also came out for professional reasons."

"Jake—" I started.

"Helen, I don't want to hear anything right now. I don't blame you for what you did. What I want is to be able to limit the damage. I have my own life. Manny is your story. I won't bring him up, and I don't know about him. What happens, happens as far as any of that, but I'm not willing to cast blame."

We drove on and made our way to Phoenixville Pike. We passed by Natalie's house. Hamish's car was in the drive. By the time we passed the girls' old high school, I was pissed.

"So you want us to get away with it, but you don't want to think of real ways for that to happen," I said.

"You killed her, Helen, not me. There isn't an *us* involved in this."

"She was *my* mother!"

"There's your *us*—the two of you, K-I-S-S-I-N-G!"

We crossed 401 and drove by Haym Salomon Cemetery, which stretched along the road for a quarter of a mile. It had turned into a perfect fall day. The air was crisp but cool, and the sun glinted in and out behind a light veil of clouds.

"When you started working outside with ice and leaves, I thought it was because of me."

"It wasn't."

"You stopped drawing me. It killed me. It was like you'd slammed a door in my face and didn't think twice about it."

"My work took me different places, Helen, that's all. Drawing was always just a way into other things."

"I don't understand how you go from drawing nudes to building ice huts and shit dragons."

"For the millionth time, it was dirt, not shit, and Emily loved it."

"Perfect little Emily," I said. The moment I said it, I wished I could take it back.

To our right a partial barn was collapsing in the middle of a graded field. I wanted to run toward it and disappear as all of us eventually would, as my father and now mother had, sinking into the region's unsung history.

"I'm sorry, Jake," I said, desperate. "I didn't mean it. I take it back. I love you."

"Do you know what you put her through? How you clung to her? She told me you used to crawl into bed with her at night and cry."

I saw myself. I was twenty-seven, twenty-eight, twenty-nine. Emily was only seven when we separated. Emily was all I had. She was a warm body I needed to hold.

"You left us," I said, trying futilely to defend myself.

"We left each other, Helen. Remember, we left each other."

"And you left the girls," I said. "I may not have been perfect, but I didn't take off to become some sort of art-circuit fuck god. Meanwhile Emily seems to have granted you a lifetime-achievement award."

"I never wanted it," he said.

"What?"

The car slowed, but Jake did not look at me.

"The divorce. I never wanted the divorce," Jake said. "I gave it to you, but *I* never wanted it. Your father knew that."

He looked down at the steering wheel between his hands. Something had collapsed inside him. I could see it in his shoulder blades. I reached over and placed my hand in the middle of his back. I thought about touching him, about how he had liked to rest his head on my chest and talk to me about what he wanted to shape and build and make. I took my hand away. We had been going in circles. I needed to focus.

"Okay," I said. "What did we do this morning? Why wasn't I at the house for the last hour or so? We need to agree on all of this now."

"That's my Helen, come out swinging."

"They'll want to know."

He turned his face toward me. "We went out to breakfast?"

"Someone would have seen us. No, we drove somewhere and made love. It was unexpected," I said.

"Are you nuts?"

"I think I've answered that resoundingly," I said.

I cautioned Jake to wait for a car coming in the opposite direction over a one-lane bridge and then directed him to the turn for Westmore.

"We drove to my favorite spot overlooking the nuclear plant and made love," I said.

"And how did my prints get on her window?"

"You came by yesterday. She asked you to fix a few things for her, and you did, for old times' sake."

"It's pretty baggy. They'll check it out, I'm sure."

"Can you think of anything better?"

By the time we reached the college, it was 9:15. I had forty-five minutes to kill until Tanner Haku's Life Drawing class. I was to do a series of three-minute standing poses, most of which I found ludicrous, from holding a towel to my side to pretending I had just stepped from the bath and was combing my hair.

"I'll be back to pick you up, just as if you weren't going to hear any news that would change our plans."

"And if the cops come?"

"Act as if this is all new to you. You don't know who killed your mother."

"And hope that Mrs. Castle told them about Manny."

Jake bowed his head. "Don't tell me those things."

"Right, I'm alone in this."

"Yes," Jake said. "I mean, I don't know."

We were double-parked outside the student union. Behind us, a car blasting hip-hop pulled up.

I put my hand on the latch.

"Good luck," Jake said.

I did not go into the student union, where there was a chance I might run into Natalie having a liberal breakfast before modeling for the Lucian Freud wannabe. Instead, I walked around the low, flat building and down a well-traveled dirt path to the sole remaining patch of earth Westmore owned that had yet to be developed. The problem was that every time it rained, the field of weeds would flood. It sometimes remained swamped for half the year. There was one large oak tree in the middle of it. It must have been more than two hundred years old before its roots had rotted through.

Perched on the edge of the field, as I thought they might be, was the Senior Center's watercolor class. In the fall and then again in late spring, you could see a group of older people in different scenic spots around the campus, with their huge painting boards out and all of them wearing sun hats and matching red Windbreakers. Their teacher was a woman my age. A volunteer who loved to work with the elderly.

I sat down in the grass far enough away from them that I would not be noticed. All of them except the teacher had their backs to me, and she was intent on her task of going from senior to senior and offering brief encouraging commentary.

I put my hands up underneath my sweater for warmth and felt the silk of the rose-petal-pink slip. I could have been watching a herd of zebra on the African plain—that's how different these older people felt from my mother. I saw these people as won-drous, as the fantasy types that I wished had raised me. What had they been in their first lives? Lawyers, bricklayers, nurses, fathers, mothers? It seemed surreal to me that they would choose to come to the Senior Center, see classes offered in watercolors, and then sign up. I knew that I would never fall among their number. I was raised by a solitary woman to be a solitary child, and that was, I now saw, what I had hopelessly become.

I had to eat something, and Natalie or no Natalie, the student union was the only place within walking distance to get food at this hour. I stood, regretfully, and bid good-bye to the Sunday painters I had been taught to condemn.

ELEVEN

I walked through the gathering crowd of students outside the student union. Westmore was not known for its intellects or even its sportsmen. It was known for being an affordable commuter school, good for a four-year degree in subjects such as marketing or health-care consulting. The Art Department, like the English Department, was a condescended-to anomaly staked out by a variety of types whom Natalie and I alternately thought of as losers or geniuses. The school's founder, Nathaniel Westmore, had been an artist and writer before his Thoreau-like disappearance into the woods of Maine. As a result, both departments had remained comparatively independent from the rest of the campus.

Westmore students wore the off-price version of the clothes that were worn in New York a decade ago. On the few occasions I'd brought Sarah with me to the campus, her presence had caused a stir. I had always been proud that my daughters lived in other states and chose to make their lives away from home even if, very often, I wished I could drive down the street and sit in their houses. But I would never do that to either one of them. One saving grace in my own life was that my mother was never capable of a pop-in.

I walked up the wheelchair-accessible ramp and passed through the heated momentary hush of the double doors, and there was Natalie, among the sea of students thirty years' our junior. She was sitting at a round booth by herself, over near a wall of windows that looked out on the swampy undeveloped land. From the student union, the old oak tree wasn't visible, only the reedy grass that soon, after the next frost, would turn color and, as winter came on, make an ushering sound as the dried-out stalks beat against one another in the wind.

She was looking out into the distance, perhaps out over the highway, where the large traffic signs were nothing but small green flecks and the cars were impossible to see.

I would not tell her, I realized. How would I phrase it? I had said the words so far only once. "I killed my mother." I wondered at this new lexicon I had entered. *I killed my mother. I fucked your son.*

I walked over to her, barely aware of the students bearing food on trays as I passed.

"Natalie."

And there were her eyes, Natalie's light-brown eyes, which I had looked into since childhood.

She was dressed in one of her faux Diane von Furstenberg dresses that Diane von Furstenberg would never have put her name on. The material consisted of an inscrutable pattern that seemed to adorn many women's bodies at middle age—a sort of dazzle camouflage designed to keep the eye from being able to focus on the actual shape inside. The wraparound dress was in a style we'd agreed was perfect for disrobing but that I had abandoned. At some point, seeing those dresses hanging in my closet had begun to depress me—their light cloth and indistinguishable patterns made me think of endless suits of wasted flesh.

"Hi," she said. "You can finish this. I'm stuffed."

I sat down opposite her, and she pushed the pale orange-flecked cafeteria tray over to me. On it was half a cheese danish and a yogurt left untouched. We had always been like this. She ordered too much, and I ate what was left.

"Where were you yesterday?" she asked. "I called your number half a dozen times. I even called the Bat Phone twice."

"At my mother's," I said.

"I had a feeling. How is she?"

"Can we not talk about it?"

"Coffee?"

I smiled at her.

Natalie stood with her cup. The cafeteria cops never stopped us when we walked backward through the line and got a refill. We were tacitly granted the same privileges as the teachers.

I wolfed down the half-eaten danish and peeled back the foil on the top of the yogurt. By the time Natalie returned, I was half-way done with my secondhand meal. The coffee—hot, watery, weak—obliterated what was left of my appetite.

"What's with you?" she asked.

"What do you mean?"

"You seem sort of nerved-out somehow. Is it Clair?"

I thought of deflecting mechanisms. I could have commented that not everyone ends the night with half a bottle of wine and a sleeping pill or that not everyone was secretly fucking a construction worker from Downingtown . . . but I didn't. I would tell as much of the truth as I could.

"Jake showed up," I said.

It was as if she'd heard a gun go off. She slapped both her hands down on the table and leaned in toward me.

"What?"

"You know how I told you he used to wake me when the girls were sleeping? With pebbles from the neighbor's geranium pots?"

"Yes, yes."

"He woke me up this morning at about five a.m. He was standing inside the fence of my backyard, tossing rocks. We spent the morning together."

"Helen," she said, "it is now my opinion that you are not acting nerved-out *enough!* What's going on?"

"I don't know," I said. "How's Hamish?"

"Since when do you care? How's *Jake?*"

And so I told Natalie that he currently lived in Santa Barbara on the estate of a software mogul whom he had never met. That he was doing some sort of installation there. That he had a female dog-sitter for his dogs, Milo and Grace, and that he planned to travel to Portland soon to see Emily and the children. I realized, as I said the few things I knew, that I didn't know very much.

"But why did he come to see you?"

It rang in my head: *I never wanted the divorce.*

"I'm not sure yet," I said. I held the cup of hot coffee in my hands and pretended I was warming them up. When Natalie looked at me, a certain lifelong look that said "You're not telling me the whole story," I could feel the shakes start where my elbows met the table. A second later, I had spilled the full and scalding cup.

Natalie stood up from the booth. The coffee had gotten on the sleeve of her dress, but most lay pooling on the table or seeping into my jeans. I did not move. I felt the hot water burning my thighs. It felt right to me. I saw the clock across the room. It was 9:55.

"Time to go to class," I said. I heard it in my voice. It was suddenly flat. I had always told Natalie everything, and now, within twenty-four hours, I had done more, I saw, than it might be possible to repair between even the oldest of friends.

Briefly I thought about what it would be like if I asked Natalie to come with me somewhere, to go away together, move to another city, maybe open the clothing store she had always dreamed of. She was adjusting her dress and daubing off the coffee from where it had splashed onto the outside of her purse. "Remember riding bikes together?" I wanted to ask. "Remember that nerdy guy who lived on your corner and had a bell on his handlebars? How he used to ring it all the time?" I thought of having seen Mr. Forrest that morning. And suddenly saw Mrs. Castle talking to the police, her arms arching in the air as she spoke. Had I seen that? Or had she been calmly talking to them? Were they taking notes? Or just listening to her talk? I tried to remember the number of police cars that had been there. Two on my mother's side of the street and one around the corner. The coroner's van and the ambulance that had pulled up to Mrs. Leverton's. I could call the hospital to find out what was wrong with her, but Jake wouldn't approve of that. It would tip my hand.

"He's really gotten to you," I heard Natalie say.

I looked up at her. My vision was fuzzy around the edges, and her voice suddenly seemed a long way off.

"Well, it's time to go get nude," she said. She was reaching for my hand. We had said this phrase to each other for fifteen years.

"Yes," I said.

"I'm leading you, woman," she said, "and we are going to sit down after this and talk men. I've got some news of my own."

This helped. It made me feel good that Natalie planned to tell me about the contractor. It was what I used — that still-to-come confidence of my friend — to make my legs work and stand up.

We walked from the student union, down the sloping asphalt pathway that led from it to what was commonly called the Art Hut. I had never understood this nickname because, more than anything else, the building itself looked like a failed attempt at an industrial office complex. One that had never gotten past the first two floors and then had been cruelly sheared off and roofed with a patchwork of composite and tar. Inside, however, were the huts. Dark, warm corners in the large studios, where many of the art adjuncts would spend the night, as the conditions in the art building were often better than the places they rented in the surrounding neighborhoods — especially as winter came on. In the Art Hut, you could crank up the heat, and the bill went to the university. As we were walking through the doors and up the three stairs to the first-floor hallway, I thought that maybe I would come and live in the art building. Surely there had to be a blanketed warren to spare. What I hadn't quite put together yet was that I was already churning. Half of my mind had now begun to plan an escape.

I saw Natalie retreat with a wave into Room 230 — the Warm Room. I thought it was unfair that Natalie so often lucked out and got assigned to it, and had wondered if there was a silent favoritism shown toward my friend on the part of the room assigners at the start of every semester. I could see why. Neither Gerald, the other model, nor I brought muffins or wine over to the administrative offices. We never put Halloween pencils, with erasers shaped like counts or pumpkins or ghosts, in the secretary's mailbox.

Gerald, I suddenly thought, was someone I did not want to see. He had lost his mother in a fire the previous year. She had gone to bed and left a cigarette lit, and the next thing Gerald knew he was falling to the floor and gasping for air. He barely got out alive, and his mother, they said, was dead from the smoke before she burned. Since then, when I ran into him, he would say, "My mother died," in the middle of talking about the weather or about what poses we were doing for various classes. Natalie had always thought he was a little dim-witted, and this new habit seemed finally to have confirmed it, but as I walked down the hall to my own classroom, all I could think of was his genius. How did the firemen know it was *her* cigarette left burning on the bedside table?

"Hi, Helen. You look great!" one of the students greeted me. She was a girl named Dorothy, the best student in the class even if also an insufferable suck-up.

I could feel one or two other students take note of me then. They were adjusting their easels, which were battered and stained from years of undergraduate use.

I made my way to the three-panel screen, behind which I dressed or undressed. I noted only vaguely what was set out on the platform or pinned to the curtain that lay to its rear. There was a basin. There was a washcloth and comb. And on the curtain there was a large picture of an old-fashioned bathtub. It barely made an impact. I thought, *Bathtub,* and then I stepped behind the screen and sat down on the painted black wooden chair to take off my shoes and find my bamboo flip-flops to place on the floor.

Just as I had clung to the idea that Natalie was planning to tell me about the contractor, I now was helped along by the sharp scent of bleach coming off the former hospital gown hanging from a metal hanger on the back of the screen. The woman who did the laundry for the art building was afraid, Natalie and I both thought, of live-model disease. As a result, she used so much bleach that it quickly ate through the gowns we used and left them as thin as tissue paper after a very short time. But the scent of her fear, made palpable in the bleach, served to startle me to my task. I heard Tanner Haku, a Japanese printmaker who had ended up in Pennsylvania after twenty years of teaching around the globe, enter the room and greet his students. He began talking to them about individual style in the depiction of the nude.

I took my sweater off over my head and shoved it in the small hutch beneath the window beside me. I placed my shoes in the hutch below. I sat in the chair in my mother's slip and my black jeans. On the other side of the screen, I heard Tanner Haku quoting Degas: "Drawing is not form; it is the way we see form."

But he did not credit Degas. If he credited Degas, he would have to explain who Degas was and what Degas meant to him personally. It would be that much more of his soul he would have to sacrifice to the classroom.

I unbuttoned my jeans and stood to take them off.

"That doesn't make sense," I heard the reed-thin voice of a boy say.

I could feel the thud to Haku's chest. After this many years, even though I was only the model, I could usually feel the thud to mine. But this boy's confident assertion in the face of a hundred years of history made no impact on me now. In a way it made me see that no matter what happened, things would go on just as they had been, with or without me. Gerald would come, and he would say, "My mother died," and the students would nod uncomfortably, but he would stand on the platform, and they would do slightly altered assignments—*Man on a Pedestal* instead of *Woman at the Bath*—and then they would turn them in and Tanner would listlessly grade them as he blasted opera and drank gin.

"And Helen will do a series of poses of women at their toilet," he said.

I heard a few titters as I put my rolled-up jeans beside my sweater in the hutch. *Ah, he is baiting them,* I thought, and this gave me another jolt to stay on my feet.

As he explained what this meant, I knew he would be pointing to the basin and washcloth on the platform and to the picture of the old-fashioned tub. I knew I should hurry to disrobe. In just a moment, Tanner would say, "Helen, we're ready for you." But I stood in my mother's slip. I felt the old silky fabric against my skin. I stepped out of my underpants and then undid my bra, pulling it through the spaghetti straps of the slip. Briefly I thought of Hamish waiting for me. Pictured him stretched out on the couch in Natalie's living room. Then the vision changed, and his head was awash in blood. I put my underwear in the hutch just above my pants and sweater.

Everything about disrobing at Westmore had a rhythm. I walked into the classroom, said hello to a few of the students, glanced at the platform, and went behind the screen. I started undressing as the professor arrived, and continued as he began the patter that preceded my posing. Each article of clothing had its place in every room. In the room where Natalie posed, there was an old metal locker salvaged from the renovated gym. In my room, there were hutches and a painted straight-back chair. As I ran my hand over the material of the rose-petal-pink slip and felt my chest, my stomach, the slight curve of my hip, I thought of my mother. I thought of what a refuge Westmore had always been. I came, stripped away everything, and stood in front of the students, who drew me. I had never been quite so foolish as to believe that this meant they actually saw me, but the methodical disrobing, the stepping up on the carpeted platform, even the shiver in my body, often felt revolutionary to me.

I heard the students opening up their large sketch pads to a clean page. Tanner was coming to the end of his useless mini-lecture. I took the slip off over my head and stepped into my bamboo flip-flops. I placed the slip on the chair for just a moment and took the hospital gown from the hanger. Quickly, I covered myself.

"Helen, we're ready for you."

I saw the slip. It was my mother in the chair. I wanted to cry in horror, but I didn't. Was I thinking self-preservation at that point? What was it that made me do what I did? As if it were one of the small objects in my house that I discarded, I balled up my mother's slip in my hand and shoved it behind the hutches against the cinder-block wall. There it would stay, I knew, for a long time. Natalie had lost a ring there once, and months later a professor, bored to the point of rearranging the furniture in the middle of his own class, had found it.

I walked out from behind the platform, holding the hospital robe closed at the waist, my flip-flops and the shifting of the students the only sounds. I climbed the two stairs up to the carpeted platform, and Tanner handed me a little book. It was one with which Natalie and I were very familiar. Not much larger than my palm, it was part of a series of small art books from the late 1950s and had been kicking around the classroom for years. This one featured fifteen color plates of Degas and was titled simply *Women Dressing*.

"I'm good," I said, keeping the book held out so Haku would take it away again.

"We'll cycle then," he said. "Give them a three-minute pose. Ten, Nine, Seven, Four, and ending on Two, which you can hold a bit longer if you like. You know the plates?"

"I do," I said. Ordinarily I would have shot back their names in the order he'd asked me to do them, but I was not paying attention to him anymore. Instead, I set my energy toward Dorothy, the best student in the room. I decided that for Dorothy, I would wear my mother's murder on my skin.

For my first pose, my back would be turned almost all the way to the classroom, so I pivoted around as Tanner stepped away from the platform. I saw the picture of the tub pinned to the curtain behind me, peeled back my robe and placed it in my right hand to pretend it was the towel in *After the Bath, Woman Drying Herself.* I leaned, as she did, to the side and tilted my head down to a half profile. Immediately the room was filled with the sound of furious undergraduate sketching, as if they were cameras and I a subject to be caught in flight. Very few, like Dorothy, had the skill of consideration.

Three minutes was a concession to the students. Eventually, by the end of the semester, they would be working in two. But I was fine with much longer poses, and always had been. Staying completely still was something I'd taken to from the start.

"It's like you were born to do this," Jake once said.

He was my teacher then. He was my Tanner Haku, and for all I knew, I was his Dorothy. But I did not have Dorothy's talent.

"You have such lovely skin," Jake had said.

And I clung to it. Almost as if, if he said it again, something would break inside me. And he did. He said it when he noticed I had grown so cold that I was almost shivering. He'd come over to me—I had been lying down and had a cramp in my side—and had stood, watching me. I worried every moment that he was going to say, "You know, I was wrong. You're hideous. This was all a mistake."

"You're turning blue with cold," he said.

"I'm sorry," I said, keeping the chatter out of my teeth as best I could. I was eighteen and had never seen a man nude, much less been nude in front of one.

"Relax," he said.

He went behind the screen in the studio and threw a blanket over the top of it. It landed on me. The scratchy wool was like an assault, but I was too cold to complain.

"I've turned the kettle on," he said. "I'll make tea. I've got some ramen noodles if you want."

Ramen noodles as aphrodisiac. I had asked Jake later if he had known he would make love to me.

"I had no idea. When you walked in in that silly pink suit, I almost laughed at you."

"It was coral," I corrected him. It had taken all the money I had.

"When you took it off," he said, "I fell in love."

"So it was a good outfit?"

"When it hit the floor," he said.

I was huddled in the scratchy blanket when he returned with two mugs of tea.

"Thank you, Helen," he said, and placed the mug by me. I remember I was still too cold to even reach for it. "You did an extraordinary job today."

I was silent.

"And your skin," he said. "It's lovely, really."

I started crying. Something about how cold I was and how much snow there was piling up outside and how far away I was from home and from my mother. He put down his tea and asked if he could hold me.

"Um-hmm," I said.

He wrapped his arms around me, and I put my head on his shoulder. I was still crying.

"What's wrong?" he asked.

How could I say what seemed ludicrous even to me? After having dreamed of getting away from her, I missed my mother. It haunted me during that first semester like an ache.

"I'm just so cold," I said.

"Change!" Haku barked.

The students put their final touches to what was most obvious in *After the Bath, Woman Drying Herself* but not to what many of them were still too self-conscious to sketch — my ass. Whenever I looked at the drawings from freshman classes, the attention to detail was always focused on the props. On the one occasion I modeled for the Senior Center, there was no such fear. Both the women and the men dove right in, knowing time was limited.

"Woman at Her Toilet!" Tanner announced proudly. There was no laughter now. The students were serious, and I, dropping the towel née robe onto the platform, leaned over the metal basin that had been left upon a chair and took the sea sponge in my right hand. I pivoted now toward the classroom and cupped my breasts in my right arm as I reached the sponge up under my left armpit, as if I were washing myself.

I had always found this pose awkward. It forced me to look toward my armpit and made me all too aware of my own body. As the years went by, I could see more sunspots on my chest and shoulders, and the resilient skin with which I had been blessed had slackened no matter what inverted poses I was able to do in yoga. Flexibility did not, in the end, trump gravity. I lived on the borderline between a Venus just holding it together and Whistler's mother in the buff. I thought suddenly, as the dry sea sponge scraped against the tender skin of my armpit, that if I were less flexible, less in shape, I would not have been able to commit either of the crimes of which I now stood guilty. Lifting and hauling my mother would not have been possible. Being attractive to Hamish, unthinkable.

"Helen?" I heard Tanner say. He stood close to the platform, I could smell the garlic capsules he took every day.

"Yes?" I did not break my pose.

"You seem to be shaking. Are you cold?"

"No."

"Focus," he said. "Two more on this one," he announced to the class.

Five years ago and very late at night, Tanner had wanted to draw the skeleton of a rabbit he'd seen in a dusty showcase of the old Krause Biology Building. He had taken me to an art opening, and the evening had ended with us stumbling around without a flashlight in a building that had yet to be renovated. We found many a display case but not the right one, and we had frozen like misbehaving children when we heard the creak of the exit door below us, and Cecil, the elderly security guard, calling into the darkness, "Is anyone there?"

During the renovation of Krause the following year, I walked by and saw bones sticking up out of a Dumpster. Not caring who might see me, I hiked my skirt up and climbed onto some cinder blocks that had been lowered by crane and were still bundled in steel ribbons, so I could see inside the Dumpster. There lay the rabbit skeleton on its side.

It sat now, as pristine as I could have hoped, as the centerpiece of a collection of found objects that Tanner had placed on the long, high windowsill that ran the length of the room. It was the first thing I saw sometimes when I entered the space—the delicate bones of the rabbit next to rocks of various shapes and sizes, a God's eye made by a student's child, and an endless collection of sea glass he picked up on his solo journeys to the Jersey Shore.

Now I felt the menacing bones of this rabbit behind me and could not strike the image of my mother rotting in layers until she too was bone. There was something in the idea of it, this slow molting toward yellowed calcium that must be pinned together to prevent collapse, that I found both frightening and comforting. The idea that my mother was eternal like the moon. I wanted to laugh in my awkward pose at the inescapable nature of it. Dead or alive, a mother or the lack of a mother shaped one's whole life. Had I thought it would be simple? That her substance, demolished, would equal myself avenged? I had made her laugh by playing the fool. I told her stories. I paraded around as a fool at the mercy of other fools, and by doing this I guaranteed that she did not miss anything by choosing to turn her back on the outside world.

By giving up my life to her on a global basis, I bought small moments away. I could read the books I liked. I could grow the flowers I wished. I could drive to Westmore and stand nude on a platform. Only by thinking I had freedom had I come to understand how imprisoned I was.

"Change!" Haku barked. I could hear in his tone an admonition to work harder on my pose.

A godsend, this one, after the awkwardness of the last. I sat down sideways on the chair, knowing that the students would have to imagine the edge of the tub beneath me. How my ass would be rounder instead of squared off by the seat of the chair. Again, I reached for the hospital gown and used it as a towel. *After the Bath, Woman Drying Her Neck* always allowed for a quick massaging squeeze or two to my shoulders before I grew still.

I heard a few students grumble about a lack of time. How they wanted the poses to be longer. There was one boy I particularly disliked, even if I knew myself to be uncharitable. When I was introducing myself in the first week and telling them about myself, describing my daughters—where they lived and what they did—the boy had said, "So you're, like, as old as my mother." I had answered, because my pride knew no danger, that I was forty-nine. His two-word response, I told my mother, laughing, was "Vomit city."

"I tried to seduce Alistair Castle once," she had said to me. I stopped and stared. Early in her eighties, she'd begun to tell me things I'd never known. How she was touched inappropriately by a friend of her father's. How she had stopped having what she called "relations" with my father after his accident. How she didn't care much for Emily, though she enjoyed Sarah's failed audition stories. "Imagine having to audition to be a waitress," she'd said, loving that in New York a restaurant job could be so competitive it involved callbacks.

With each of these unexpected revelations, I grew numb, an art I had perfected over time in order to extract the truth behind the flashes.

"And how did your seduction go?" I had asked my mother, my head spinning with the pain this must have caused my father if he'd known.

"Vomit city!" my mother responded, looking into the empty fireplace, whose bricks were painted black. "Marlene Dietrich had it right," she said. "For about ten years, you can glue rubber bands to your head and pull your skin tight, but after that, it's about hiding out. At least then you have mystique."

I wanted to tell her that in terms of mystique, she'd won the lottery. From Billy Murdoch to her blanketed escapades, her mystique was bulletproof, even if it was more about being creepy and strange than unattainable.

She looked from the fireplace to me. She assessed. "You should get plastic surgery. I would if I were your age."

"No, thanks."

"Faye Dunaway," she said.

"Tits, Mom," I said. "If I get anything done, I'm going to get huge monster tits. I'll serve dinner on them, and you can eat off the right tit and I'll eat off the left."

"Helen," she said, "that's disgusting." But I had made her laugh.

I stood to draw the blinds before turning on her PBS shows for the evening. As I lowered the blinds all the way and then went to the television in the opposite corner, my mother landed her spear: "Besides, Manny and I were talking, and we both think it's your face that needs work. Your body is still fine."

What I wanted to say was "I'm glad to know Manny wants to fuck my headless body." Instead I said, "It looks like *Wall $treet Week* has been preempted by *Live at the Boston Pops*."

Days later, the rest of her story came out.

"Hilda Castle was in the hospital, having a hysterectomy," my mother said. "I offered myself."

The phrase repelled me.

"You what?"

"I tried to seduce him."

I was holding the large bath towels I used to mask her way to the car, and she was delaying us as she always did when we had to go to the doctor.

I stood just inside the front door and unfolded the first towel, draping it across her shoulders like a shawl. This was the backup. If, for some reason, the towel that was protecting her head and face should fall, she could quickly grab the shawl towel and replace it.

She peered into my eyes, the algae green of the towel darkening her papery skin.

"Does Sarah fuck?"

I knew enough to ignore her.

"We are late for your date with the machine," I said. My mother was scheduled for an MRI and was deathly afraid. For weeks beforehand, I had arrived to find her lying on the floor of the living room with a ticking alarm clock by her head. "What are you doing?" I'd ask her. "Practicing," she'd say.

Going to the doctor was one thing I could not do by proxy for my mother. It was her body they needed to poke and prod, not mine. Twice the man my mother still called "the new doctor," though he had taken over the office of my parents' original physician in the 1980s, had encouraged her to try a sedative. It was an attempt to make leaving the house not so excruciating for her. She had nodded her head as if she found this sage advice. I watched her as she creased the dutifully written prescription once down the middle and then continued folding it over and over again. By the time we reached the car to head home again, the prescription would be the size of her thumbnail, even smaller than the notes

I remembered finding in Sarah's room when she was a teenager. "Mindy screwed Owen under the bleachers," Sarah's notes said. "Xanax 10 mgs. As needed," my mother's said.

As her daughter, I could fill her prescriptions, and though she would not medicate herself, I often popped a pill before I had to wrestle her into the car. I was sanguine about it—if, by taking a sedative, I crashed the car and killed one or both of us, life would be easier as a result.

"Emily must fuck because she's married," my mother said, but by the end of the sentence I'd put the towel over her head and muffled the sound. It was actually better if she got onto a topic like this. Her aggression was strength and therefore preferable to the alternative, which was her moaning in fear as I guided her down the front steps and toward the car.

I had done this too many times to worry about what the neighbors thought. I learned from Manny that many of the newer neighbors assumed my mother was a burn victim and that the blankets and towels were meant to hide her scars.

"But she's a really nice old lady," he'd said. "I was surprised."

"Right," I'd said, and then Manny went down to the basement for some unidentified chore for which I'd have to figure out what to pay him.

"Alistair Castle just stared at me," my mother said as she sat next to me, under her towels. "He stopped coming around."

"And Hilda started," I said.

"He rejected her after the operation. We had that in common."

"A hysterectomy?"

"No, sexual rejection," my mother said. She had lifted the towel up just enough to make sure she was heard.

"Got it," I said.

"Change!" Tanner barked.

I heard the students growing restless. Three poses was usually the max of their attention spans. The adjustment for *Woman*

Washing in Her Bath was minimal. I had to lean farther over and replace the hospital-gown towel with the sea sponge, which I would hold at the back of my neck. My shoulders ached now but in ways I was long familiar with. Quickly, I glanced up to find Dorothy at her easel. She stared intently back at me.

Jake had come from a family that prayed. Emily had taken up the call by covering all bases: New Age spiritualism, Christian revivalism, and an ecumenical inclusiveness that bordered on the sublime.

I thought of my father tending the sheep in a graveyard for a church he had never been in. Churches spooked him, he said. "I prefer it out here, with the dead."

In the weeks following his suicide, I had freighted that sentence with more meaning than it had most likely deserved. I did this with everything. I remembered the particularly sweet kisses he had laid on the heads of Emily and Sarah in the days before. I was struck by how all his suits were hung perfectly in the closet, with one Jake had complimented freshly dry cleaned and ready to wear. And I went searching in his workshop for a photo I had found there as a girl.

It was still in his tool drawer. I stared at the boy who would become my father and who would kill himself in the end. How far back did it go?

I had held on to the picture as I dialed Jake's number in Wisconsin. His work was just beginning to garner attention. He was in the midst of applying for a Guggenheim to travel abroad. He had only recently left the temporary faculty housing we'd shared and was renting a house outside Madison—the carriage house of a mansion on a lake.

"Tell me everything," he said.

"I can't."

I had managed to blurt out the words, not yet able to use the more exact word of "suicide." So Jake described the water on the lake. How the back door of his house opened onto a short flight of concrete stairs that led directly to the water; how, depending on the season, the water came to within inches of his door.

"Where are the girls?" he asked.

"With Natalie," I said. "I'm in the kitchen. Mom's upstairs."

I clutched the cord of the phone so tightly that my nails turned white.

"Say anything," Jake said. "Just talk."

I moved over to stand in front of the window. I could see my father's workshop and the Levertons' backyard.

"Mrs. Leverton's grandson was outside, weeding the flagstones," I said. "It was Mrs. Leverton who called the police."

I felt the clutch in my throat but strangled the sob. I was blindingly angry and confused. I hated everyone.

"I thought of him this morning, once, just a half thought really. I was driving the girls to the Y. Emily got her Flying Fish Badge yesterday, and I heard music coming from the car behind me when I stopped at the light. It was Vivaldi, the sort of overdramatic stuff that could make my father smile. Mr. Forrest would know the exact piece."

I dragged the red step stool away from the wall and put it in the middle of the kitchen. I could sit there and look out through the dining room and across the street.

"He used my grandfather's old pistol," I said.

I could hear, if I let myself, a momentary crackle on the line or the hum of Jake's breath — the baffled noise of the distance between us. I told him everything I knew, how my father had looked when I'd come in the door; how my mother had seemed almost erased, I had such difficulty focusing on her; how the police and the neighbors had been so decorous, so kind, and all I'd wanted to do was rip off each face and throw it, fleshy and wet, onto the floor where my father lay.

Finally, when I had talked for a very long time, Jake spoke. "I know he loved you."

My mouth hung open. I thought of the vodka in my freezer at home. I wondered what medications—sedatives and pain-killers—might lurk upstairs in the bathroom cabinets and the dresser drawers.

"How is this proof of love?" I asked.

Jake had no answer for me.

I thought of the Catholic minister. My father told me that the minister had never gotten his name right. "He called my father David instead of Daniel when he saw him tending the sheep."

"Helen?" It was Tanner. He was close to me.

I heard commotion at the back of the classroom. Painfully, I sat up from my bending position on the chair.

"Here," he said, "put this on."

He draped the papery hospital gown over me. "There are men here to see you," he said.

"Men?"

"Police, Helen."

Over Tanner's shoulder, I saw into the back of the room. Standing just inside the door, and trying not to look in any one direction for all the drawings of my nude body they might see, were two men in uniform. Beside them, just as ramrod straight but in a sport coat and slacks, was another man. He had thick white hair and a mustache. He looked once around the room, his eyes coming to rest on me.

"Class," Tanner announced, "we'll end early and pick up next time."

The easels jostled while sketch pads were collected and char-coal was put down. Knapsacks were opened and cell phones were turned on, emitting songs and beeps and whistles to let the students know that yes, just as they'd thought, something more exciting *had* been going on while they'd been locked inside the classroom.

I thought of a handmade felt Christmas ornament my mother had sent me in Wisconsin one year in the middle of July. It was meticulous in every detail, from the sewn-on beads in the shapes of ornaments, no two alike, to the loop at the top, which had been braided from silk floss. The card, tucked inside the box, had said, "I made this. Don't waste your life."

As the students filtered out, the man in the sport jacket came up to the platform. "Helen Knightly," he said, extending his hand. "I'm Robert Broumas, Phoenixville police." His hand hung in the air, and I motioned toward my own hands, which were clasping the gown in front of me.

"Yes?" I said.

"I'm afraid we have some disturbing news."

"Yes?" I thought about how to prepare for it, what to say. The surprise party without the surprise was coming, and I had no idea how to behave.

"A neighbor of your mother's found her this morning," he said.

I stared at him and then at Tanner.

"I don't understand."

"She's dead, Mrs. Knightly. We have a few questions to ask."

I could not form an expression of any kind. He watched me intently, and I could do nothing but look back at him. To rise or leave the platform felt cowardly to me, an admission of my guilt.

If I could only have willed myself to faint, that small slice of oblivion would have been welcome, but I could not. I had wanted to faint upon seeing my father, but instead I had heard my mother's voice. "She'll help me clean up," she'd said to the police officer nearest her, and not knowing what else to do, I had gone straight to the kitchen, filled his old hospital sick bowl with water, and returned to the hallway to find my mother standing barefoot in my father's blood.

"He finally did it," she said. "I never thought he would."

I had wanted to hit her, but I was aware of the officers watching us, and in my hands I held the bowl.

TWELVE

When I was twelve, I found a photograph of my father in the small metal drawer beneath his workbench. He was a young man in the picture and stood outside an old brick row house. He was posed on the stairs, which were imposing and made from poured cement. On either side were brick-and-mortar pilasters. He wore a crumpled white shirt and pleated trousers, a thin brown belt holding them up. Next to the stairs where my father stood was the corner of a large square Dumpster in the scrappy patch of yard. Table legs and what looked like a chair poked up above the rim.

By twelve I had already begun to listen for when my father spoke about the place he came from. It was called Lambeth, and on the new maps, it no longer existed except as the name of a dam along the Delaware.

My mother called it the Dirty City because after they'd closed down the town and evicted the people — "relocated," a nice word for what they'd done — they had built a dam that redirected the river and was supposed to result in the obsolescence of the town.

Instead, despite the careful calculations of the engineers and draftsmen, what roared through town was a wall of mud that grew chunky with floating mowers and brittle with the skeletons of animals from backyard graves. After six months, it receded and left the upper parts of the town merely drenched in mud and ruined by water.

The official flood had happened shortly before he met my mother at the John Wanamaker shoot. "It's why I went into water," he would explain to people. The flooding had coincided with the buildup of surrounding towns, including Phoenixville. "Lambeth paid for the Holy Ghost Social Center," my father would point out when we drove by the squat brick-and-silver building.

On my thirteenth birthday, he had decided I was old enough to go with him to the drowned town where he'd grown up. He packed a picnic basket for the two of us and kissed my mother lightly on the forehead. "Be well, beautiful," he said.

Forty minutes later, I could sense the atmosphere palpably change inside the Oldsmobile as we approached the town, where low one-story cottages and five-house rows of brick homes still shared peaceable blocks until the streets dipped underwater and reappeared in the distance, a few miles on.

His house, when I finally saw it, was a ruin of the building in the photograph. It stood in a row of condemned homes that, though slated for demolition, had been left in place year after year. The only remaining access was by a patched asphalt road that fell off on either side into culverts eroded by water. Trying to avoid the yawning potholes meant that he wove the car in and out of lanes like a drunk might. To me it was a sickening carnival ride.

At last we stood outside the front door, and he took my hand as we picked our way up the rotting stairs.

"This is where you stood in the photo," I said.

"Nature takes things back," my father said. "Watch your step on the porch."

And sure enough, the planks, stripped over time of their protective paint, were all but rotten. Someone—my father, I realized—had placed a new sheet of plywood down so you could make it to the front door without falling. I saw the sawed edges of a faulty arabesque and recognized it as what remained after he had carved out the arching back of a rocking horse.

We walked into the front hall, and I spotted a propane lamp sitting on an old mule-ear chair. It was from his workshop.

"There'll be things in here," he said, "that we don't need to tell your mother about."

I had begun to vary my reading at school with squirreled-away paperbacks that did not appear on our reading lists, and I knew, I thought, what comprised "men's needs." I pictured what Natalie and I loved the sound of: a den of iniquity. There would be velvet drapes and throw pillows and some sort of women smoking things out of pipes that looked like vases but weren't. That's as far as my imagination went, but I thought I was prepared.

I wasn't.

I didn't even know what to make of them at first.

Not in the hallway or the front room but in the back rooms on the first floor and in the bedrooms of the floor above, I saw and understood what my father had been doing over the years in his workshop when he was not busy with his rocking horses. He had been making figures out of plywood.

When I walked into the kitchen and saw wood nailed to the wall—a finely articulated shadow of two adults and a child sitting at a table—I stepped back.

"Dad!" I said.

"I'm right here," he said.

And he was, standing right behind me just inside the doorway.

"That's so cool," I said.

I could sense his rare smile even though I wasn't looking at him.

"I'm glad you like them."

I went up and traced the head of the child lightly with my index finger, careful of splinters. They were rough and unpainted, and what held them fast was a variety of screws and nails.

"Is this supposed to be you?" I asked, my palm spread flat against the chest of the child.

"Yes," he said. "And that's my mother and father. This is the second one I made. You were very little then."

It must have struck me at some point that this meant he had been building a family out of plywood over a stretch of about a dozen years. At the time I felt the adrenaline rush of the shared secret between us, something my mother wasn't privy to.

"Is this where you went that time?"

"No," he said, and gave the standard line. "I was in Ohio, visiting friends and family."

By thirteen I sensed this was a lie my parents told, but I still didn't know why.

It was cold in the rooms, as there was no heat, and the plaster around the plywood people was nearly down to the boards, but I could see why he liked it here. It was deathly quiet except for the tree branches scraping against the windows. Occasionally, a pane would break, my father said, "from the trees' desire to occupy the place."

"Are you ready to go upstairs?" he asked.

"This is so weird, Dad," I said.

"I can count on you, can't I?" he asked. His eyes drew together in anxiety for just a moment.

"I'll never tell if you don't want me to," I said.

We climbed the stairs together, as if on the way to an important party just beyond the landing up above. Here there were more people. In a room to the left, there was a bed with a figure propped up. I could see the space between the angle of the elbow and the wall. A figure was standing at the end of the bed.

"That's my mother, coming to wake me up," my father said.

"And who's that?" I pointed to a gaunt plywood figure holding up something that, without paint or shading, looked like a cord or snake.

"That's the doctor. He had come to sound my chest."

I turned and looked at my father.

"I was often sick," he said. "It was hard on my mother."

In another room I thought I spotted myself, and without speaking, I pointed to a figure tacked to the wall.

"Yes," he said.

There were two other figures in the room—the smallest room on the second floor—and I did not ask who they represented. If I was the larger one—the size of myself at eight or nine—then the two bundles on either side of me were my unborn brothers or sisters.

In the middle of the largest room, where two adults stood with their arms gesticulating in the air, was a rocking horse like the one he had once made me and those he made and painted each year for the Greek Orthodox Children's Fair. This one was plain, save for the pencil work that would mark out the separations between colors.

"Why didn't you paint it?" I asked.

"I thought about it," he said, "but I wanted it to feel at home here. Go ahead and ride it if you want."

"I'm too big, Dad," I said.

His eyes saddened behind his heavy glasses.

"Not in this house," he said. "In this house, you're ageless."

I looked at my father and felt a pain right in the center of my chest, as if all the air in the room would not be enough, could not fill me up.

He smiled at me. I did not want to disappoint him, so I smiled back.

"I'll show you," he said.

He took off his glasses, folded the stems carefully, and handed them to me, his thumb and forefinger on either side of the nose bridge. I took them in both hands on the outside of the frames. His world without them, I knew, was merely fuzzy shapes and colors.

Carefully, he got on the rocking horse.

"I have to admit," he said, "I haven't tried this before. I don't know how much weight it will support."

He sat on the flat back section of the horse and kept his feet on the floor instead of curling them up to the dowel that stuck out on either side. I was grateful that I held his glasses. If I winced, it might look like a smile.

He rocked the horse back and forth gently, keeping his weight, I saw, mostly in his legs. "Hilda says I put so many screws in them that these horses would hold a horse!" He laughed at Mrs. Castle's joke.

The plywood curve mashing against the wooden floors didn't sound right to me. It went against everything my mother had taught me about putting furniture on rugs and coasters under cups.

"I'm going to go farther up," I said.

My father stopped rocking the horse.

"No, sweetie," he said. "This is it."

"But there're more stairs," I said.

"That's just a cramped attic space. No people there."

He stood but still straddled the rocking horse, and I knew he had another secret.

"I'm going up!" I said gleefully, and turned and ran, his glasses still in my hand.

I could hear my father stumbling as I put my hand on the newel post and gained the bottom stair.

"Honey, don't!" he called out.

At the top of the stairs, there was a closed four-panel door. I put my hand on the cold porcelain knob.

"You won't like what you find in there."

"Oh, well," I said over my shoulder. "Such is life." It was an expression Mr. Forrest often used when talking to my mother in the living room. She would complain, and he would say, "Such is life," and steer her back to a discussion of Trollope, whom they read in tandem, or of Edith Wharton's *The Glimpses of the Moon,* a first edition of which Mr. Forrest had given my mother as a gift.

I turned the doorknob and stepped into the room.

It was much smaller than the floor below, and there were windows only at the back, which looked out over the sunken yards of Lambeth. Unlike that of the first and second floor, the view from the third floor still cleared the trees. In the distance I could see the menacing inward curve of the Delaware.

My father stood in the doorway now. He had taken the stairs slowly, giving me time to see what there was to see. His eyes without his glasses looked lost.

"Here," I said. He fumbled for them and put them on.

"The front is a storage space. You get there by crawling into that small doorway."

But I was looking at the mattress, covered in blue ticking with balled-up blankets and a pillow, that sat in the middle of the floor. I thought of all the days he spent away from us.

"Sometimes I sleep here," he said.

I shifted my feet so that all my father would see from where he stood was my back. There were paperbacks on the floor beside the head of the bed. I recognized a photographic history of trains. It had once been on the nightstand in my parents' bedroom. And a huge anthology of love poems was there too. It had been a gift at Christmas from my father to my mother. And I could see, peeking out beneath a scattering of detective novels, one fleshy thigh of what I knew was a nude photograph of a woman in a magazine. Her skin looked orangey to me.

"I like being able to look out over the yards at night. I feel like I'm hidden away up here in a nest."

"Did you really go to Ohio that time?" I asked.

"I went to a hospital, Helen."

I took this in.

"And the business trips?"

The question hung in the air. He walked up behind me and put his hands on my shoulders. He leaned over and kissed the top of my head, the way he did with my mother.

"I go on business trips," he said, "but sometimes, on my way home, I spend a night here."

I tore myself away from him and turned around. My face felt hot.

"You leave me alone with her," I said.

"She's your mother, Helen."

I stumbled over the edge of the mattress and fell down. He came toward me, but I quickly leaped to my feet and walked to the head of the bed so that we would have the blue ticking and the smelly wad of sheets between us.

"Just for a night or two at a time," he said.

I kicked the anthology of love poems and the detective novels aside and uncovered the rest of the orangey woman. Her breasts were larger than I'd thought it possible for breasts to be. Even then they struck me as preposterous.

We both stared at her.

"She's gross, Dad," I said, forgetting, for the moment, my anger.

"Admittedly," he said, "she's a bit top-heavy."

"She looks like a freak," I said. Inside my head I heard the word "hospital" over and over again. What did it mean?

"She's a beautiful woman, Helen," he said. "Breasts are a natural part of a woman's body."

Without thinking about it, I crossed both arms over my chest. "Gross!" I said. "You come here and stare at gross freak women and leave me with Mom."

"I do," he said.

What I didn't ask, because it was never a question in my mind, was *Why?*

"Can I come here with you?"

"You're here now, sweet pea."

"I mean, can I sleep here?"

"You know you can't. What would we tell your mother?"

"I'll tell her about this place," I threatened. "I'll tell her about the magazines. I'll tell her about the plywood babies in that little room!"

Each sentence hit nearer the mark. He didn't actually care much if I told on him about the mattress or the *Playboy* bunnies or visiting the house. It was the plywood people he cared about.

"I didn't raise you to be cruel."

"What hospital?" I asked.

My father looked at me, considering.

"Why don't we go on our picnic and I'll tell you about it."

For the remainder of that afternoon, my father showed me the still-visible parts of the town where he'd grown up. We had a picnic of egg-salad sandwiches with cucumber, and chocolate chip cookies that he'd made himself. There was a thermos of milk for me, and he drank two Coca-Colas end to end and burped as loud as I'd ever heard anyone. He couldn't get me to stop laughing after that. I laughed so hard I ended up coughing, like a bark, over and over again.

"Why don't we wait for the darkness here," he said.

It was a gift, and I did not have the heart to ask again about the hospital. Part of me was happy with the fib. It made him seem normal, even if it was just pretend. Where is your father? In Ohio, visiting friends and family. I decided that day that I would never blame my father for anything—his absence, his weakness, or his lies.

THIRTEEN

Jake and I had been married for little more than a year when I began having nightmares. They involved boxes, the empty gift boxes that occupied space on tables or were circled under the Christmas tree. But these boxes were sodden and the cardboard darkened. What was in these boxes were pieces of my mother.

Jake learned to wake me slowly. He would put his hand on my shoulder as I mumbled words that in the beginning were too garbled for him to figure out. "You're here with me, Helen, and Emily is safe in her crib. Let's look at Emily, Helen. You're here with us." He had read somewhere that repeating the name of the sleeper helped usher her into the present. He would speak to me like this as he saw me surfacing. My eyes would open but remain unfocused until I heard him saying his name, Emily's name, mine. My pupils were like camera lenses, adjusting, readjusting, zooming in. "Cut-up dream?" he would ask then. Slowly I rose out of the land where I was the person who had cut my mother up and labeled the boxes. My father was in our house at large in the dream. Whistling.

As the remaining students left and Tanner futilely shouted out a homework assignment to their departing backs, I stepped behind the partition to get dressed.

"We'll wait for you outside the room," Detective Broumas said.

I heard them go and the door shut, but I was not dressing. I was sitting on the wooden chair, shivering and holding the hospital gown tighter and tighter against myself. I had finally done it, and now the world would know.

"Helen?"

It was Tanner.

"Are you okay?"

"Come around," I said.

Tanner came behind the partition and knelt in front of me. We had tried to have sex once but instead ended up getting drunk and depressed about how our lives had turned out. As he knelt before me, I saw that he had begun balding on top.

"You have to get dressed," he said.

"I know." I stared down at my knees, which suddenly seemed as marbleized as my mother's skin. I saw my joints, fat sheared off at a rendering plant. Scarsdale patties made of my thighs and arms and stored in a meat freezer, waiting to be broiled or pan seared.

"It will be okay," he said. "Cops are always freaky, but they'll just ask you things about your mother's routines and such. It happened when my landlady died."

I thought about nodding my head, for a moment I even thought I was nodding my head, but my brain seemed to have broken itself in two. I looked at Tanner.

"I'm not crying," I said.

"No, Helen, you're not."

"It's over," I said.

Tanner did not know the details of my life. But drunkenly, I had mentioned how I felt my mother was sucking the life out of me day by day, year by year. I wondered if he could possibly know what "it's over" meant, or if he, despite his anarchist habits, was still moved by the sentimentalist portraits of mothers that were created all over the world.

"Let me help you," he said. "Is this your sweater?"

He reached over to the hutch and pulled out my sweater, along with my bra, which I had tucked inside. Hurriedly he snatched the bra off the dirty floor.

"Sorry," he said.

Though Tanner had seen me nude week after week for years now, as I peeled back the top of the hospital gown and let it fall around me on the chair, I felt as if I had never really undressed in front of him. He held out my bra as if it were a dress for me to slip into. Seeing his attempt to dress me, I realized that no matter how hard it was, I would have to wrest control of myself and perform.

I took the bra from him and held it in my lap. I managed a small smile. "Thank you, Tanner," I said. "I'll take it from here."

He held out his left hand, and I put my free hand in his. When I was standing, he very gently leaned over and kissed me on the head.

"I'll see you Monday morning at ten a.m.?"

This time, I nodded my head.

I was zipping up my jeans when Natalie came in.

"Are you back there?"

"Yes."

She came around the partition in her Diane von Furstenberg

and a cloud of newly applied perfume. Her face was splotchy. Tears had recently moistened her cheeks.

"They came in Room Two Thirty looking for you. I dressed as fast as I could. Can I hug you?" she asked. Always, even now, I radiated that permission had to be granted.

Her warmth made me melt into her, want her in the way I had always wanted a mother. But inside my animal brain, I thought how dangerous this was. The very things that would comfort me could make the necessary coil unwind.

I wanted to claw at her. At her ample breasts and what we recently had read was called a "menopot." I wanted to take her ridiculous dyed hair and pull it out at the roots. I wanted these things because I could not have what I wanted most—to crawl inside her and disappear.

I let her move her hand through the short bristle of my hair and down the back of my neck. I let her rub me across my bony shoulder blades. And I cried, just a little bit, unable to know whether it was because I should, given the circumstances, or because Natalie's comfort was painful to me.

"Where's Jake?" she asked. She pulled herself away from me and held my shoulders in her hands. I looked at her. I was happy to have tears at the corners of my eyes. Would this make me more sympathetic? Could I manage it again when necessary?

I remembered our backstory. "I don't know. He's supposed to pick me up. He was going to hook up with a former student who works at Tyler now."

"So he'll be here soon? He can go with us."

"With us?"

"To the police station," Natalie said.

"What?"

"Your mother was killed, Helen."

I sat down with force.

"Didn't the police tell you? I thought you knew."

I tried not to wince. "By who?"

"I thought they told you, sweetie. I'm sorry. Listen, get your shoes on. They'll tell you everything they know."

"Do they have a suspect?"

"I don't know. I was talking to one of them, and then another guy, in a sport jacket, cut him off."

"Detective Broumas," I said. My voice enunciated each syllable in a monotone. I thought of Jake and of our wedding vows: *Do you promise to take this man in marriage, as long as you both shall live, in sickness and in health, in murderous extravagance?*

"Shoes," Natalie said, and pushed them toward my chair with her foot.

The door opened, and I heard Jake's voice in the hallway.

"Is she almost ready in there?" an unfamiliar voice asked.

"We're coming," Natalie trilled. "Just one more minute."

"Her husband's here."

"He can come in."

"The detective is asking him a few questions."

Natalie and I looked at each other. My shoes were on, and for all intents and purposes I was as ready as I'd ever be.

I grabbed my bag, for a moment confusedly thinking my mother's braid was still inside. Jake had known. Without him it would still be on the bed, curled like a snake.

"Lipstick?" Natalie said.

"Kiss me," I said. Without hesitation, she did. I rubbed my lips together, spreading out the gloss.

"Ready?"

"Let's go."

"It's horrible, what's happened," Natalie said as we approached the door. "But Jake is here. The Lord works in mysterious ways."

I could not tell my friend it had nothing to do with the Lord but everything to do with a chain of events that my own hands had set in motion less than twenty-four hours ago. Pushing down on the towels, the blankets wrapped around her broken body, her rose-petal-pink slip wedged between the hutch and the wall, traces of the silver braid clinging to my toilet bowl. All of them, like the phone call to Avery that had alerted Jake, had come from the hands that now held my purse, now reached for the door as it swung open, now shook the meaty palm of Detective Broumas.

I saw Jake sitting on the teacher's desk in the classroom opposite. He made a move to stand up, but a hand on his shoulder stopped him.

"Your husband is answering a few simple questions for us," Detective Broumas said. "I'd like you to do the same."

I focused on his shoulders. Flecks of dandruff were scattered over the midnight-blue wool. His eyes, a deep hazel surrounded by long lashes, reminded me of a therapist I'd gone to five years after my father's death. "Probe, probe, probe," I had said to this doctor. "Is that all you ever do?"

A student, late for class, headphones blaring, walked by, turning her head like an automated camera, then passed on.

"We're ready to leave," Natalie said.

"Leave?"

"Yes, Detective," she said. "I would like to accompany her to the station."

The detective smiled. "Nothing so fancy," he said. "We'll just find an empty classroom and make the best of it."

I was watching Jake. His feet dangled over the edge of the desk. For all his height and maturity, he seemed to me, in that moment, a child. By coming to help me, by climbing through that window, he would be inextricably linked to whatever happened to me. I remembered our story. He had tried to fix my mother's window, doing me a favor for old times' sake.

"Shall we go in here?"

"Here?" I said, pointing to the door Natalie and I had just stepped out of.

"That is, if you don't mind."

Natalie was asked to wait outside. Detective Broumas called for one of the uniformed officers, and the three of us went into the classroom.

"It was a very confusing morning for the neighborhood," Detective Broumas said.

Surveying the room and seeing few places to sit, he pointed toward the platform.

"There's a chair there, I guess. Does that suit you?"

"Sure. There's another chair behind the partition," I said.

"Will you get that, Charlie? We can move them over here."

"Actually," I said, "Professor Haku would prefer that you didn't move that one chair. He has it set up so the pose can continue on Monday."

Detective Broumas smiled. He removed his navy blazer and hung it off the back of one of the easels in the first row. "We were talking to your husband in there. An artist. Is that how you got into this line of work?"

"Yes," I said.

The policeman named Charlie brought the chair I'd just been sitting on and put it in front of Detective Broumas.

"Put it up there with the other one," he said. "Shall we?"

As I stepped up on the platform and took the seat that was meant to substitute for a tub in *Woman Washing in Her Bath,* Detective Broumas turned to retrieve a notebook from the pocket of his blazer.

I remembered finding a small notebook that must have fallen from Jake's jacket pocket. Inside he kept a sort of journal of his time outside in the cold.

Dripped icicles for forty minutes in snow. Used tree as cover.
Can I break up ice and solder it together by melting it with my
*   hands?*
Leaves as thin as parchment. How to embellish what is already
*   perfect?*

"Are you ready?" Detective Broumas asked. He sat across
from me. The uniformed policeman had taken up his post near
the door. I noticed, as I glanced at him, a certain boredom, as if
this were a day like any other.

"My friend says my mother was killed," I said.

"Somebody had a hand in it, yes."

"Who?"

"We aren't sure yet," he said. "She was found in the basement
by a neighbor of hers."

"Mrs. Castle," I said. "She has a key." Answering, for myself,
my own open question.

"Actually, she doesn't. She found a window open in back that
had been jimmied and asked a young lady to help her."

Detective Broumas referred to his notebook. It was a small
leather bound book with a red ribbon to mark his place.

"Madeline Fletcher. Her father lives next door."

For a moment I thought of the tattooed wonder snaking into
my mother's house, how it would have upset her.

"Yes," I said, "that's the window my husband tried to fix yesterday."

"It was wide open," Detective Broumas said.

"It shouldn't have been."

"Mrs. Castle also said that you were there last night. That she
saw your car as late as seven p.m. outside the house."

"That's right."

"What were you doing there?"

"She's my mother, Detective."

"Just go through what you did and how you left her, if you can. Was she sleeping? Up? What was she wearing? Did you get any phone calls? Hear any strange noises? Had your mother been frightened of anyone or anything?"

"My mother has been declining for some time," I heard myself say. I used the passive vernacular I so hated in reference to the elderly. "She had a grim bout with colon cancer a few years ago and never really recovered. Her doctor says that if people live long enough, cancer of the bowels gets them in the end. It's his little joke."

Detective Broumas cleared his throat. "Yes, well, that sounds difficult. We've talked to Mrs. Castle, and I know she assisted her a great deal. Was there anyone else who frequented the house?"

I looked down at my hands. I had stopped wearing jewelry of any kind. I didn't like the weight of it on my body, and whenever I found myself out at a restaurant, by the end of the meal I would have piled everything, from rings to earrings to watch, to the left of my place mat. I was unable to talk with it on.

"Not recently," I said.

"Mrs. Castle mentioned an incident in the house not too long ago," he prodded.

I looked back up at him.

"I found a condom in my old room."

"And?"

"We all assumed it had to be the boy who ran errands for my mother and sometimes did things around the house that she couldn't manage herself."

He referred to his notebook. "Manny Zavros?"

"Correct."

"Fifteen twenty-five Watson Road?"

"That's his mother's house," I said. "He disappeared after Mrs. Castle put the congregation on him."

"Disappeared?"

"Do you think it was him?"

"We're following every lead."

"I don't want to get Manny in trouble, but . . ."

"Yes?"

"There's something else that I didn't share with anyone."

"I'm the person to share things with," he said.

I knew this was the moment to plant the seed. As I spoke, I felt my face flush.

"Around the same time, the contents of my mother's jewelry box went missing."

"You didn't report it to the police?"

"I didn't notice it for a few weeks, and by that time Manny was gone and I'd had the locks changed. Anyway, I didn't want to upset my mother. She hadn't worn most of the jewelry for years."

"I see. By the way, your mother isn't the only one who died in the neighborhood in the past twenty-four hours."

I knew what he was going to tell me and tried quickly to hide any expression that might indicate this.

"It wasn't Mr. Forrest, was it?"

"Why do you ask about him?"

"Because I'm very fond of him," I said. "I've known him since I was small."

"And Mrs. Leverton?"

I drew a quick inhalation of breath and covered my mouth with my hand. The action—too calculated—made me immediately self-conscious.

"She was found in her bedroom this morning by a cleaning woman."

Though I knew what I had seen—Mrs. Leverton alive and leaving in an ambulance—I couldn't help thinking that at least I'd been present when my mother died.

"How did they die, exactly?" I asked. I felt a light layer of perspiration spread beneath my sweater. My hands grew clammy. Why hadn't I asked this at the start?

"Very differently. Mrs. Leverton was unconscious but breathing when the maid found her. She died in the back of the ambulance on the way to the hospital."

"And my mother?"

"What time did you leave your mother's house last night?"

I sat up straighter and looked for signs that he was on the verge of accusing me. But he glanced at me mildly and pulled at the crease of his right trouser leg with the same hand that held his pen.

I remembered a phrase Sarah had taught me. *Weak Handsome.* It was a show-business term that stood for men who were shadows of truly handsome men. They held all the proportions and qualities — hair color, height, etc. — but there was just enough flat or off about them that they were never cast as leads. A weak chin, eyes a bit too far apart, ears that stood out from the sides of their heads. I decided that Robert Broumas was *Weak Handsome.*

"I want to know how she died," I said.

"I'll answer that in a moment. What time did you leave your mother's house?"

"Shortly after six," I said. I stopped short of flinching. Mrs. Castle had said she'd seen me at seven.

Detective Broumas flipped back a few pages in his notes. He adjusted himself in the chair, cleared his throat.

"Did you go straight home?"

"No."

"Where did you go?"

"Mrs. Castle may have told you how badly off my mother was," I said. "That she hadn't recognized her yesterday."

"She did."

"I knew I would have to call the hospice. That once they took her away, she would never see her house again."

I found myself crying now. Tears rolled down my cheeks, and I wiped them with the sleeve of my sweater. *She never had to leave her house,* I wanted to say. *Do you realize how important that was to her?*

"I drove around a lot," I said. "I went to a spot I go to, to think."

"Where is that?"

"It's near farmland up near Yellow Springs Road. You can see the Limerick nuclear plant from there."

"And you stayed there for how long?"

I calculated in my head how long I had been with Hamish and added the extra hour or so I'd still been at my mother's.

"About three hours."

"You sat and thought for three hours?"

"I'm afraid to admit that I fell asleep. My mother can be very exhausting."

"And you went home after that?"

"Yes."

"Did you make any phone calls or talk to anyone?"

"No. Will you tell me how my mother died?" My lies were mounting, and I knew it.

"Her body was found in the basement."

"The basement? Did she fall?" I stopped. Even to my own ears, I sounded false.

"We aren't certain yet. We have an autopsy scheduled for this afternoon. What was your mother wearing yesterday?"

I mentioned the skirt I had cut open, the blouse I had ripped, and her putty-colored bra. They must have already collected them from the kitchen floor.

"Was she in the habit of dressing herself?"

"Yes," I said.

"Did your mother go outside the house much?"

"She was agoraphobic," I said. "It was very hard for her to leave the house."

"I mean around the yard or, say, taking the trash down the steps outside the kitchen, that sort of thing."

"She was very willful. She wouldn't let Mrs. Castle and me do everything."

I thought we had barely begun, but after placing the thin red ribbon on the current page, Detective Broumas closed his notebook. He visibly relaxed, waving a sort of postural off-duty flag.

"Can I ask you a personal question?" he said.

"Can I see her?"

Detective Broumas stood. I stayed in the model's chair.

"Tomorrow, after the autopsy," he said. "What's this like?" He gestured to indicate the room.

"What's what like?" I asked.

"Doing what you do for a living?" His smile came easily. I hated it. I hated it because I could not tell him to fuck off, because I knew the kind of interest he had. There was sincere and there was prurient.

"Like any other job, but that much more exposed," I said.

He chuckled to himself and stepped off the platform. I took this as my cue that I could stand.

"We have a few people we still haven't tracked down who we want to talk to. Neighbors at work, that sort of thing." He took his jacket off the easel and slipped it on. "There are fingerprints and a footprint to run. We found a small bit of blood on the side porch. It could be your mother's. Her body had been moved."

I stepped down from the platform. I felt myself floating.

I pictured myself nude and curled up in the bathtub of my father's workshop. The tools and hooks that had fallen from the walls were sticking halfway out of my bloodless flesh.

Coldness kills. I saw it as an entry in Jake's journal, scribbled in his hurried hand. I thought of my mother leaning out my bedroom window when I was a teenager, to braid and rebraid the vine outside. Protecting me from Mr. Leverton had seemed so crucial to her that she had regularly risked falling from the second story of her home. Why hadn't she been frightened? Had she loved me that much or had it had nothing to do with me? Had my birth merely created an extension of her fear?

The uniformed police officer opened the door.

"I'll let you get back to your friend and your husband. Oh," Detective Broumas said, "I'm sorry. Your ex-husband, correct?"

I nodded my head. I had gotten down off the platform only to find myself desperately in need of a chair. I leaned, as nonchalantly as I could, into the carpeted edge of the platform.

"Yes."

"And how long have you two been divorced?"

"More than twenty years," I said.

"That's a long time."

"We have two daughters."

"You're close enough that he would come and repair your mother's window."

"Yes."

"All the way from Santa Barbara?"

"Actually," I said, "he's in town to meet his—"

Detective Broumas cut me off. "Yes, yes, he gave me a name. Let's go, Charlie."

I stood then and walked toward the door. I thought of the game of shadow the girls had played when they were small, in which one of them walked right behind the other, turning left when the other turned, leaning right when the other leaned, so that the one in front could never see the shadow girl.

I could see Natalie and Jake talking in the room opposite. Both of them had taken seats in the front row of what was a more traditional classroom used for art history and Western thought classes. The desk part of the molded chairs was a light lemon yellow and curved around their bodies.

I saw the policemen walking down the hallway, Detective

Broumas slightly behind the two uniformed officers. He was talking on his cell phone. I heard him say "hair ribbon" to someone in a directive tone and then the word "braid."

Jake, who was facing toward the door, spied me first.

Natalie turned awkwardly around in the school chair and looked at me. "I don't even know who you are sometimes," she said.

I felt my stomach drop. I started to speak but then saw Jake vigorously shaking his head side to side and mouthing, *No.*

There was only one other thing Natalie could be referring to. Why would he have told her?

"I'm sorry," I said.

"You've known him since he was a baby."

This didn't matter to me. Plenty of fifty-year-old men slept with thirty-year-old women, and I was certain that among their number were those who had known their conquests as infants. Unfortunately the only person I could think of just then was John Ruskin and a ten-year-old named Rose la Touche.

"It was mutual," I said.

"Jesus," Natalie spat out. She looked away from me and toward the blackboard. I followed her glance. One of the students had taken advantage of an emptying classroom to draw a giant penis on the board. The caricature fellating it looked an awful lot like Tanner.

"You slept with Hamish?" Jake asked, incredulous.

"Last night, in her car," Natalie said. "I called home to tell him about your mother, and he comes out with that! He says he's in love with you."

"Did you tell the police I was with him?" I asked, knowing that it conflicted with what I'd just said.

"That's what you care about? That's all you have to say?"

Jake was staring at me now. "You took him to the Limerick spot." It was not a question.

I nodded my head.

Natalie's dress, as often happened, had loosened, and the deep overlapping *V* of the neckline now hung low and open, revealing her bra and her ample cleavage.

In comparison I felt like a twig that could be snapped underfoot—brittle, insubstantial, combustible. Fodder for fire or lust. "There's an autopsy scheduled for this afternoon," I said. "She was killed somewhere other than where her body was found."

Natalie stood. She walked over to me.

I bowed my head, avoiding her gaze.

"I guess I should congratulate him," she said. "Hamish has wanted a run at you for a long time."

"And me?" I asked.

"Truth?"

"Yes."

"I'm tired. I'm tired of living in that stupid house and of this job, and I'm seeing someone."

"A Downingtown contractor," I said.

"Of course you don't approve."

"I'm not in a position to judge anyone right now," I said.

Natalie brought her hand up to my cheek. A gesture, I was aware, that Hamish also used. "But you do."

The three of us left the Art Hut. In my joints I felt the ache of tension—the accruing of the previous night's deeds with posing and the police questioning. I wanted desperately to go and sit where I had that morning, overlooking the rotten oak tree behind the building.

"Remember my father's plywood people?" I said to Natalie. We stood in the parking lot. Jake's red car glistened in the sun.

"Yes." She had seen them only once, shortly before they'd finally been demolished. Jake had only heard about them.

"They were more real to him than my mother and me."

"I feel sick looking at you," she said.

She dug in her shoulder bag for her keys. They were easy to spot. After she had lost them dozens of times, Hamish had presented her with a key chain topped off by a giant red cat.

Jake tried to fill the space. "Sarah is coming on one of her visits today. We won't have the happiest news to greet her with, I'm afraid."

He had put his hands in his pockets, which he had always done to keep himself from fidgeting. Out of nowhere I thought of the shirt he was wearing beneath his sweater: "Life is good."

"I'm headed up to York with my contractor. I'm meeting his mother for the first time," Natalie said to Jake. She would not look at me. I had suddenly become the unstable one to their upright citizens. Had I killed the only person who, in comparison, made me appear sane?

Moments later I was lying curled up in the backseat of Jake's car just as I had the night before in my own. Natalie had turned from me with no good-bye.

"Take care," she said to Jake.

"It was nice to see you again, Natalie."

"I guess it was," she said. Jake started the car, and I closed my eyes. I would ride in the back the way I had as a child, with my father driving and no one in the front passenger side. I hadn't told Natalie about my mother, and now I never would.

After the remaining parts of Lambeth were destroyed to make way for a new bypass and an outlet mall, I had written down a line for my father: "All of them are gone except for me; and for me nothing is gone." I couldn't remember who had said it or in what context.

*　　*　　*

When Jake stopped drawing me, I thought his fascination with the way ice coated a leaf or the way crushed berries mixed with snow could make a dye was a temporary fancy. I thought he would come back to me. But then he began building things out of earth and ice, sticks and bones, and left all human flesh behind.

Emily found one of his first crude sculptures and marveled. It was made out of grass and dirt woven together, the grass of winter acting as a thatch to keep the mud from disassembling. If it were not for Emily's delight, I would quickly have grabbed it with a covered hand and flushed it away. It looked like a particularly nuanced piece of shit to me, sitting as it did on the floor behind the toilet. But because Emily made me get down on my hands and knees first, and called it "him," I had a chance to see.

Jake had made a small sculpture. As I stared at it, open-mouthed, Emily launched, as only a small child's body could, in one swift motion from bent knees to sitting with legs stretched out in front of her and began to bang the flat of her palms on her fleshy thighs with joy.

"Daddy!" she screamed.

"She's afraid of the toilet, Helen," Jake said later, after I had brought out the offending object and placed it on the small ceramic dish where he put his keys and change at the end of the day.

"And this is how you propose to cure her? By making donkeys out of shit?"

"It's mud, and it's supposed to be a dragon."

If I wanted to talk to him in those days, I had to stop him between the front door of the small house we rented and the shower. He would begin to disrobe in the hallway, peeling off the layers of scarves and hats, parka and vest, and heavy wool plaid shirts so that by the time he hit the bedroom, he was dressed like a normal man about to sit down to dinner.

That day I had chased him from the front door to the bedroom with the sculpture held aloft on its ceramic dish.

"Did she like it?" he asked as we reached the bedroom.

He wore his rag-wool sweater over a turtleneck and, I knew because I watched the routine in the dark each morning, hidden layers of T-shirts and long underwear. First to come off before entering the house were always his boots, but still on his lower half were the old army pants from the surplus store and huge wool socks that looked as prickly as cacti and that necessitated liners between them and his humid, winter-tenderized feet. On his hands he wore nothing, swearing that as they acclimatized to the cold, he would ultimately become more dexterous, able to stand more hours outside and capable of finer detail work.

"Of course she liked it," I said, not wanting to concede what was so obvious, that any child, even a fearful one, would love an animal made out of mud and found at the base of a semipristine toilet.

He turned to me. His cheeks were permanently ruddy where the wind got to them between his wool cap, which sat low over his eyebrows, and his scarf, which he knotted up above the tip of his nose. His eyes, watering a bit from the shock of the baseboard heat inside the house, seemed liquid blue to me.

"That's all I wanted for her," he said. "To make her laugh when she was face-to-face with that thing."

I could not say that I was jealous, not of my child but of the objects that he'd begun making, nor could I bring myself to beg him to keep drawing me.

He peeled all the underlayers of T-shirts and thermal underwear off together and threw them on the bed, then walked into the bathroom to turn on the shower. I followed him inside the shower stall, fully clothed.

"What are you doing, Helen?" he asked, but he was laughing.

"Fuck me," I said.

I did not think about what was happening to me. I had begun to chase my husband as I had once chased my mother, toe to toe, a shadow girl trying to be what I thought they wanted me to be.

I felt Jake take the speed bump just before exiting Westmore's front gate.

"Sit up and talk to me," he said. "I know you're awake."

I pushed myself up with my arm as if I were in yoga class, about to come out of the all-too-fitting corpse pose.

He caught my eye in the rearview mirror.

"So after suffocating your mother, you decide to seduce Natalie's son? Is that the timeline?"

"Yes."

Jake shook his head. "Now you're diddling with children."

"He's thirty."

"Well, mine is thirty-three," he said.

"Yours?"

"Her name is Phin."

"Fin? What kind of name is that?"

"The best she can do, having been named Phineas by her father and called Phinny. She works at the art museum in Santa Barbara."

"What's she like?" I asked.

"Shouldn't we be talking about other things?"

"Like prison?" I said.

"Or what we're going to tell Sarah?"

He pulled the car into a lot across from the Burger King. There was a store there I'd never been inside of called Four Corners.

"Do you want anything?" he asked.

I shook my head.

As I watched Jake hold the door for a young mother pushing a stroller with another child in her arms, I thought of my mother giving my phone number to the man who'd dug new sewer lines that spring.

"I've told you not to give out my number without asking first," I had said. The sewer man had already called me three times by that point.

"Your sordid life is your sordid life," she had said. "You shouldn't live it if you don't like it."

It had been as easy as that. She had stood in her kitchen and issued her riddle-me-this invitation to end my life. When was she, and when was she not, aware of what she said?

I wondered what specific rhythm had been playing inside my father's head as he lifted the pistol. He had plunged down the staircase face-first, blood arcing up and splattering in a diminishing wavy line along the stairwell. He had done it in front of her. Had she begged him to stop or had she begged him to go, directing the thoughts in his head like a traffic cop?

I got out of the car and closed the door. I watched Jake exit the store.

"Cigarettes," Jake said. "This is what you do to me. Get in."

This time I sat beside him in the passenger seat.

He closed the car door. "I saw a park off the highway between here and the house this morning. We need someplace to talk."

I nodded my head as he started the car.

"Mrs. Leverton would have been a witness," I said after we merged onto the highway. "She saw the two of us last night out on the side porch. I sat there with Mom before I used the towel."

Jake was quiet. I felt the breeze from the night before. I saw the tops of the trees bending in the wind, the light outside Carl Fletcher's back door, the muted sounds of his radio. Had his daughter, Madeline, been there last night? Had she seen anything?

"There, that's the park I saw," Jake said.

We pulled off the highway and took the access road until we came to a sad little park of picnic tables and trash. The wrought-iron barbecue grills set in cement looked like they hadn't been used in years. We parked in the slanted spaces and got out.

"Pennsylvania depresses me," said Jake.

"I may spend the rest of my life in Pennsylvania," I said.

Jake stood in a scrubby patch of weeds and grass, and tore the cellophane off his pack of Camels.

"Do you want one?"

"No, thanks," I said. "I'll have plenty of time to pick up the habit in Graterford or the women's equivalent."

"Christ." He took a long drag off the cigarette, almost as if it were a joint, and let it stream through his nostrils instead of his mouth. "I think they know, Helen. We need to figure out what to say."

"Will you marry Phin?" I asked.

"Helen, we're talking about our future incarceration."

"Mine."

"The window, my apparent collusion. Hello?"

"You'll tell them why if you have to," I said. "You'll be fine."

"No."

"It makes sense," I said. "I'm the one who killed her. You just broke in to make sure I was okay."

"They asked me about your mental state," he said, absent-mindedly looking at the cigarette as if someone else had put it in his hand.

"And you said?"

"That you were fearlessly sane."

He moved closer to me and put his arm around me. He drew me over to him so I stood snugly against the side of his body, my shoulder fitting into his armpit as it always had.

"You are," he said.

"What?"

"Incredible. Always have been."

In front of us, between two disused grills, stood one small sapling that the township had recently planted. I remembered reading about a fight, pro and con — beautifying through trees versus more money for the schools. A wire support surrounded the sapling's trunk, and I wondered if anyone would remember to cut it off before the tree slowly strangled.

"Poor fucker," Jake said.

"Me or the tree?"

"Your father, actually. Did you think you were marrying him when you married me?"

"I wanted your attention."

"You had it," he said.

"For a little while."

"That was my work. It had nothing to do with you."

He leaned his head down, and our lips met. We kissed in a way that lifted me, however briefly, out of the world where discipline and temper, grit and resolve, carried me through my weeks and years. Afterward he looked at me for a long time.

"I'll have to tell them what I know."

"I think you should," I said.

"What about the girls?"

"I'll tell Sarah," I said. "And Emily."

"Emily won't understand, you know."

"Do you think it matters that she was so old?"

"To Emily?"

"To the police."

"There's no special dispensation I'm aware of. I'm sure it depends on how a lawyer frames it."

"I don't even know any lawyers."

"Let's try not to think about it, okay?"

"I should have stayed in therapy," I said.

"Why didn't you?"

"His shelves were full of I. B. Singer, and the statues on his tables were that lost-wax Holocaust style. Lots of dismembered trunks of tortured people wrapped in barbed wire and mounted on poles. I would be talking about my mother, only to look up and see a legless, armless torso reaching out for me."

Jake laughed. The two of us moved toward the sapling and sat down in the scrubby grass surrounding it. He lit another cigarette.

"Plus, he loved wordplay. I told him about my father's town, the drowning of it, and he just looked at me, bugged out his eyes like he was a cat with a mouse, and said, 'Swoosh!' "

"Swoosh?" Jake said.

"Exactly. What was I supposed to do with that? He cost me thousands of dollars and did nothing but put me off Philip Roth."

"There are other therapists."

I started to pull up the grass beneath me, as I'd once told Sarah she should never do.

"I saw someone for a while," Jake said. "Here's a hint: she wore Pippi Longstocking tights."

"Frances Ryan? You went to Frances Ryan?" I stared at him in disbelief.

"She helped me after you left."

Frances Ryan had been a graduate student at U–Mad when we were there. Everyone knew her by her trademark hose.

"Does she still wear them?"

"It's been ten years, at least, since I saw her. I don't think those hose work over forty."

"I don't think they ever worked."

"Better than martyred torsos," Jake said, passing his cigarette to me.

Other than murder and seduction, I'd limited my vices to such an extent recently that from just one inhale, I felt an immediate rush. I had worked in therapy on my issues of control, until one weekend I was in the grocery, thumping melons. I held a cantaloupe in my hands and felt as if I were holding my head. The therapist had been poking about inside of me, turning my brain into so much mush.

"What do we do now?" I asked.

"We pick Sarah up. We put one foot in front of the other. I think that's all we can do until they contact us."

"Or show up."

Behind us, we heard a car pull in. Both of us turned around. It was a panel truck with sheets of mirrored glass strapped to either side. The man inside shut off the engine but kept the radio on. It was a talk station. Rancor poured forth from his open windows.

"Lunchtime," Jake said.

I watched Jake smoke until he had finished the cigarette. He had always, I thought, looked silly with a cigarette, somehow too feminine, as if he were declaiming from a divan.

"So will you marry Phin?"

Jake took a moment to consider.

"Probably not," he said.

"Why?"

"She's efficient."

"Meaning?"

"She's very good at organizing dinner parties and trips."

"And feeding dogs?"

"I transferred my affections to them a long time ago."

"Milo and Grace?"

"Animals in general."

"That doesn't sound like you."

"It's where I ended up." He smiled. "Besides, I'm too attracted to struggle. You know that."

"Poor fucker," I said.

He looked toward me. His eyes were as I had never seen them, as if they'd been crushed somehow, flattened by my existence in the world. "I loved you, Helen."

What I had done, not just to my mother but to everyone, seemed suddenly bottomless.

It was out before I could stop it. A loud, broken caw close to the sound of retching, and then out of nowhere I was flooded with tears. My sinuses let go, and saliva and phlegm flooded my mouth and nose. There was nowhere to hide, and so I put my head into my hands and leaned to the side to bury my face in the ground.

"It's okay, Helen," Jake said. "It's okay."

I could feel him kneeling over me, his hand lightly touching my back and then my shoulder. I did everything I could not to respond to his grip. I felt like I could barely breathe, but I took huge drafts of air. I was crying and coughing and grinding my fist into the dirt.

"Helen, please."

He took hold of my wrist, and I stared at him.

"I ruined everything!" I said. "Everything!"

The man in the panel truck had turned up his radio. Calls for the ban of illegal immigrants issued forth.

"You have to control yourself," Jake said. "For the girls' sake, for mine. Who knows, nothing might happen."

Nothing seemed worse to me somehow. That there would be so little evidence of the loss of my own life to my mother that I could even get away with killing her. I was, at the end of the day, that insignificant. Was it this that chastened me? Or that when I sat up and Jake daubed at my face with his shirt, I saw that the man in the truck had pulled his vehicle to the side and across three parking spaces, in order, I imagined, not to have to look at us while he ate his lunch. I noticed this, and then I saw the woman in the mirrored glass held fast to his truck. It was me. I was sitting on the ground in a desolate park in Pennsylvania. A man I had once been married to, had had children with, was trying to pull me toward him. I saw the sapling and the broken grills and the edge of the highway behind me.

FOURTEEN

Jake went immediately for the vodka, and when he lifted the pillow from the bar, I saw that the Bat Phone was blinking madly with messages.

"Should I play this?"

"Yes."

Following the messages from Natalie that she had left the day before was one from Emily, who said she had also left a message on my other phone.

"But this one seems more appropriate somehow," she continued. "Remember, you are entering a new and exciting period of your life. I'll try later tonight after I've put the kids to bed."

"I always hear half of what she says as 'blah, blah, blah,'" I said.

Jake walked into the kitchen in order to retrieve his glass.

Sarah came next. Her voice hit the still house with its usual force factor.

"Mom? Fuck, leave me alone, asshole. Sorry, Mom, some jerk likes fat asses, apparently. Listen, your other phone is busy. I'm on my way to Penn Station, and I'm taking the earlier train. I'll get in around two thirty, okay? If you can't meet me, I'll cross over and sit in that hideous T.G.I. Friday's, if that's what it is anymore. Maybe get some cheese fries. Die, asshole! I mean it. Sorry, Mom. Two thirty, okay? Bye."

I paused over the liquor cabinet and waited for the machine to tell me what day and what time the message had been left. This marked the before time, I thought, before my children knew I'd killed their grandmother.

Jake stood in the doorway of the dining room, drinking straight vodka out of a juice glass.

"That's your second round today," I said.

"No rules apply."

I thought of the box in my basement, the one that held my father's letters, which he had written to me when Jake and I had spent two months overseas right after Emily was born. Jake had been awarded a travel grant by the university, and we'd chosen the most obvious place to visit: Paris.

While he went off to museums or met with other painters, I walked around the streets with Emily in a sort of Central-American infant sling across my chest. I remembered how hot it was and how alone I felt. I learned to order a plate of cheeses and a beer in one café and go to the French-American bookstore. I walked the same fifteen blocks every day and spoke to no one, bleary with cheese and hops, the sling wearing a sore on my shoulder. The highlight, for me, was not the chance to visit the Louvre or to plumb the depths of Le Bon Marché, but the letters my father sent me describing his days, telling me about the progress of his herb garden or whether there was only one owl or two, the first having been joined by a mate in the trees between Mrs. Leverton's house and theirs.

*　　*　　*

"That gives us two hours," Jake said. "I'm going to shower. What are you going to tell her, Helen?"

"I don't know yet."

"You better figure it out. Sarah's no idiot, and this isn't over the phone."

"Emily," I said.

"Call her back."

"I can't."

"Do it," Jake said, and left the room.

Once, when I was in Seattle, Emily had shown me how she took vitamins out of their original jars and placed them in beautiful porcelain containers on a handmade cherrywood lazy Susan in the middle of one of the multiple islands of their kitchen. When I was foolish enough to ask how the children could tell where their chewables were, Emily told me that color entered a child's memory more fluidly than text, and so Jeanine knew that the jar with the eggshell-blue glaze held her chewables.

Emily had been just out in front of me her entire life. She learned to dress herself and tie her shoes before I was ready to relinquish these tasks, and she became absolutely adamant about taking responsibility for herself as soon as she could. If I tried to read her a story or pour her cereal into a bowl, she would rip *Harold and the Purple Crayon* or the box of cornflakes from my hands and shout—quite bossily, I always felt—"I do!"

I heard Jake above me in the girls' bathroom. I remembered how he would leave his pants on the bathroom floor where they fell. I listened for the sound of it, for the belt buckle and pockets, heavy with change, hitting the tile floor. When I heard it, I picked up the Bat Phone and dialed Emily's number.

It rang three times.

No one said hello, but I heard breathing on the other end.

"Jeanine?"

Nothing.

"Jeanine, it's Grandma. Is Mommy there?"

I heard the phone being dropped on a table or on the floor and the sound of small footsteps walking away.

"Hello?" I said.

I waited for what seemed a reasonable amount of time.

"Hello?" I called again. Louder this time.

I heard the water in the pipes above my head. Jake was taking his shower. I noticed that the vodka bottle had not been put back. I thought about how four years ago I had found my mother curled up on the floor of the linen closet after I had called for her throughout the house.

"What are you doing?" I'd asked.

"Hiding," she'd said.

I had hauled her out like an animal that had gotten stuck under the house. She had a line of heavy dust from the closet floor along her left side. I had batted at her gown in order to clean it off.

"Stop hitting me!" she'd shrieked. "Stop hitting me!"

And I had had to remind Mrs. Castle to keep the linen closet locked.

"I only wanted to change the tablecloth."

Why hadn't I told her, *"You don't understand—my mother hides in there"*?

I pressed the phone to my ear. I heard voices. They were the voices of TV. In Seattle, Jeanine was watching television—a DVD, I imagined. Emily and John kept the shelves that I thought should hold books stocked with them. When I'd asked John where they kept their books, he had shrugged his shoulders. "Who has time to read?"

I listened for a while. I pictured the rooms. Judging by the nearness of the television, it had been the phone in the kitchen Jeanine had picked up. I wondered where Leo was. Emily. I knew that John would be at work, lecturing nonenvironmental types on the endless joys of plastic fabrication.

"I suffocated her on the side porch," I whispered over the phone. There was no response. "I cut off her braid and took it home."

Cartoon music filled the air in Seattle. A chase was on.

I hung up the phone. I thought of the line that traveled through me and reached all the way to Leo and Jeanine. How Leo almost uncannily had my eyes. How Jeanine seemed to possess a trace of my father in her jawbone. Her laugh had me in there somewhere, and when she sang, as she often did, I remembered my mother singing in the quiet house when I was a child.

I walked upstairs to my bedroom. I had told Emily when she was little that we were descended from the Melungeons of Tennessee. When she was much older, she realized I had been pulling her leg, but for a brief time I had her believing that she sprang from this strange, lost group of people cut off from the rest of the world in the mountains of eastern Tennessee. I had passed by the bathroom to find her looking for the telltale signs of bluish skin. In Sarah, she said, she saw the high forehead and cheekbones and the "almost Asian look," but in herself she saw nothing.

Along with my father's letters in the basement, there would be the paper Emily wrote in junior high, on which a teacher had scrawled a failing grade. I no longer remembered the woman's name, Barber or Bartlett, something beginning with a *B*. I had marched into the junior high in a mock-mommy outfit I'd composed for effect — corduroy bag jumper and deranged Mary-Jane flats — and lit into Emily's teacher with all my might. This had succeeded in gaining Emily a C and me a plea from my daughter never to do anything similar again. I still saw these moments spent in defense of my children as the finest of my life.

I heard Jake gargling on the girls' side of the house. The faint scent of his musk-based aftershave reached me as I turned to lock the door.

I walked into my long closet. Most of the luggage was kept on the other side of the house, in the closet that had slowly gone from keeping shoes and clothes that Emily could use when she visited to a place where I could stash items I might never use again but did not feel like throwing out. But the many lopsided, ill-measured sweaters and scarves my mother had made over the years, I kept in my closet in an old duffel bag of Jake's. It sat, an army-green lump, balanced perilously on top of two other boxes on the shelf above the clothing rack.

I stood up on a small step stool that Sarah had made in wood shop. I batted at the bag with my right hand until it came tumbling down. I did not think about what I was doing. I knew we were going to pick Sarah up at the train. I knew the police knew more than they were saying. Jake was right, there was still a sliver of a chance I would get away with it, but I had realized sometime during the morning that it did not matter whether I did or not. It was my children who would ultimately sit in judgment of me, and the two of them *would* know. I could never fool them, and I didn't want to.

I unzipped the heavy gold zipper of the canvas bag and took out my mother's sad pile of knitting.

"Why is it that everything she knits resembles vomit?" Sarah asked one Christmas. The girls were just entering adulthood, and that year, my mother had outdone herself, knitting a full-length sweater coat for each of them. She had used a variety of yarns in a striated design, and sure enough, though it was meant to be autumnal in effect, the result seemed more intestinal.

I found one of these coats easily enough and placed it back in the bag before shoving the remaining knitting on top of a file cabinet I kept in the corner. Then I looked at my jumble of shoes and chose the ratty sneakers I wore for gardening. I heard Jake walking down the hall toward my door. Three shirts. Over to my dresser, long underwear, underwear, one cashmere sweater. I had my good jeans on, and I put a second pair into the bag. In the bottom drawer were the slips and a nylon running suit with reflector stripes that I had thought was stylish in the store. I shoved the nylon suit in the duffel bag and zipped it up.

Jake knocked very lightly on my door.

"Helen? Are you awake?"

I left the duffel on the floor and closed the closet.

"Of course," I said.

I saw the doorknob jiggle.

"It's locked," he said.

When I opened the door, Jake was bleary-eyed. He swayed slightly to the right.

"Did you shower with the vodka?" I asked, and led him by the hand across the room, where he slumped into a sitting position on the bed.

"You lie down and close your eyes for a while," I said. "I'll wake you when it's time to go get Sarah."

He nodded his head up and down. "I *am* tired," he said.

"Of course you are. Where's the poison?"

"Don't have any, Helen," he cautioned. "You need to stay sober."

I smiled.

"I know. I just want to put it away."

"We should call Phin. Phin could help us."

I put my hand against his chest and pushed. He fell backward on the bed.

He brought his knees up and curled up on the unmade sheets.

"You've been wonderful," I said.

"Milo and Grace love to lick faces," he said. "Phin doesn't like that."

I grabbed a pillow from the headboard for him to put under his head. "You sleep for a bit," I said.

A moment or two later, I heard his breathing shift into light snoring. I reached out to touch him. I realized I had forgotten socks, but I didn't want to risk waking him. I tiptoed to the closet, grabbed the duffel bag, and crept down the stairs through the back hall — *Who knows, Caracas?* — and out into the garage. I tucked the duffel behind the lawn mower and a few empty plastic pails that were left over from the last time I'd had the house painted. It would go unnoticed there.

I had prepacked a bag for the hospital before Sarah was born. I had made a day of it. New toothbrush, new nightgown, even a powder compact, because all the pictures of me holding Emily had featured my face flush with perspiration. I had been the rare mother, the doctor had said, who had had a more difficult delivery the second time around.

"My big head," Sarah would concede.

"Your big, beautiful head," I would correct.

I noticed that the sticky trap I'd set out early in the week was no longer in its place near the trash cans. I stood very still and listened. Wherever the mouse had dragged itself, it would have to be dead or close to dead by now.

Back upstairs in Sarah's bedroom, I saw the vodka bottle on the windowsill. There was still at least a third left. Jake had always been an easy drunk. On our first real date, he had slipped under the table within an hour after a salty full professor had challenged him to a drinking contest.

I did my best to straighten the room in preparation for Sarah. I had kept her room the lavender she had wanted years ago. All the other rooms had been repainted a stark white, even Emily's.

I moved my hand briskly against the deep-purple coverlet, smoothing out the wrinkles from where Jake must have sat to put on his shoes. I adjusted the alarm clock by one hour, having failed to do so at daylight saving time, and I used the bottom of my sweater to dust around the items on her bureau.

In this room, three years ago, I had unleashed a violence I had never thought myself capable of. Sarah had come home with a boy named Bryce, whom I had been suspicious of as soon as I met them at the train. He was an ultra-WASP who, he claimed, came from an old family in Connecticut. None of this meant much to me, and after a dinner during which he talked mostly of himself, I'd gone to my bedroom so the two of them could have the run of the house.

The first slap was like a distant gunshot. On the second, I sat straight up. I heard Sarah in that way that you do when a person is trying not to make a sound but can't stop themselves. By that time I was halfway across the house in my nightgown, with the baseball bat my father had given me for protection.

It was something Sarah had sworn me to secrecy about. Emily and Jake were never to know that she had allowed a man to hit her. Bryce fled the house on foot after I had brandished the bat and then slammed it as hard as I could into the doorjamb.

I sat down on the floor of Sarah's bedroom and then lay back on the rug. Without thinking, I went through the series of stretches I had done every morning for fifteen years.

At half past one, I went back to my bedroom to find Jake asleep in the same position he had been. I whispered his name, but I had already decided to go without him. I left a note on the kitchen counter saying I would return with Sarah. I tucked the vodka bottle in the liquor cabinet, and just as I was about to put the Bat Phone back in with its companion pillow, I stopped myself. I yanked the cord from the wall and carried it out to the garbage cans.

I debated taking the duffel bag with me but decided against it. I was not ready yet. If I could, I wanted to cook dinner for Sarah and wake her the next morning by bringing up a pot of hot coffee for the two of us to share.

I had never gotten used to the official rush hour of the suburbs, which revolved around school's letting out and parents in their cars lined up outside. In the years since I'd had children coming and going, the curbside pickup, fueled by stories of abduction, had increased in popularity. Still, as I edged my way down the street where Lemondale Elementary School sat, I was happy to see at least three or four yellow buses pulled up to the curb.

At Crescent Road, I was stopped by a matronly crossing guard with a white sash and a whistle—the full effect. I watched a mass of children—the "primaries," they were called at Lemondale— walk in front of my car in a swirling pattern that reminded me of shifting clouds on a TV weather map. Only a few kids walked by themselves, heads bent, knapsacks towing their shoulders down. The others ran or pulled at one another's coats and shirts, dropped their knapsacks, and yelled names and taunts across to those on the other side.

I drove on.

I passed the old music store, which was now a shop called The Ultimate Cupcake, where I had once purchased Emily's much-despised clarinet. I thought of how when the girls were growing up, their friends would thunder through my house and think nothing of having me make sandwiches to order. This one liked mayo, but this one would have only mustard. One of Emily's friends, disappointed in her sandwich, had stood in the kitchen and pointedly explained the difference between jelly, which she had requested, and jam, which I had given her.

The most convenient train for Sarah to take from Manhattan stopped in Paoli. This way she could avoid switching in Philadelphia and arrive via Amtrak. Instead of crossing the bridge to the side where the passengers were let out, I checked my watch. I counted out the minutes and double-parked outside Starbucks.

I walked briskly into the station and over to the Amtrak counter. I asked for a current schedule for the Northeast Corridor. On the way past the local SEPTA booth, I took two or three of their schedules as an afterthought. I did this by rote, as I had done my stretches, as I had packed my duffel bag and stowed it in the garage. My brain had divided in half, half focused on the tasks of normalcy—picking up my daughter from the train—and half focused on escape.

I got back into the car and turned it around. Driving the red rental car made me feel even more conspicuous, but it had sat in the driveway, blocking any other choice. I thought of the promise I had made to Hamish—that I would see him tonight—and wondered if I was insane. I pictured Natalie in a crossing-guard outfit, holding a stop sign and blocking my way.

Sarah was standing at the top of the platform stairs, scanning the parking lot. She had on a ratty sheepskin coat, beneath which I saw an old pair of my Frye boots that she had confiscated on her last trip home. "These are so urban hippie retro," she'd said. "I can't believe you wore these." When I told her that apparently she was now going to be wearing them, she said, "Yeah, but not *seriously*."

Her hair was braided into two pigtails that reached to her waist, and clustered about the crown of her head were what seemed an infinite number of rhinestone barrettes. She would not recognize the car, and so I cruised up beside her, ducked my head across the passenger seat, and called her name.

"Mom, oh my God, this is a horn-dog car!" she said as she threw her bag in the backseat and got in beside me.

She leaned over and kissed me on the cheek. It carried a shock, as if she had been rubbing her feet on carpeting.

"Sorry," she said.

We left the parking lot.

"How was the train?" I asked.

"Is this, like, a midlife crisis thing?" she said. "Go out and get a sports car? I thought men did that."

"Women get Botox," I said.

"Right, so what gives?"

"Actually," I said, "this isn't my car. It's a rental."

"The smell. I should have guessed that! Where's yours?"

We were stopped at a light across from Roscoe Automotive and the Mail Boxes Etc. store. *Cars and mail,* I thought. *Trains.*

"Your head looks like a disco ball," I said.

"Don't avoid the question."

"My car is in the garage, and your father is asleep in my bed."

I could not help baiting her. It was a game we had played since her childhood, who could get the other's goat, who could create the best exaggeration. Sarah, I knew, had hoped to make this early skill into an art. She was a child of embellishment and stylish turns. What Emily had in stolid substance, Sarah possessed in her ability to distract everyone from the main topic of conversation. That way, no one ever thought to get a real answer to the question of how she was doing. It was what she'd carried into voice classes like a blank check. She could sing well enough, *but*—and the "but" held everything, both a buoyant magnetism and what I feared might be her incipient version of the family's insanity.

"Tell the story," she said.

We passed the hospital, and I picked up speed. I could tell she was feeling good. Her cheeks were flushed as if she had just come from a run. But Sarah didn't run. She didn't exercise. Not for her what she called my "gym crucifixion." She starved sometimes, and sometimes binged. She drank and smoked, and I was sure did other things.

"There is a lot to tell," I said. "I'd rather not go home just yet. Your father needs to rest anyway. It might be easier if it's just the two of us."

"I sense intensity," she said.

"We'll go somewhere," I said, "then I'll tell you all you want to know."

"Yow!" she said, but she did not follow up with anything else. As we passed Easy Joe's Restaurant, I saw her check each rhinestone barrette with her hands. She took its shape between her thumb and forefinger and then tested it to make sure it held.

"Why the braids?" I asked.

"Oh, I don't know. My hair was wet. Like or not like?"

"They remind me of your grandmother."

"Not like, got it."

I knew where I was headed. Hamish had been the first person I'd gone there with in years. In the daytime the farmland invited the eye, and then the towers between the treetops stopped it cold.

As we passed by the Ironsmith Inn and turned left to crest the hill, Sarah sighed loudly.

"No Schlitz?" she asked regretfully.

Without looking in my rearview mirror, I threw the car into reverse and swung backward into the general store's lot.

"Cash and carry," I said. "Make it quick."

"I'm liking this new you," Sarah said, all lit up. She grabbed my purse from the floor and headed inside. No one could claim that when I broke bad news, I didn't make sure people had some-thing to prop themselves up with.

I could see her through the window, talking to Nick Stolfuz at the counter. She was using her hands to make a giant circle over her head. Nick laughed and handed her a six-pack with her change. When she reached the door, she turned to wave good-bye.

"What was that all about?" I asked.

"I was telling him about the Macy's Thanksgiving Day Parade."

I backed out of the lot and got onto the road. Sarah popped the tab on a can of Schlitz and slurped the foam with her mouth.

"What led you to that?"

"I told him I lived in New York. He's always wanted to go up for the parade."

"The things you don't know."

We passed under the keystone tunnel and onto the other side.

"You have to take an interest, Mom. Nick is single, you know."

"No, thank you," I said.

"Damn," she said, and punched her thigh. "I could have had my own bar. Are we going to the towers lookout?" she asked, getting her bearings.

"Yes."

"Whatever floats your boat," she said. An expression I had taught her.

I pulled off the road and onto the gravelly patch where last night Hamish and I had had sex in my car. I was glad for the rental, for the swinging scented tree that hung from the cigarette lighter.

I turned off the ignition.

Sarah sipped at her beer. "Can you open the windows?"

"Better yet, let's get out," I said.

"Beer?"

"No."

She stashed an extra in her coat pocket anyway.

When I stood up, my legs buckled, and I stumbled, whirling around to put my hands on top of the car to steady myself. Sarah came rushing over.

"Mom, are you okay?"

I had seen a detective show on television in which the trademark maneuver of a tough-talking cop was to slam the criminal's chest so hard into the roof as he pinned him to the car that it made a thumping sound. I watched this show with my mother, and every time this happened, the two of us would giggle. "They call them 'perps,'" she said one night, and I had thought how our moments of ease were so rare anymore that even this stupid television show was something I was grateful for.

"I'm weak, Sarah."

"Weak? What are you telling me?"

"A weak person," I said.

I gained my breath. I had begun.

"Let's go for a walk," I said, and crossed the road. I had never set foot on Forche Lane in all the times I had driven here, but I decided that's where Sarah and I would walk. It was a one-lane road that was privately owned and full of gaping potholes, from which weeds and wild grass poked out.

"What are you talking about, Mom? Slow down." She caught up to me, holding the open can of beer in her hand.

"I have to keep walking if I'm going to tell you everything."

"I hate your exercise shit. Don't make me pump my arms."

"I'm weak morally. And who I am does not reflect on you and Emily. That needs to be said up front."

Sarah ran in front of me and spun around to block my path. The Schlitz foamed up, and a few drops spilled on the ground.

"Don't," I said.

"Mom, what is it?"

"Move."

"No."

I pushed her aside, then moved to my left a bit to regain the road. Sarah joined me a moment later.

"Okay, I'm listening," she said.

"I don't know where to begin."

On our right, a flock of grouse fled the bushes where they'd been hiding. The air was filled with the beating of wings.

"How about why Dad is here?"

"I called him. He flew out from Santa Barbara last night."

"Why?" She took a preparatory slug of Schlitz.

I could not do it. Not yet.

"Remember Hamish?"

"Of course."

"I slept with him last night in my car. Twice. Once in his driveway and once back there, where we parked."

"No shit!" Sarah said.

"No shit."

"Hamish, our blond-god doofus?"

"Yes."

"That's your moral weakness? Granted, not the usual thing, but cool, very very cool."

We walked on. Forche dropped down after the part of the road that I had always been able to see from my car. Here the pavement gave way to dirt.

"So is that it?" Sarah asked.

"No."

"Well, what?"

"Your grandmother is dead," I said.

"What?"

"She died last night, and I called your father."

Sarah grabbed my arm.

"Mom, that's huge. Were you there?"

"We're not walking," I said.

"Were you?"

"Yes."

Sarah dragged me toward her and tried to hug me. Despite her bloodline, she had always been one for touch. Emily had called her "Face Invader" when they were teenagers because Sarah didn't know when close was too close.

"You're all bones," she said.

I pulled back and looked at her. I felt the tears in my eyes and knew they would fall.

"And you're my beautiful child," I said.

"Mom, it's okay. You did everything for her." She offered me her beer, but I shook my head.

"I killed her, Sarah."

"That's ridiculous. She sucked you dry."

"Don't."

"I'm sorry. And I'm sorry she's dead, but come on, you sacrificed yourself to her."

"You're not understanding me," I said. I turned out of her embrace and looked back in the direction of the car. We were so far down in a hollow I could not see the main road.

The fields were wheat or barley. I had spent my life surrounded by them, but they were only various colored patches of earth to me, things that were good mainly because they were not buildings being built. I'd never known a farmer in my life.

"Listen. I'm sorry. I know you loved her, but Emily and I both think she's why you never had a life."

"I had a life," I said. "I had the two of you."

She paused. "Dad came all that way because Grandma died?" Something had twitched in her brain.

"Yes."

"But he hated her."

"That's not why," I said.

"Then what?"

"I've been trying to tell you. Because I," I said, pointing to myself and waiting a beat, "*killed* her."

I could see it begin to sink in. I could not make it go away. No Bactine for this wound, no soothing salve or spray.

"You what?"

"I suffocated her with a hand towel."

Sarah backed away from me and dropped the beer can.

"She was very out of it," I said. I thought of my mother's eyes looking up at me, of her ruby rings flashing in the porch light, and of the sound of her nose as it snapped. "I don't think she even knew it was me."

"Stop talking," Sarah said.

"The police are investigating. Mrs. Leverton died this morning after they took her away in an ambulance."

"Mom, shut up! What are you saying?"

"That I killed my mother."

Sarah picked up the beer can and started walking back toward the car.

"Sarah," I said, "there's more."

She pivoted.

"More?"

I felt suddenly heady with it.

"Your grandfather killed himself."

"What?"

"My father committed suicide—your grandfather."

"You're smiling," Sarah said. "Do you know how sick you look?"

"I'm just happy to finally tell you the truth." I walked toward her. A butterfly-shaped barrette was coming lose from her hair. "Your father knows, but we agreed never to tell you and Emily." I reached up to fix her barrette. She flinched.

"Honey?" I lowered my arm.

She felt for the barrette and ripped it out, a clump of her hair coming with it.

"Don't do that," I said.

"How?"

"He shot himself."

"And you blamed her for that?"

"At first."

"And later?"

"She was my mother, Sarah. She was ill. You know that."

"I don't know anything," she said. "You said something about police."

"The thing is," I said, "Mrs. Castle found her, and she was, well…"

"Yes."

"I washed her."

Sarah's face distorted, her lip curling as if she might soon be sick.

"Before or after?"

"After."

"Oh, Jesus," she said. She walked away from me but this time across the potted road and into the edge of the woods on the other side.

"Ticks," I said.

She walked quickly back. "You killed Grandma, and you're worried about Lyme disease?"

"She had soiled herself. I knew she wouldn't want anyone to see her like that."

She stared at me. It took me a moment, and then I realized.

"Not afterward," I clarified. "She soiled herself that afternoon. I was trying to figure out how to clean her before I called hospice. That's why I had the towels."

"I want to see Dad."

"I wanted to tell you myself. I thought it was important."

"You've told me." She threw the beer can down, smashed it flat with her foot, and then tucked it inside her coat pocket. "Now let's get out of here."

She turned too sharply and a second later was down on the ground. I saw her lying there. I thought of my mother. I thought of tiny Leo bouncing off the back of the chair.

"Honey," I said, stooping over her.

"It's my fucking ankle."

"Is it broken?"

"No," she said. "That is, unless you're in the mood for more."

"Sarah?"

"It's a joke," she said flatly. "Get it? Ha-ha."

"You can lean on me until we get to the car," I said.

"I sort of don't want you touching me right now."

I helped her to stand regardless, but within three or four hops, I knew we should sit.

"Can you make it to that log? We'll rest awhile first."

It would be dark soon, and the animals, who had slept all day in the woods behind us, would come alive. I had always preferred the fall. In providing shorter days, it was more merciful than spring or summer.

The two of us sat on a long fallen tree that looked as if it had once blocked access to the road but had been shunted to the side. Part of me wanted to keep walking, to see who or what lived at the end of Forche Lane.

We were quiet. Sarah took out her stowed beer and popped the tab. While she sipped, I looked at the ground between my feet.

"Emily doesn't know yet," I said. "Your father told her that Grandma was dead but not how. I went to Natalie's house afterward, but she wasn't there. She's dating someone pretty seriously. Hamish thinks they'll get married. He was home. I needed someone, Sarah, and so I made love to him. I'm not proud of any of these things."

I could hear her breathing beside me. Imagined what my life would be like if she chose never to speak to me again. Thought of the pain I had once put my own mother through.

"But I'm not ashamed either. I don't know how to explain it. I knew that she was at the end, and when I realized that, it just seemed a very natural thing to do. Her eyes opened, but it wasn't her; it was her amphibian brain — pure survival instinct. I know it was wrong, but I'm not sorry."

"Do the cops know?"

"I think so."

"I'll stay here if you want me to," Sarah said.

"What?" I looked over at her. She too was keeping her eyes trained on the ground.

"Things aren't working out for me in New York."

"But your singing," I said.

"I'm broke. I could help out and be here for you. The cops and stuff."

In a day or two, I would slip out of the house, put the duffel bag in my car, and back out of the driveway, claiming I would soon return.

I had a flash of myself walking down the streets of some foreign city. Children frayed by poverty were begging me for money by holding out old plastic bags. Slapping against my emaciated body underneath voluminous clothes would be bags too, bags of all kinds, holding my fluids, giving and receiving, an in/out system of effluvia, shit and urine, saline and blood, and illegal remedies — the ground bones of animals, the pits of stone fruits mixed with liquids in someone's mortar and pestle, and broths that I would drink that would never slake my thirst.

"I think we shouldn't make any decisions just yet," I said. "We'll see how the next few days play out."

I stood and offered her my hand. She took it and wobbled up.

"Better?" I asked.

"Good enough."

As we walked slowly up the incline and back to the car, I felt as if we were being watched from behind. As if Mrs. Leverton and a thousand ghosts were standing in the woods, advancing as we left, wanting to get a look at the woman who had killed her mother in the same way you would turn the light off in an empty room.

"I never really knew Grandpa," Sarah said as we came within sight of the car.

"I hate the phrase 'You never get over it,' but that's a hard one. It stays."

"And Grandma?"

"She lost her connection to the world," I said. "And I replaced it."

"No, I mean, did you love her?"

We stopped for a moment before crossing the road.

"That's a hard one too," I said.

"If you had to answer it," Sarah said. "If you were asked in a court of law."

I don't know, I thought. "I will say yes," I said aloud.

I led her to the car and opened the passenger-side door. I heard a musical gurgling sound.

"That's me," she said, retrieving her phone from the pocket of her coat.

"Your grandmother thought the cell phone I gave her was a grenade."

"I know."

I went around to my side of the car and got in.

"It's from Dad," she said, after getting into the passenger side. "A text message."

She held up the phone so I could see the screen. I ignored her face and focused instead on Jake's words.

"Helen—search warrant," it said.

I imagined Jake standing in the downstairs bathroom, unable to speak for fear he might be heard.

Sarah slipped the phone back in her pocket. "We should go home."

"Do you think you could drive?"

"Not with my ankle."

"Right."

I started the car and did a U-turn, taking us back in the direction of the Ironsmith. *I can drop Sarah there* was my first thought. I would tell her what? That I wanted to face the police alone? She would never buy that. I knew her well enough to know she would not let me out of her sight, not for one moment. For reasons that I feared could only spell her doom—because I was her mother and because I needed her—she would stick to me like glue.

Natalie was in York. This meant Hamish would be alone. Jake had told me he had friends in Switzerland in a town called Aurigeno. He had gone to the trouble of spelling it out. But I no longer had a passport. It had expired years ago.

"You're taking the long way," Sarah commented.

"I always do," I said.

"Are you frightened?" she asked.

When I didn't respond, she volunteered, "I am."

We passed a new corporate complex whose landscaped lawns still had the checkerboard pattern of freshly laid sod. They did them better now than when the girls were growing up. No more metal boxes surrounded by wide loops of easy-access road. Now there were mature trees brought in by the truckload.

People came out of the buildings and approached their cars.

I would wait until very late at night, when no one but the security guards were about. I could park my car and walk around unnoticed. Virginia Woolf walked into the River Ouse. Helen Knightly, into the Chester Corporate Center's false pond.

I did not want to leave my children. I had loved them both immediately. They were my splendor and my protection, both something to safeguard and something to safeguard me.

I saw a familiar neon sign up ahead.

"I have to go to the bathroom," I said. "I'm going to pull in here."

Easy Joe's was full of the silver-haired happy-hour crowd that filled up on cheap booze to mask the flavor of their meals. The arrival of someone my age, unaccompanied by a parent, was an event. When Sarah followed, it caused a hush. It was the opposite of a biker bar, but it could make you feel just as unwanted. What I knew about Easy Joe's was that they had a pay phone by the bathrooms and an exit opening onto the back.

I set Sarah up on one of the plush leather stools, facing a mirror lined with booze.

"I may be a while. I need to collect myself."

"Should I order something?"

I opened my purse. I would need all the money I had, but I had never been stingy with my younger child.

"Will a twenty do?" I asked.

"Do you want anything?"

"Just to wash my face. I'll come back for you," I said. I placed the keys to Jake's car on the bar.

"Mom?"

"I love you, Sarah," I said. I reached out and touched her hair and cheek.

"It will be okay, Mom. Dad's here to help."

"Hey, do you have that butterfly barrette?" I asked, brightening.

She dug into her pocket and brought it out. I took it from her outstretched hand.

"For luck," I said, holding it up. I knew I would cry then, so I turned and quickly rounded the corner of the bar.

At the phone, I put in my change and dialed.

"Hamish, it's Helen," I said. "Could you come pick me up?"

"Where?"

I thought quickly. It was a walk I could easily make.

"Vanguard Industries. Twenty minutes."

"You know," he said, "Mom told me about your mom."

I leaned my head into the reflective surface of the phone. Pressed it hard into the return-change knob.

"Yes. Vanguard, okay?"

"I'll be there."

I hung up. The voices in the restaurant area behind me grew louder.

I did not turn but proceeded down the back hall toward the "Heifers" and "Bulls" rooms, as if it weren't clear by a bit of translation that this meant women were cows. The back door was propped open with an ancient gray milk crate turned on its side. Carefully, I stepped over it, opening the door only a little further to squeeze past. There were a few beat-up cars parked at odd angles in back — *The kitchen staff,* I thought — and a Dumpster on the edge of the lot before it turned to grass and trees. As I climbed up the hill out back, I saw a large paper sack on top of the Dumpster. The top was open. Inside were rolls of bread, perhaps a day old. I thought for the first time, *How will I live?* and saw myself in a month, two months from now, grabbing a bag like this and ferreting it away.

I paused at the edge of the trees. I saw Sarah, marking off days on a calendar and living in my house alone, waiting for me to come home from a prison term for manslaughter or accidental death. She would need work, and my job would be open.

Perhaps Natalie would drive her that first day. The students would be pleased—new meat—and she could talk to Gerald on her breaks. "My mother died," he'd say. "My mother rolled a decade," she'd say. I knew Sarah well enough to know she'd love the lingo—a paltry consolation prize.

But none of this was the picture in my mind that scared me most. What scared me was the one where I was home again, where Sarah and I lived together, where she ran errands and massaged my feet while they sat begging on a leather ottoman. She'd bring me broths in bed and draw a shawl over my shoulders, rub at the caked-on food at the corner of my mouth with a damp cloth. And I would begin to forget her, to scream at her, to say cruel things about her body and her love life and her brain.

I bushwhacked through the trees along the property line and entered a patch of roadway forest. The ground was strewn with litter as I cut farther in, beer cans and condoms being the trash du jour, and I winced each time I accidentally stepped on them.

I had forgotten the red hair ribbon on the porch, leaving it to Bad Boy to have his fun with, and my fingerprints were on every surface of the kitchen. How many children bathed their mothers on the floor, sliced their clothes off with scissors, or quite literally dragged them outside to get fresh air? There would be no evidence of Manny Zavros anywhere.

On the arm of my desk lamp at home, I had hung a ribbon from my mother's hair. It too was red. But there were other ribbons, as well as a magnetic cat, a Mexican Day-of-the-Dead skull, a snail figurine, and the felt Christmas ornament my mother had sent. Why would any one thing in my home draw more attention than another?

I had not squirted the bleach into the toilet that morning. The hair from her braid might still cling there—might have scattered, unbeknownst to me, across the tiles of the bathroom floor. Would it have a time-and-date stamp if examined in a lab?

I reached Elm. Traffic was intermittent on the back roads, and I waited for my moment to rush out of the trees and across to the other side—ducking into another patch of abandoned forest.

The police could easily discover enough evidence. And if faced with direct questions, I knew I would tell the truth. Either way, when I thought of returning home with Sarah, I could see only one destiny, and it was hers, not mine.

I reached the place where I would have to scramble down a steep embankment in order to meet Hamish. I looked down the gravelly berm that they had built on all three sides of Vanguard. More than anything, the place itself looked like a high-voltage electrical plant. In the lot below, separated from the berm by a high metal fence, was a row of shiny black SUVs—top-of-the-line. I would pass within a whisper of them.

I took precautions not to injure myself, descending the steep slope from a seated position, crawling like a crab all the way. I strapped my purse over my neck and left shoulder and rested it in the center of my stomach for the descent. It would not be the last time, I knew, that I wished I could trade my discipline for Sarah's youthful resilience. My youngest could still beat the shit out of her body and go to her job the next day—if she had a job.

At the bottom I stopped for five whole luxurious minutes, daring the men inside Vanguard to sense me radiating human heat on the other side of the corrugated fencing that shot up ten feet high. It was utterly sterile. Not an ant or a blade of grass. Not a weed. Just gravel and more gravel. An endless gray sea lit up by spotlights posted along the fence.

I did not want Hamish to come and look for me, so I pushed myself up and walked hurriedly along the wall toward the parking lot.

About two hundred feet away, I could see Hamish's car near the entrance. He hovered next to the giant illuminated *V* that sat on the edge of the property.

I stepped briskly across the pavement and slipped inside the car.

"Let's get out of here," I said.

"No argument," said Hamish.

As we backed up into the road, I saw a guard come around the opposite side of the building and glance our way with a quizzical look. I could have met Hamish outside the VFW or the Mini Storage, but I hadn't thought of them quickly enough.

"Where's your car?" Hamish asked.

I could smell the heavier-than-usual application of Obsession and remembered that Mr. Forrest had once given my father cologne from Spain that smelled like pot. Oblivious, my father wore the cologne until it was gone, saving the bottle on his dresser, where I found it the day after he'd shot himself.

"Sarah borrowed it," I said.

This seemed to satisfy him. He stopped at a four-way stop and leaned over to kiss me. I shrank back, but he remained undaunted.

"Where shall we go?" he asked.

Paris and the Ritz, I felt like saying, and thought of the maudlin song about some sad woman realizing at the age of thirty-seven that she would never drive in an open car in a European capital. If that was the limit of her deprivation, she was one lucky bitch.

"The thing is," I said, keeping my hands on my lap and avoiding his gaze, "I need to borrow a car."

He pressed the accelerator. "Is that it?"

"I'm in a weird place," I said.

"Your mom?"

"Yes."

"Do they have any idea who did it?" he asked.

"I think so," I said, and I decided it couldn't hurt. "A boy who used to come over and do things for my mother," I said. "His name is Manny."

"The one who fucked someone in your old bedroom?"

"Yes."

"My mom told me about that."

We passed the quarry, where mountains of gravel and shale sat waiting to be borne away on trucks. They glimmered under the low argon lights spaced throughout the property.

Twenty years ago, there had been a boy Sarah's age who was playing captain-and-pirate on top of a giant pile of gravel dumped at the end of our block. He climbed up, brandishing a balsa-wood sword made the night before with the help of his father, and quickly sank inside.

"Do you remember Ricky Dryer?" I leaned my head into the window. I saw the reflection of my tired eyes come toward me and then disappear.

"The kid who died. Man, I haven't thought of him in years."

"Let's go to your house, Hamish," I said. "We can have a drink and talk."

"That's more like it," he said. I could tell he was looking over at me, but I did not look back. "You don't need to borrow a car," he said. "I'll take you anywhere you want to go."

I felt he deserved it: my body for a car.

We arrived at the house. I had made sure that Natalie would not be walking in at any moment. Hamish confirmed she was off with her contractor.

"It's like she has a whole other life now," he said. "I'm not part of it."

I steeled myself. I had had sex I didn't want before, and Hamish was a loving, wonderful—I couldn't get the word "boy" out of my head—man.

My entire body crawled with the desire to get on with it. Get on with the preamble, get on with the act, the sweet-nothing words, the faux regret at completion, the anticipated cleanup, and finally, finally, the car I would drive away in.

He held my hand and led me up the heavily carpeted stairs. *Thump,* my father's body falling. My mother cradling his skull as I walked in. The blood everywhere.

I had passed by Hamish's room countless times on the way to the upstairs bathroom when I was visiting. Once, when the children were in high school, Natalie had brought me inside and implored me to inhale deeply.

"This is the funkiest room in the house," she said. "I can't get rid of it, and he never opens a window."

"Hormones," I'd said.

She smiled. "It's like living with a bomb about to go off."

But the scent of teenage lust had been replaced with a whirring air filter in the corner of the room, and the bed was no longer a twin.

"You bring girls here?" I asked.

"Some girls," he said, and put his hand at the base of my skull. We kissed.

"I just want to make you feel better, Helen," he said. "I'm not expecting anything."

I remembered what Jake had said once, after Emily was born and I could not relax. *Let yourself fall in.*

We leaned back on the bed, and I shut my eyes. I had made my living striking poses at the instruction of others. Whenever it was hard, I would think of the smudged charcoal drawings in the basements and storage spaces of former Westmore students across the nation and of the few artists who had done something more than this.

In the Philadelphia Museum of Art, there was a painting by Julia Fusk. She had hired me to do a series of sittings for her when I was thirty-three. The painting that resulted was of a dynamic torso that bled off the page. It was only because I'd modeled for it that I saw where Fusk had taken certain liberties—made me more muscular, less lean.

As Hamish made love to me, I thought of Fusk's painting. Eventually the girls would find it again. Jake would lead them to it or Sarah would remember me taking the two of them to see it. She had stared at the blues and greens and oranges that waved across my thighs and lower stomach. Emily had excused herself and gone to the gift shop.

Fusk's work was my immortality. The fact that it was headless had never bothered me.

Hamish stopped suddenly.

"You've got to give me *something,* Helen."

I reached for his penis, hoping this time for the ejaculation that I could wipe off of my stomach and pretend was disappointing.

After his initial pleasure, he stilled my hand.

"I'm more than my dick," he said. "Touch me."

I could feel how small and desperate my eyes had grown. "Don't ask too much of me, Hamish. I can't give too much right now."

"You're doing this for the car."

I did not contradict him.

Something changed then. He parted my legs farther than was truly comfortable. He worked at me roughly, as if I were one of the action figures that had littered his floor as a child.

I tried to help him along. I pulled my own string and spoke to him in phrases I'd heard myself say in the midst of actual passion dozens of times. I stared at the small tattooed dragon below his collarbone and mimicked my former self for him.

Finally, just as the muscles on the insides of my thighs felt strained beyond recovery, the joints in my hips the dry ball bearings of a woman my mother's age, he came.

He shuddered and fell on top of me with all his weight. My

breath went out of me, and for a brief second I thought of the prostitute in Arthur Shawcross's car, how she had spent the next three days doing speedballs.

I pushed at Hamish's chest.

"Car," I said.

"You're a good fuck too," he said bitterly.

As he zipped up his pants—chinos, I noted, instead of his usual jeans—I thought how I could ruin anything.

"Give me a few minutes to check everything out," he said.

I lay undressed on his bed and listened to him take the stairs down to the first floor, walk through the family room, and go out the garage door.

I did not move until the air filter cycled on, making a light breeze cross my body. I turned on my side and propelled myself up with my left arm. I sat on the corner of Hamish's bed and began to clothe myself. I was staring at the louvered doors of his closet when I thought of it. Because it was not his house but his mother's, he must store everything that mattered to him inside his room. Hurriedly I stood and pulled open the doors. I reasoned that it would not be down low or even immediately accessible. He was not the type to show off that way. I pulled out a milk crate stuffed with CDs and turned it on its side—so much for stealth. On the shelf above his clothes, he had an extra blanket, a sleeping bag, and a shoe box, inside of which were shiny wing tips he had worn the day of his father's funeral. I did not find what I was looking for.

I was crazed now. During sex I had barely broken a sweat, but now I felt perspiration spring up along my brow. How long Hamish would take and when he would come looking for me, I could not predict. I scanned his room. I assessed. Where would he have put it?

And then, of course, I knew. He would see himself as the man of the house. He was not a freeloader; he was his mother's protector. It lay in the drawer of his bedside table, still in the Crown Royal bag my mother's father had kept it in, and beside it was an unopened box of bullets. I picked up the bag by its braided rope and grabbed the bullets before closing the door.

I saw the jumble of the bed, how our sex had made the fitted sheet pop off its corners and collapse into a jellyfish in the center. At another time I would have corrected this, but that was when I was not trying to leave behind everything I knew.

I took the stairs slowly, my thighs aching, knowing they would ache more the next day and wondering where I would be by then. Sarah and Jake would be together, perhaps still watching the police go through my house. I hoped Sarah had enjoyed her drink at the bar and only then gone looking for me in the ladies' room. I had to get the Crown Royal bag back to my purse before Hamish saw it. I sat down at the bottom of the stairs. My purse was in the kitchen. I knew I had to move but couldn't.

No one would be at Mrs. Leverton's, I realized. Her son had always avoided coming to the house, and if he was there, his Mercedes would be prominently displayed in the driveway. I could rest there, and given the food stores I was sure she must have, I might hide there for days.

I heaved myself up and walked through the hall and into the kitchen. I found my purse on the dining table and plunged the gun into my bag. I breathed.

Natalie had had the back wall redone that year. Now a long window ran across the kitchen, above all the counters. "He's convinced me," she'd said, "to have only under-counter cabinets to create an indoor-outdoor feel." She called him a charmer. What was his name?

I could see a reflection of myself in the glass. I turned my back on my spotlighted ghost and walked to the fridge. I was as hungry as I'd been the night before and realized that except for what I'd managed to eat of Natalie's breakfast in the student union, I had not eaten all day.

I grabbed what seemed easiest and most full of protein — hot dogs and cheese sticks — and methodically stuffed myself with them, one after another. I ate mindlessly, looking blurrily at the items tacked to Natalie's fridge. There was an invitation to a wedding for someone I did not know. She had yet to RSVP. The little card and envelope were under the magnet with the invite. It was a Christmas wedding, and I wondered if Natalie and her contractor would go. If the ceremony might put thoughts in his head or if, like Hamish said she hoped, they were already there.

Beside this was a picture of Natalie and me at a party at Westmore eighteen months ago. I remembered the day. Emily and John and Leo and Jeanine had left the day before, three days earlier than originally planned. I had kissed Leo good-bye on the one bare spot of his forehead that was not covered by gauze. I had tried to hug Emily, but her shoulders were stiff and resistant, and reminded me of me.

In the photo there was no sign of any of this, or the argument I'd had with my mother before I'd doubled back to pick up Natalie. Natalie looked radiant, and I, I felt, looked as I always had, the dutiful sidekick.

Hamish walked in just as I was pushing the last of the hot dogs into my mouth. He came over to me and turned me around to face him. My cheeks full of food.

"I'm sorry for up there."

I chewed and made a waving motion with my hand to indicate that it was fine, that it hadn't meant anything.

"It's just that you can be so cold, and I know you're not at heart. I've always known."

I looked at him. My eyes bulged as I swallowed.

"It wasn't Manny, was it?"

I saw the phone hanging on the wall near the kitchen table. Wondered who I could call to help me if Hamish refused. And I saw my purse sitting upright in the middle of a gingham place mat. Why had I taken the gun? What did I think I was going to do?

"It just makes sense. I was out working on the car and I thought, *What is she doing here? Why is she borrowing a car?* Mom told me Jake was here, and you said Sarah was too. The only reason why you're not with them is because they don't know where you are."

"You're very smart today," I said.

"Chalk it up to postcoital genius," he said. He turned and opened the fridge. "Besides, it fits. You came looking for my mom last night."

He grabbed a quart of chocolate milk and brought it over to the counter, where he stooped to get a glass.

"Are you going to tell?" I asked.

He poured his milk and faced me again, leaning back into the counter.

"You asked me yesterday if I ever thought of killing my father. Well, I did. I think a lot of people do," he said. "They just aren't honest about it. You actually went ahead and did it."

He took something from his pocket, a set of silver keys, and threw them at me. They landed at my feet.

I squatted down to get them.

"My mom won't forgive you," he said. "She's turning very moralistic in her old age."

I could feel already that I would be outside soon, that I would put the key I held in my hand into the ignition and back the car out of the driveway.

"Maybe it's Sarah I'm meant to end up with," he said. He took a swig of his milk. "After all, I love her mother."

It was like a sock in the stomach, and he saw it.

"Too much," he said. "I know."

"I have to go now, Hamish," I said, wishing I could leave him with some perfect phrase.

"Where?"

"I haven't figured that out yet," I lied. "I'll leave the car somewhere. I'll call you and let you know where it is."

He turned. I grabbed my purse from the table and followed him through the kitchen and then the living room. I saw a vase I'd given Natalie countless years ago. It was filled with store-bought flowers.

Behind the garage where Hamish kept the extra cars he worked on, he got inside a nondescript late-'80s Ford and signaled for me to wait. He turned the engine on and backed up until the nose of the car was facing toward the street, then got out with the engine still running.

All I could see was the open car, waiting. All I could think was with each leave-taking, those who remained behind were safe from me.

"I wish I was enough to make you stay," Hamish said. He hugged me, and for a moment he was my father and I was his child.

He stroked my hair and then squeezed me one last time for emphasis. I felt the increased heft of my purse on my forearm.

"I'm here if you need me."

I nodded my head. Words had begun to desert me for the first time.

"Take care of yourself," he said. "I'll wait for your phone call."

"Phone call?"

"About the car."

"Thank you, Hamish. Tell your mother I said good-bye."

I got into the driver's seat and tucked my purse beside me. Only the final click of the car door shutting made me sure that I could go.

I did not look at him again. I put the car into gear and started down the driveway, passing to the right of Hamish's car and onto the grass. As I reached the road, I turned on the radio. Swing music, when I had expected heavy metal or alternative rock. I listened to the muted cheer, then shut it off. I tucked in my chin and made the left toward Phoenixville.

FIFTEEN

It was still early in the evening. The clock on the dash read 7:08, and traffic along the road outside Natalie's was such that I felt the need to concentrate. I saw minivans and SUVs pulling off into driveways and versions of these same cars disgorging men or women carrying grocery bags and dry cleaning. Lamps went on in downstairs windows, and blue lights flickered from large-screen televisions.

When I reached the end of this new prosperity and took the still more abandoned stretch of road toward my old neighborhood, I felt myself calm a bit. Here the land had begun to be sold and quartered like so much meat, but there were also dilapidated houses tucked up between trees or, more sadly, so near the road that they would never be able to escape the influx of population despite shut-up windows or white-noise machines. The occupants of these old houses wouldn't even know what a white-noise machine was. Things such as noise-cancellation headphones or expanded cargo holds were foreign concepts to them. As members of my parents' generation, they sat and suffered until death, and I had reached the age where I glimpsed why this seemed preferable to keeping up.

There was one man who had taken matters into his own hands and built a ten-foot cinder-block wall around his entire property. He regularly sprinkled the top with broken beer bottles, which spilled over the side. No matter how many fines or threats of demolition came from the county, he would not tear the wall down. The war between the city officials and this homeowner had been going on for a decade with seemingly no end, and though he had made the local papers repeatedly, there was never a picture of him. I had begun to think of him as a homunculus who contained within him all the fears of modern man. There were no pictures of him because he looked like all of us. His fear had made him into a phantom who changed shape behind his walls. He was my mother, hiding in the linen closet. He was my father, drawing shadows on sheets of plywood. He was Natalie, afraid of loneliness, or Sarah, stealing change. He was me as I passed his house at 7:23 on a Friday night, going to Mrs. Leverton's. I hoped, as he roared and thundered and fought off every lawsuit or claim, that he would survive forever or, if not, would at least die thrashing and spent long after all our deaths.

I drove into Phoenixville proper, the old part of town, where revitalized businesses still shut down at five p.m. and the streets were empty except for small clusters of activity that revolved around insular community projects. I saw Antipode, the sculpture gallery, all lit up. It was a hub for the arty in the area, and I had gone there more than once. It had been the scene of my drunken date with Tanner. He and the owner, surrounded by people much younger than they were, had engaged in a one-upping concerning each other's relevance.

"That was the saddest display I've seen in a long time," I said as the two of us stumbled out onto the sidewalk.

"Oh, shut up!" he had cried. "What have you ever done?" And our companionable misery began.

Antipode was bright but quiet tonight. I saw movement toward the back. A show was being hung. Down the block, the wheeled carts of the Paperback Shack, which were brought in each night, had been knocked over onto the sidewalk and into the road. The owner, a lone old woman, stooped to pick them up, no doubt regretting her attempt to stay open longer for the sake of attracting after-work customers.

I pulled over into an empty spot and got out. I gathered up a group of tattered romances strewn in the road, their busty cover art faded from long days in the sun. But what caught my eye was a heap of moldy poetry books, seemingly adhered to one another, that had fallen as one. The names appeared Russian to me. Quickly I scanned the titles and knew immediately: these were the books Mr. Forrest had donated to the local library thirty years ago. "They are deficient in their Russians," he had said to me.

I startled the woman when I said, "Excuse me," and held out the two stacks of paperbacks.

She spit toward me, spraying my hand as well as the books.

"I'll put them here," I said, and laid them on the trunk of a stripped-down Lincoln Continental.

As I walked back to my car, I could hear her muttering. I had read about the poet Marina Tsvetaeva and how she had hung herself from a coat hook. *How was that possible?* I had thought at the time. Ceiling fixtures, trees — yes. But doorknobs or coat hooks?

Shooting yourself in the head was, I'd been told, a message suicide, but what kind of message had my father been leaving? I had scoured the house for a note afterward, looked in his drawers and under his pillow, and ended up washing down the stairwell with old rags, determined to erase the only marks he'd left.

*   *   *

I neared my mother's neighborhood, and a hot wave of dread began to prickle across my spine and back, tiptoeing along my shoulder blades and turning into gooseflesh. I could not explain why, exactly, but I sensed I should not even pass through the place, much less stay the night. I was also tired. It was easier for me to attribute the strange shifts in my body to a forlorn exhaustion—the futility and ruin of the last twenty-four hours taking over my heart, my limbs, my mental firings—than to know I was merely a robot that had gone off the rails and that, after serving its master faithfully for years, had turned back predictably to the place where it was made.

A few of the houses were still dark, waiting for their owners, but most had one or two lights on. There were young couples with children in my mother's neighborhood, but these were not the same sort of couples who bought the faux manses near Natalie's house. These were couples who cleaned their own houses and fixed their own leaks. They set aside weekends to replace the rotting shingles or paint their chimneys, trim their trees, or wash their cars. The children helped and were rewarded with ice cream or special TV shows.

I drove by Mrs. Tolliver's house as I rounded the bend toward my mother's and Mrs. Leverton's. There was no light on, and I wondered where Mrs. Tolliver had gone. It had been a summer night, I remembered, when Mr. Tolliver, screaming at her from his position on the lawn, suddenly clutched his chest.

"He fell over like a pillar of salt," my mother said. "Blam! The sprinkler shifted before anyone had thought to shut it off. They drove him to the hospital sopping wet."

I had seen Mrs. Tolliver six months later, when I was home visiting my parents with Emily and Jake. We were shopping in the Acme. She lit up at the sight of Emily.

"How wonderful!" she said. She was animated in a way I hadn't remembered. Overwhelmed to see me in the deli aisle, she had gestured with a package of boneless chicken in her hand.

I asked after her, her house, how she was feeling.

"It's too late for me," she said at some point. "Not you. It's not too late for you." She looked at Jake and smiled, but the smile contained a wince, as if she were afraid of being hit.

I was lost in thoughts of Mrs. Tolliver when I saw him through his giant, still-uncurtained window. Mr. Forrest sat in his front room, as he always had, for all the world to see. I pulled the car over to the side of the road opposite him. I was not even aware of what was to my right—a house, a horizon, or the pope out for a stroll.

I lowered the window and let the night air of my old neighborhood flood in. I breathed. I smelled the scent of the lawns and the asphalt. And I heard faint music. It was coming from Mr. Forrest's; he was listening to Bartók.

He and my mother had argued in the months following my father's death. There had been no funeral, and Mr. Forrest found the omission unforgivable; he didn't care whether she could leave the house or not. "And why, Helen," he had asked me, "were those guns allowed to remain?"

Without reflection, I got out of my car and hurried across the road and up the sloped concrete walk. He had never favored vegetation, and decades on there was barely a bush or branch on his lawn. Two chubby untamed boxwoods were the exceptions. They stood on either side of his stoop.

But I did not make it there. Halfway up the path, I stopped to watch. There was something in Mr. Forrest's lap—an animal—and he was petting it. I thought for a moment about all of his dogs, but then I realized that it was Bad Boy, the marmalade tom. He was upside down in Mr. Forrest's lap, allowing himself to be scratched.

How smart Mr. Forrest had been, I thought, how incredibly smart to remain alone as he had.

My knees felt as if they were made from hollow glass, and I knew I might collapse, but I did not move.

I had no doubt why my father had liked him; Mr. Forrest had shared the burden of my mother. He had a way of revealing her beauty to her that she trusted. His conversation was like a sparkling cocktail held aloft. In his eyes, my mother had been the neglected Garbo still in her slip, forever young, unspent.

I wondered if he would look up and see me standing on the path. Over the fireplace, I saw the painting he had bought from Julia Fusk. Finished the same year she'd painted me, the portrait Mr. Forrest had chosen was of a clothed woman whose face you could see. With her eyes shut, she was leaning to the left and pointing down toward the mantel, where my glance now fell. Spaced along it were three almost-perfect wooden globes made by my father. He had become obsessed with how these anonymous globes represented the finest woodwork he had ever done. Sitting in his workshop in the last few years of his life, while I gave birth to children and went to wine-and-cheese parties as Jake's wife, my father would sand these spheres for hours. He came in at night only after he saw the lights in the house go off. He would step quietly across the backyard and into the kitchen, climbing the steep wooden steps to his room, where the guns were kept.

I had blamed my mother. I had blamed her for everything. It was easy. She was crazy— "mentally ill," Mr. Forrest had said.

For years I had done my penance for blaming someone who was essentially helpless. I had warmed baby food and fed it to her with long pink spoons pilfered from Baskin-Robbins. I had carted her to doctors' appointments, first with blankets and then towels to hide the world from her. I had even stood and watched her drop my grandchild.

I would not disturb Mr. Forrest; I would not ask him for money or confess my sins to him. I would leave him with his portrait, with his spherical pieces of wood, and with Bad Boy, who had scratched my mother's cheek.

I turned and regained the sidewalk, walked to the car in order to fetch my purse. I could not bring myself to get back in the car. I could not imagine the sound of the engine. It would destroy the music I heard and the hush of the dark, abandoned lawns. I took the keys out of the ignition and walked around to the other side. I would leave them in the glove box.

I reached my hand inside the open window on the passenger side and quickly opened and closed the glove box, tucking Hamish's keys away. I grabbed my purse. *From braid to bullets,* I thought. How this would have satisfied my ill-fated therapist. He would delight in the alliteration until I would want to smack him silly. Perhaps I would give him a call sometime. A little ring-a-ling from hell.

I heard the Bartók go silent. I placed the purse firmly on my shoulder. I would walk to Mrs. Leverton's, let myself in, and— was it possible?—calmly shoot myself.

As I stood, I noticed that Mr. Forrest had shut off his lights. I saw Bad Boy bounding across the lawn and heard the front door close. I turned and walked at what I considered a normal pace, down to the end of the block.

I did not look at my mother's house—never my father's, though it had been his earnings that had paid for it. His earnings that had set me up, allowed me to raise two daughters on live modeling and occasional secretarial work. I had moved, married, had children, my own home, a job, but just like my father, I had seen the yawning tide that was my mother's need and fallen in. Jake would say I had dived in, that it had been my choice to return.

Mental illness had the unique ability to metastasize across the generations. Would it be Sarah? Would it be tiny Leo? Sarah seemed like the most obvious candidate, but that didn't mean much. And always, always, it had been left undiscussed, as if the geographical cure that Emily had taken would be enough. But I had tried that myself. I thought Madison, Wisconsin, would mean escape, but it did not. Nor did marriage or motherhood. Or murder.

I crossed the street again. I saw police tape stretched across my mother's front stairs. It zigged and zagged all the way to the top, through the iron rails. I kept walking. The holly my father had planted when they'd first moved in obscured the house from the side, but even so, I knew where the three slate stepping-stones were. During my father's life, he had kept these shrubs trimmed back so he could carry large sheets of plywood back to his workshop. Now the stones were hidden. They had been the three slate steps Mr. Forrest had backed over that day in the yard in the months following Billy Murdoch's death. I bent down where I remembered them and pushed my way into the prickly hedge. Small, rigid branches caught at my hands and face.

I had grown to believe there had been countless signals left by my father. I thought of my mother and me counting down the days until he returned from what Natalie eventually helped me realize must have been a mental facility.

"What do you remember?" she had pressed me.

"Only that he hurt himself in his workshop, and he went to the hospital for a long time."

And Natalie had looked at me long enough for me to realize what that had meant—not an accident with a screwdriver or skill saw as I'd initially thought, but that he had been the agent of what had happened to him.

"And the guns," I'd murmured.

Natalie had merely nodded her head.

*   *   *

I heard my father say the universal words again: "It's a hard day, sweetheart."

It was the afternoon. My mother was still in her nightgown. My father had retired from the Pickering Water Treatment Plant and spent his days at home, conscientiously leaving at least once a day on either real or created errands. He found it helpful as a way of staying connected to the outside world.

He bought stamps. He stopped by Seacrest's on Bridge and High to buy a paper or have a briny coffee at the lunch counter. He kept the house well-stocked with cleaning supplies and bouillon, instant Jell-O, and eggs from a farm stand run by an Amish family. He waited patiently on the old wooden benches that ran along the walls of Joe's Barbershop, chatting to Joe about items from the paper. Eventually, he would have to get in his car to come home.

By the time he shot himself, he must have known that leaving the house each day was not enough. Standing in the sun—if he could find it—for his required fifteen minutes of vitamin D was not going to do the trick, whatever that trick was.

My mother came out of the kitchen. She'd taken to eating Marshmallow Fluff on carrot and celery sticks in the afternoons, craving sugar and licensing it with vegetables. My father had left the house that morning but had returned quickly and gone upstairs to lock himself inside the spare room.

"I slept in," my mother had told the police. "He was in his room when I got up. I read. We mostly talked in the evenings."

I watched the policeman silently nodding his head. At some point during the questioning, Mr. Forrest arrived, then Mrs. Castle.

He had stood at the top of the stairs, my mother said, and called her name three times.

"I was rereading *The Eustace Diamonds.* I was two paragraphs from the end. I called out for him to give me a minute."

He waited. Then she laid down her book on the round table next to the wing chair and went to the bottom of the stairs.

"Are you done?" he'd asked her. The gun was already at his temple.

"I reached my arm up," my mother told us—and there on the carpet was a celery stick with its Marshmallow Fluff now pink instead of white—"but he..."

I held her as she shook, and I shook too. I would not allow myself to wonder what exactly, if she had baited him, she might have said in the end. Her head was against my chest, and mine was tucked over her shoulder. I had vowed to hold her more from that day forward and to come and care for her, because we were what remained.

The police asked her if she had a mortuary she preferred, and Mr. Forrest mentioned Greenbrier's on Route 29. I nodded my head. In that moment, I could not have realized what had just happened to me. My father had exited stage right, and in I had walked, seeing it not only as my duty but as perhaps the greatest gift I might give him posthumously, to take forever the burden of my mother.

Now as I left the border of my parents' property, I knew that it had been *his* house as well as hers. It had been *his* illness as well as hers. She just garnered more attention. She was always—day in, day out—*there*. My father had been pity to her blame, warmth to her cold, but had he not, in the end, been colder than she? She had fought and blubbered and screamed, but hadn't the two of us sat together for years?

Last night I had left her rotting in her own basement, and now she was in a metal locker somewhere, having been autopsied. Sarah knew. Emily would know soon, if they had not already told her. And Jake—Jake had even seen her body and stayed.

There was no Mercedes in the driveway. Only the timer lights along the front walk and at the four corners of the house shone out from Mrs. Leverton's lawn. Why not call her by her first name now that she was gone? Beverly Leverton and her late husband, Philip, neighbors to my mother for fifty years.

Unlike my mother's house, where single-pane glass still prevailed, which I could easily have smashed with a tap of a good-size rock to each corner, Mrs. Leverton's house had windows fitted by her son with thick thermal glass and a trigger-point alarm. But Mrs. Leverton had disconnected the alarm, and Arlene, her Jamaican cleaning woman of long duration, had kept a key in the basket of a concrete bunny statue under a pine tree just off the back porch. I often stood in my mother's backyard and saw Arlene carefully bending to retrieve the key. I had even noted recently that doing this was getting harder and harder for her. As old ladies grew older, so did their maids.

The bunny key was there, under a loose concrete egg. I looked to my left and right; the roof of my father's workshop was barely visible through the trees. It was odd to be in a neighboring yard from mine, where completely different lives had been lived, and to know almost no one now but those who had died.

Ultimately, even with a valid passport, I could never have escaped to Jake's converted mill house in Aurigeno, or even hitch-hiked west. I had told Jeanine that Greenland was a big piece of land and was composed of nothing but greens. Green people eating green food on green chairs at green tables in green houses. And then we moved on to Iceland, where everything was ice. And China, where the people and the places all had a porcelain sheen. I had made her scream with laughter as I spun the globe. "In Oman," I said, "there are men shaped like Os! Australia is 'ausome' and India, in!" *In Madagascar,* I thought...

I opened the screen door, turned the key in the lock. No alarms went off. I stumbled in the dark of what I knew to be

Mrs. Leverton's kitchen. I could see dark shapes around me, and with ease I saw the phone, its old-style cord twirling down to the floor and back. Tsvetaeva could have hung herself easily enough. I thought of Arlene wiping down the counters, the stove, the sink, each week entering and leaving another person's house, learning that person's habits and regimes. *At least,* I thought, *she was smart enough to get paid.*

I knew I could not turn on the lights for fear of being seen. I would take a moment and adjust. That's what I thought, but I heard a mewling outside, and I jumped.

I took my purse into the half bath to the side of the kitchen and closed the door. It felt safe to risk a light inside the window-less room, but I was unprepared for who I saw.

There I was in the mirror, the strap of my purse cutting into my shoulder, weighing me down. The gun heavier with each step I'd taken since leaving the car. I saw my face, puffy from lack of sleep, my hair jutting out in all directions. My lips were dry, the creases above them puckered and hard. I looked into the mirror, and I saw the thirteen-year-old Helen. I touched the plywood figures along the walls of a once-drowned house. I looked at my father on the rocking horse, saw the solitary mattress on the floor.

"There are secret rooms inside us," I had said to my therapist.

"A relatively benign construct," he said, and so I did not bother with the rest of it. That in my house we never left them, that in my house my mother and father preferred them to everywhere else.

My eyes staring back at me were small and black, and behind them was a room I'd avoided all my life. My parents were waiting for me, I thought, and in the small wallpapered bathroom of Mrs. Leverton's house, I could, if I wanted to, blow my brains out. My father had killed himself, I had killed my mother, and I could join them both. If I hustled, perhaps I could be interred with my mother, head to toe—our own jumbled version of *The Lovers of Pompeii.*

Quickly, I shut the light off. I set the purse down, and in the dark I washed my hands and face, splashing the water cupped in my two palms against my skin, running the tap ice-cold. I saw her then, Emily racing up to me beside the pool at the Y. She was holding something out to me and smiling widely.

"My Flying Fish Badge," she said. "I got it!" In the weeks leading up to my father's death, she had mastered the butterfly.

I did not turn on the light again but stood over the sink, breathing heavily. I willed myself to open the door. I picked up my purse as if it were some stranger's bowling bag and made my way into the kitchen and over to the round dining table, where I sat down in a wicker-backed chair. I moved my hand over the smooth grain of the table. Mrs. Leverton had left no crumbs from her evening meal.

I thought of the girls.

Once, when the three of us were visiting my mother, and Emily and Sarah were still small, we had been walking down the street on the way back to the house from the park, where a new jungle gym had been installed. The girls were excited and wild. Sarah had run up Mrs. Leverton's walk and started stamping on the concrete with her foot.

"See, it's not like Grandmom's!" she yelled.

"Sarah, get back here. That's not your house."

She had stared at me, nonplussed. "I know that," she said. Emily looked up at me to see what came next.

Mrs. Leverton was what. She tapped on her front glass—single-paned back then—and as I hurried up the walk with Emily to retrieve my errant child, the front door opened fast.

"Why not come in?" she said. "Daughters must be lovely things."

And though my mother hated her and she disapproved of me, we went into her house and sat in the living room, which Arlene cleaned every other Friday. We had store-bought cookies from a tin, and Sarah told her about how, at her grandmother's house, there was a hollow spot under the front path.

"The sound changes when you walk on it," Emily clarified.

"And Mom says there are tiny people who live in there," Sarah said.

"Does she?" Mrs. Leverton looked at me and made an effort to smile. Crumbs from a shortbread cookie sat at the corner of her mouth.

"A whole village," Sarah said excitedly. "Right, Mom?"

I did not say anything.

"Like *Gulliver's Travels*," Emily said. "Sarah likes to imagine them."

There she was, I thought, at nine, already a better mother than I was. She had taken the lead with Mrs. Leverton so that Sarah would not notice my disappearance. I had wondered if all mothers shared a fear of how vibrant and alive their children were.

I put my hands together.

"God, forgive me," I said softly.

I had set my purse on the floor beside me, and I leaned over to pick it up and place it on the table. I pushed back my chair a foot or so and reached my hand in. There was the felt between my fingers. I searched for the braided gold twine and pulled out the Crown Royal bag. It made a loud clunk against the table. Next I took out the box of bullets. I put the box beside the bag. I stared at the purple felt. Even taking the gun out seemed unfathomable.

I stood up.

The clock over Mrs. Leverton's sink had a blue neon circle surrounding it—a faux diner clock. They had the real McCoy at Easy Joe's.

It was only 7:45 p.m. It felt like three o'clock in the morning. Finally, I thought, I had reached the future that was no future.

I saw the teapot on the stove and decided that I would make a cup of tea. A stalling tactic, no doubt, but what was and wasn't reasonable had left me. Everything was reasonable if killing your mother was. Everything was reasonable if giving up your life was second nature.

I did not want to think. I became methodical. I filled the tea-kettle and made sure not to replace the blue whistling bird on its spout. I pushed back images of my father in his terry-cloth robe and my mother wrapped in the Mexican wedding blanket, top-pling to the basement floor.

I brought the water over to the stove and turned on the flame. I could not leave this way. Not, I thought, without a letter, not as my father had left me, had left my mother. I had chosen Mrs. Leverton's because it made sense. It was empty. But I also knew now that it was a house they would never have to enter, my head blown off a sight they would never have to see.

I opened one cabinet and then another, finding the cups in this second one. Mrs. Leverton did not have hooks with mugs or pots hanging on them. She had good china and everyday. Mugs, to my mother, had also been abhorrent things. How nice it would have been if they had known each other. Visited. Done something besides send cards at the appropriate moments—the birth of grandchildren, the death of men—but it was my mother who had pointed out their reality. "Just because we're old doesn't mean we change into friends."

I knew that, like my mother, Mrs. Leverton would no doubt have a drawer in the house that held stationery—perhaps a whole chest of drawers. It was one of the fallback gifts for an old lady. How many shawls or boxes of note cards had Mrs. Leverton been given in her ninety-six years? "Cash," Jake reported his father had said to him near the end. "If it isn't cash, I'm not interested." He joked with Jake that he wanted to die clutching a thousand-dollar bill in each hand. "I didn't have the heart to tell him they didn't exist anymore," Jake said.

I left the water to boil. Who cared if I burned the house down?

I went to the door that led to the living room. In the center of the wall across the room, there stood a highboy desk. The bottom edge was illuminated slightly by a light-sensitive night-light. I looked to my left and saw another of these lights. Green circular disks jutted out of random outlets so that Mrs. Leverton or a happy burglar could pick his or her way through her downstairs rooms.

Once, my parents had fought about the light bill. My mother insisted that every light in the house remain on even when it was sunny out. Even when I was at school or my father away on a business trip.

"Why? Why all these lights?" he had asked, waving the bill in her face as she sat on the couch, unraveling a thread at the hem of her dress.

"I'm not a bank," he said, before grabbing his hat and coat to go out.

Later I told him that it must have something to do with the operation—her mastectomy. That she thought the light was helping her heal, and that if he was patient, I was sure she would return to using lamps only in the rooms where she sat. Four months later, she did. I never knew what had caused it. I had made up the lie to keep things as they had always been.

In a drawer under the foldout desk, I found the stationery. I would write the first letter to Emily. She deserved what she had never gotten from me, what she so much wanted: an explanation.

Why I was the way I was despite what she thought of as free will and the endless possibilities that she had never seen me grasping.

I could not make out the designs of the paper or the colors, and I did not want to write my suicide note on card stock lined with Holly Hobbie dolls. I grabbed the three boxes of stationery in the narrow drawer and stacked them in my free arm before shoving the drawer closed with my hip and opening the one below it. I smiled. On one side was a soft lump, and when I touched it, I could feel the looped wool of what must have been a shawl or blanket. To the left of this were more boxes. I lifted one out — cribbage — then replaced it. Another — a deck of cards, still in cellophane. I threw it back. The next box was obviously a vestige of her grandsons: a Crayola one-hundred pack with built-in pencil eraser. I took this.

I could not go back to the kitchen.

I carried my spoils carefully through the hallway, picking out the dark shapes of a grandfather clock and a half-circle table, on which objects of different sizes sat. I heard my mother's voice: "Tchotchkes is the woman's middle name."

I saw a small light on at the top of the stairs — enough to write by, I thought, and climbed. Her stairs were padded with plush carpeting. I wanted to take off my shoes and walk about, but I had what countries called an exit strategy to pursue.

I spilled the boxes of cards and the crayons at the top of the stairs near a hope chest, on which the brass reading lamp illuminated the hall. I knelt down in front of it. Fanned across the surface of the hope chest were back issues of *AARP,* with an occasional *Woman's Day* or *Ladies' Home Journal* as bright spot. I felt I was kneeling at a foreign altar and then imagined myself flailing around, stuck to a giant glue trap.

I needed a pen. I could not write to Emily with a crayon. For Sarah, yes, the rainbow effect seemed appropriate, but for Emily, no. I needed ballpoint. On the windowsill behind the hope chest, there was a light-blue cup—the blue of my mother's Pigeon Forge bowl—and in it there was an emery board, a tire gauge, and three Bic pens.

I extracted a pen and grabbed an *AARP*. I crawled back to the boxes and crayons, three feet away, and sat with my feet two stairs down, using the magazine as my desk. Quickly I chose a piece of ecru-colored paper with gilt edges—elegant for Em—and bent to my task.

Dear Emily,

How can I begin to explain to you what you already know? That though I am prouder of you and your sister than anything else in the world, I have found myself at the end, with no other choice.

I stopped. I knew how she scrutinized. She spent hours in front of a mirror, finding flaws. Her house was spick-and-span, and she had once pointed out to me that the best thing about having a cleaning woman was that they did what she called the "first wave" and left her free to focus on the details.

I cleared my throat. It echoed in the hall.

By the time you get this, I will be dead. I hope you are spared having to see me. I had to see my father, and it never left me. Sarah will have told you by now that my father killed himself. That he did not fall down the stairs, or rather he did, but only after shooting himself.

I don't know why he left me.

Did you know my mother kept her hair long for your grandfather? He loved it. He would brush it every night one hundred times. In hindsight I came to think of it as their nightly Prozac. Yes, I know, I know—meditation, not medication. In theory I agree, but sometimes... don't you think?

What I want you to know is that I did not kill my mother out of vengeance or even, really, pity. It was the right thing to do, though I didn't plan it. If I had, I obviously would have thought of where I am now. All day today, I've been thinking of you and your sister.

It was unforgivable—how I forced you to grow up, to take the place beside me that your father's absence left.

I applaud you in your life. That's what I really wish to say. You have your own house and family, and you live very far away. Keep it like that. Never come back. With me gone, there will be nothing to come back to. That's the gift I want to give your sister. Don't let her live in the house, Emily, or fritter her life away. Sell both houses. Your father will help.

I paused. I thought of my father, sitting beside me the day we cosigned the papers for my house. He had made sure to set me up as firmly as he could, had mentioned that day that his will and other important documents were in the Malvern branch of the bank, and had told me where he hid the key. Only later did I realize why he had been so explicit in this, making me repeat back to him each fact.

I wrote again.

When I close my eyes for a moment, as I've done just now, I see my father, but then I see you. Remember that day at the Y? I'm so proud of you, my Flying Fish!

I'm in Mrs. Leverton's, and it's dark outside. I have to write a note now to your sister. Take care of Jeanine and Leo, and God bless any positive memory of me you are able to entrust to John. Do you remember how much Sarah has always loved the color green? I do.

I love you, Emily, no matter what.

Remember that over everything.

I sat back. I let the pen fall from my hand and silently tumble to a stop. For years after his death, I had gone around jealous of the moments with him I'd missed, staring at Emily and Sarah, thinking of the grade-school chaperoning or the jungle-gym monitoring I'd been engaged in instead. Once or twice he came to sit at the edge of the playground and join me. I had that. That, I clung to, but when I tried to remember what we had talked about, I couldn't. I had wanted something to keep with me; even my mother had hurriedly clipped a lock of his hair when we'd first heard the men from the mortuary coming up the front walk.

I stared at her, horrified, while she tucked it inside her shirt.

"He was my husband," she whispered.

When the doorbell rang, I felt it would be my job to assist the men with their task. Lift my father onto the gurney. Strap him fast.

But in reality, at the mortuary director's urging, I had excused myself. I had taken my mother into the dining room, where we stood by the large corner cabinet near the kitchen, huddled together—not exactly touching each other so much as hovering helplessly in proximity.

"I'm sorry for your loss," the director said when they'd come back up the stairs with the paperwork. They were trained to say that.

The younger one had just started at the funeral home. "Yeah, me too," he'd said, and shook my hand.

Something was digging into my side. It was sharp. I felt it stabbing me. Became aware that it had been poking at me for some time.

I leaned back and put my hand in my jeans pocket. Sarah's butterfly barrette. I took it out and held it in the palm of my hand, making the light from the hope chest pick up its blues and greens, the thin gold rhinestones on the blunted antennae and legs.

It was almost nine. I wondered if Sarah and Jake were looking for me or if they'd thought to speak to Hamish yet. I wondered when Hamish would open his bedside drawer.

I closed my hand over the rhinestone butterfly and pressed, thought of all the discarded items over all the years that had made me feel free. I had not thrown out the weeping Buddha Emily had given me. I would not throw out the butterfly.

I stood up on the landing and pinned the blunt clip of the barrette through the weave of my black sweater until I heard the closure snap.

Mr. Forrest will be asleep now, I thought, *or listening to music on his treasured Bose.* We had talked about it when we'd run into each other a year or so ago.

"It gets the best sound. I can lie in bed and listen. I have a special velvet sleep mask. It used to be if I wanted to listen to music, I had to sit in the front room."

I bent down to retrieve the letter to Emily and the box of crayons. I tucked them under my arm like a clutch. I was in the house, finally, of the Other. The Levertons and their holiday cruises, their intricate "On Donner, on Dancer" display at Christmas, their elaborate barbecues out back — the laughter of the guests pushing through the trees and across our lawn. All of that was over forever.

I knew exactly where I wanted to go, and so I walked down the short hallway that in my mother's house ended in the only upstairs bathroom. In Mrs. Leverton's, it led to another hall, off of which was the bedroom where she had been standing the night before and seen my mother and me outside.

A humidifier had been left on in the corner of the room, and the overwhelming scent of Mentho-Lyptus filled the air. On the table beside the bed — the wood protected by a thick sheet of glass, cut to fit — there were rows and rows of prescription bottles and a notepad made from strips of paper held together with a clip. Beside this sat a chewed-up pencil. It seemed the prompts to off myself were endless.

I put the crayons and Emily's letter down on the bed and sat by the table. There was something written on the notepad. I picked it up.

She had a shockingly spidery hand.

I realized that almost all the pages of the tablet were filled up, not with lists of chores or groceries needed but with the names of the presidents, the capitals of each of the fifty states, and the names of doctors who had treated her, coupled with their nurses' names. I looked at page after page.

On her good days, her hand was stronger, and she remembered Frankfort, Kentucky; Augusta, Maine; and Cheyenne, Wyoming. On bad days, her hand shook more, and she forgot Johnson through Bush. My knowledge paled in comparison. I knew nothing of Rutherford Hayes.

I was about to lose it anyway, I could feel the tears waiting to fall, but then I saw a drawing she had made—a scribble really—of a woman's figure. I knew it was a woman because it wore a skirt, and all around it, in a hand shaky with frustration and fear, were obsessive misspellings of her daughter-in-law's name. Sherill, Sherelle, Cherelle, Shariwell, Charille. She never got to Cheryl no matter how many times she tried.

I wondered what Cheryl thought of her. I had seen her only once or twice. Was Cheryl someone Mrs. Leverton loved or an ogre she had to befriend in order to get to her son?

I looked again at the figure Mrs. Leverton had drawn next to the butchered spellings of her daughter-in-law's name. *Every day,* I thought. Every day, Mrs. Leverton wrote again the things that kept her tethered to the outside world. No matter how frail, she had not relinquished her hold.

I knew what held me.

I found my note to Emily by the crayons. I ripped it lengthwise once. I ripped it this way again. I was determined now to explain what I could to my children and to carry the shame of my mistakes.

I let the confetti I had made fall to the floor and thought distractedly of the water I'd left boiling on the stove. I smiled at the memory of Jake calling Sarah his "Little Gadhafi" because of her penchant for green clothes. I could take the Crayolas and melt them into lumps in a pan. I could mark the capitals of the countries I had never been to and never would. *Green for Nuuk,* I thought, *the capital of Greenland, where everything is green.* I could teach art classes in prison. One day I'd be released, and I'd stand in the field at Westmore, coaching old people to paint the rotten oak tree.

I got up. In the kitchen there was a gun on the table and a fire on the stove, but I walked to the casement windows in the corner. One faced the rear of the Levertons' property, and the other faced my mother's house.

The trees had grown even thicker in the years since my father's death, but fall had arrived early, and leaves were dropping fast. I could see my father's workshop and, beyond this, the house lit by the moon. I saw the window of my bedroom and imagined the vines lacing up, my mother's front half hanging out the window while my father held her and I sat quietly on my bed.

It must have been then or a moment later that I saw the lights. They were blue lights that seemed to be pulsing from somewhere out in front of the house. Blue lights and red.

I did not understand, and I wasn't sure I ever would. What my mother's fear was comprised of, why my father felt he had to leave us the way he did. Or the blessing of children and the love — once, then twice, because Hamish had to be counted — of a more-than-good man.

I stood at the window and edged off my shoes. My feet sank into the plush carpeting. I opened the window ever so slightly, and a breeze rushed in, bringing into the sealed-up room a blast of cool night air. I listened. I heard the branches creak against one another in the wind, and then, coming from my mother's house, I heard voices and saw dark shadows armed with flashlights spread out across our lawn and enter my father's workshop.

I would do what I did best, I thought. I would wait. It was only a matter of time, after all.

"She's not here!" I heard a policeman yell. "There's no sign of her."

ACKNOWLEDGMENTS

THE BLOOD:
Bender, Cooper, Dunow, Gold

THE CIRCLE:
Barclay, Doyle, Elworthy, Fain, Goff, Muchnick, Nurnberg,
    Pietsch, Snyder

THE UNEXPECTED:
Charman

THE MASTER MECHANICS:
Bronstein, MacDonald, Schultz

THE CITADEL:
The MacDowell Colony

WILD CARD:
Wessel and the Italian Contingent

WILD DOG:
Lilly (woof!)

picador.com

blog
videos
interviews
extracts